Caffeine Nights Publishing

No Doves

ANDY BOOT

Fiction aimed at the heart and
the head...

Published by Caffeine Nights Publishing 2015

Copyright © Andy Boot 2015

Andy Boot has asserted his right under the Copyright, Designs and Patents Act 1998 to be identified as the author of this work

Published in Great Britain by Caffeine Nights Publishing

www.caffeine-nights.com

British Library Cataloguing in Publication Data.
A CIP catalogue record for this book is available from the British Library

ISBN: 978-1-910720-92-2

Cover design by
Mark (Wills) Williams

Everything else by
Default, Luck and Accident

For Anita

Acknowledgements

'Thanks to Darren for taking it on,
and Sandra for the edit'

NO DOVES

NOTE: As with many of the crimes in London, this was silenced. Spoken about only in whispers, the official line is that it never happened. But it did. It made 1991 a very bad year for justice. Even now, if you ask officially, everything that follows will be denied.

CHAPTER ONE

The body was found at 9.15am on a Sunday morning. It was at ebb tide, and the waves of the Thames lapped gently on the old stone steps leading from Wapping Old Stairs down into the filth and decay of the so-called freshwater Thames. Further down the Essex stretch of the river, where it ran towards the Thames estuary, the water was salt but cleaner. Here, the dark brown and oil-streaked liquid left deposits against the stone and earth of the river walls, eroding and exposing old oak pier beams that rotted gently in the morning sunlight.

The light and heat also rotted the corpse that bounced off the old steps and back again with every gentle wave of the tide. It was swollen, and the once expensive powder blue suit it wore was now a dark and neutral colour, with soggy sheets of old newspaper covering the stumps that used to be hands, fixed there by sticky excrescences that had long since ceased to flow.

The body was found by a chartered accountant with a pony tail and a springer spaniel. His wife had asked him to take the dog for a walk, and he wasn't happy about it. Sunday was the day he usually had a long lie-in, maybe even got to play around a little with his woman. But not today. Today the dog – still only a puppy at eight months – had wanted to go out. With a penthouse apartment on a £250,000 mortgage in the heart of the refurbished London Docklands, there was no garden to kick the dog into, and no way was it going to urinate on his expensive carpets.

He took the dog out on an extending lead, cursing it every step of the way and trying to nurse his erection for when he got back home.

The dog kept dragging him back to the top of the steps that led down into the river.

"Stupid animal," he muttered under his breath. Then louder, and in a petulant tone: "There's nothing down there, you stupid bloody thing. Come on, I want to go home." He pulled on the lead, but the dog strained against him. It turned and snarled at him. "Don't start that," he sighed. "Alright, let's see what's so bloody marvellous down there, then."

He walked to the top of the stairs, and looked down. He could only see what appeared to be a bundle of old rags and newspaper, floating near the steps. The buzzing of a small boat sounded in the distance, getting nearer. He stood back, more interested in the vessel.

"Bit small for a cabin cruiser," he said to himself as the boat passed, making the waters swell and tumble in its wake. The turbulent waters lapped the steps. Suddenly the dog started to bark again, this time with real excitement.

"Oh for God's sake, there's nothing there. Look."

He followed the dog's line of vision.

Suddenly, he forgot about his erection and started to heave. By the time he reached the nearest pay phone he had thrown up four times.

***

Daniel O'Day was a man of few words, most of them of no consequence. He stood at the end of the pier on St Catherine's Dock, resting his arms on the railings and looking across the river at the rows of new buildings and converted warehouses that lined the bank, pitted here and there with areas where the old London still shone through: dark and dank skeletons of old industry, waiting like malevolent dinosaurs for the moment when they could reach out and take back the areas that wealth had made clean.

O'Day didn't believe in the concept of clean.

The old man pushed his cap back on his forehead, inhaled deeply, then hawked up phlegm. He spat it into the river, and watched it hit the dark and calm surface before being absorbed into the turbulence beneath.

"The Thames is like life, son." His voice was harsh and guttural, ruined by a lifetime of shouting to be heard above the roar of dock machinery, followed by a retirement of shouting to be heard above the roar of a London that didn't care any longer. "It stinks because it's full of shite. And it's dark."

"What's worse?"

O'Day turned to face his companion. He was eighty-two, but his eyes still shone hard and black, piercing through the man who had asked the question.

"The dark. Always the dark."

He turned and walked back down the cobbled pier, his legs bowed and his gait awkward. Jack Goldman, Daniel O'Day's grandson, could hear his laboured breathing even from a distance of fifty yards. He doubted that the old man had too much time left.

He followed his grandfather down the pier, walking slowly to keep his distance. He wanted to leave him alone with his thoughts for a short while. When he caught up, Daniel was leaning against Jack's car, labouring hard for breath.

"You alright?" Jack asked.

The old man nodded, unable to speak for a few moments. Finally, he managed to wheeze out a few words. "Fine. As fine as I ever will be now. I just wanted to see it one last time."

"Even though they've ballocksed it?"

A grin lit up Daniel's face. "Ballocks is the word, young Jack."

Jack laughed as he opened the car door for the old man. He was going out fighting.

As they pulled into the hospice's small car park, Jack turned to his grandfather.

"What is the dark?"

"Eh?" The old man had been dozing, and looked at Jack with incomprehension.

"The dark. You were going on about it at the dock. About it being worse than the shite."

"Was I? Jaysus, I must be rambling. I swear it's those drugs they give me." His face split into a huge grin. "Last week I thought I saw God fucking the Virgin Mary." He laughed hoarsely. It degenerated into a cough.

"You blasphemous old git. If gran could hear you now –"

"She'd go and say a prayer for me," said the old man, recovering his breath. There was a tinge of sadness in his voice.

"But the dark. . ."

The old man's face took on a more sombre mien. "When I was a child, back in Cork, the priest used to tell us about the light and the dark. You can wade through shite, Jack, but the dark gets you so you don't know what you're doing. That's the worst. And maybe it's the dying of me that's doing it, but I can feel it more than I used to."

Jack nodded. There was nothing he could say.

***

After he left the old man settling back into his decline at the hospice, Jack drove straight home. He didn't feel like stopping and having a drink, having to be happy with people. He didn't feel happy. There was little enough sense of community in his family, and what little there was would die with his grandfather. His grandmother had always wanted to better herself and get out of the East End. It was an ambition that she instilled in her own children, so much so that they had all left for the suburbs and middle-class careers at the earliest opportunity, having little to do with their parents. The old man had lived most of his adult life in the area, and wanted to see out his remaining days there. He had settled into a life of pubs and betting shops after retirement, and Jack had joined him. Jack's mother hated him for letting her down: he was an only child, and she had wanted him to be something. Her siblings' children were brokers and lawyers. Jack became a policeman, and was stationed at Limehouse.

Phyllis had kept tight lipped and disapproving when the twenty-two-year-old Jack had told his grandparents about his posting. Danny had laughed.

"Jaysus, son, you'll need to watch yer arse there. I remember when I first worked on those docks. . .Y'know that the coppers had to go in pairs down there, they were that scared." His tone had suddenly become more serious. "Not that I blame them. There's the darkness for you, round that place."

As Jack parked the car, he remembered about the darkness. He hadn't thought much of it at the time, but he knew now what the old man meant. Ten years was a long time to be around an area and police its filth and degradation. Sometimes he wondered why he still did the job. His granddad had reminded him.

The darkness was more than something Catholic priests used to put the fear of God up Irish kids of his grandfather's generation some seventy years before: the darkness was something palpable that came not from some kind of supernatural source but from men themselves.

Jack had seen enough of it over the past ten years. It was more than just nicking villains.

He sat in the car for five minutes, and tears rolled down his cheeks. He didn't know if he could take seeing the old man slowly rot in front of him, fighting every inch of the way but knowing that he couldn't cheat the darkness.

**

"How long, do you reckon?"

"Hard to say. From the look of him I'd say at least two days, possibly two weeks."

"Is that the best you can do?"

"You've seen the state of this poisonous muck. You could fall in at different times and it'd either corrode or preserve you. Two days to two weeks is all I can say right now. You'll just have to be patient."

The police doctor rose from the bottom step, and picked his way up the slimy stones with care. Detective Sergeant Errol Ross squatted at the bottom of the steps, water lapping his immaculately polished shoes. He looked down at the corpse again, and wrinkled his nose.

"Thanks for nothing, Doc," he muttered in a sarcastic tone before raising his voice to the men waiting at the top. "Right, you can come and take this bugger away now. The river's got enough pollution without his sort adding to it."

He walked heavily up the steps, letting the two uniformed ambulance men pass him on the way down. He didn't bother to watch as they loaded the stinking body onto a stretcher and carried it up to a waiting ambulance. He was more concerned about the non-appearance of Jack Goldman and the fact that he'd have to question the hysterical accountant on his own. He looked over at the man with the pony tail, sitting on a low wall with a cup of tea and a uniformed constable fussing over him. When Ross had arrived on the scene the man was crying and telling anyone who would listen about how many times he'd thrown up and how his dog had run away.

Ross had him labelled immediately as gutless. Possibly literally. . . the thought brought a wry smile to his face. He'd left a message on Jack's answerphone, but whether or not he would turn up was another matter.

"I hate this poxy job sometimes," he said to himself. He looked down at his shoes. They were filthy. Ross prided himself on his appearance. "Some times more than others."

Ross walked over to the accountant, unbuttoning his raincoat as he went. He felt in his inside jacket pocket for a pen and his notebook. He walked in measured strides, and by the time he was in front of the accountant he had both notebook and pen in his hand, and had pulled his jacket and raincoat back into place, straightening them unconsciously as he came to a halt.

"Do you feel ready to talk, sir?" he said as blandly as he could, trying to keep the contempt from his voice.

"Do you think you could find my dog?" asked the accountant. Ross looked at the constable, and raised an eyebrow. The uniformed policeman gave a slight and embarrassed shrug.

"The gentleman says it was a pedigree, sir, and very valuable."

"Thank you constable," said Ross politely. "You just make yourself scarce. I'll deal with the gentleman now." It was no good, the word "gentleman" had been distinctly sarcastic. The young uniform smiled and nodded, moving off to make himself useful elsewhere. Preferably somewhere in earshot – Errol Ross had a reputation for being hard on those he considered idiots. Rumour said it was this more than his colour that kept him from moving further up the ladder.

Ross leant forward. His tones were clipped and polite, but carried an added underbite of impatience and sarcasm.

"Look sir, I'm sure this dog is very important to you. But I've just stood over a corpse that smelt like the waste product from a slaughterhouse. Someone was killed, and their hands were cut off. I just need to get a few details from you –"

He was cut short by a sudden forward movement. The

accountant leant forward, retching. A thin stream of bile and regurgitated tea shot from his lips and splattered the pavement. Some of it rebounded onto Ross's shoes and the cuffs of his trousers.

"I'm sure you'll feel better after that, sir," Ross said, with as much patience as he could muster.

***

As soon as he listened to the voicemail messages, Jack had gone back to the car and headed for Wapping Old Stairs. There was only one other message besides Errol's. Maureen, his ex-wife, had been shrilling down the phone about the lateness of this month's maintenance payment for young Danny. The boy was five now, and the old man wanted to see his namesake one more time before he died. But Maureen was being awkward, using it as a bargaining tool to get more money out of Jack. In return, he had stopped paying her until she let the boy see his great-grandfather. It was petty and childish, but he wanted to make the old man happy and there wasn't much time left. Young Danny didn't understand any of this, and kept asking Jack if Da (his name for the old man) would be better soon. Jack couldn't answer him: how can you tell a five-year-old that his favourite old man in the world is dying and that his mother didn't want him to see the old man before he died?

The traffic was light along the Ratcliffe Highway, leading away from Tower Bridge and into the heart of the old docklands. Jack always took this route when he knew it would be quiet. It was more round about, but the sight of this part of the city somehow gave him strength. All his early memories were here. He was relying on them to keep him going. In some way that he couldn't explain or reconcile to himself, it was more than just his grandfather dying that was affecting him. It was as if that was the end of an era – the end of old London. And Jack wasn't too sure if he fitted into the new one.

Too much darkness.

When he pulled up at the Old Stairs, there was no sign of Ross or the accountant, and even less of the body. It was 11.30am, and he passed pubs opening their doors on his way to the mortuary. They should have been closed until twelve, but the licensing laws were elastic in these parts.

When he arrived at the morgue, Ross was waiting for him in the pathology lab. He had one foot up on a chair, and was attempting to sponge vomit and river water from the bottom of his trousers, using several sodden tissues.

"What happened to you?" Jack asked as he came through the door.

"The wanker who found the body decided to use me for target practice," Ross replied without looking up. He tossed the wad of filthy tissues into a waste bin without even aiming.

"Very impressive," murmured Jack. "Any idea who our customer is, then?"

"You're going to love it when you see it," Ross said as he took a fresh wad of tissues and soaked them under a tap. As he squeezed out the excess water and carefully cleaned his shoes, he continued: "A regular customer, no less. I think we're in for some serious ructions."

A pasty-faced path lab assistant looked around the door. "The doc's ready for you now."

"That's big of him," muttered Ross. He threw the tissues into the waste bin and tugged the cuffs of his trousers down over his shoes before following Jack into the next room.

The corpse lay on a stainless steel table. It was stripped naked, and its puffy features were barely recognisable. The flesh was mottled blue and yellow, with open sores where it had been nibbled by what few fish manage to survive in the Thames this far up river. The stumps of the hands were ragged, and a small piece of newspaper had refused to come away from the edge of the left wrist.

Jack took a deep breath to overcome the mixed smell of decay and preservative that always haunted these rooms. He squinted at the corpse in the bright light.

Suddenly, recognition dawned. He turned to Ross, who nodded before Jack could speak.

"I thought it might surprise you," he said with a wry smile.

CHAPTER TWO

The night was never dark in Docklands. The security lights on the buildings that lay unused cast a pall over the area. Then there was the glass-sided monstrosity that was the *Financial Times* building, its presses running every night of the week, hired out on Saturday when there was no Sunday edition, pouring light into the night. Most of all there was the beacon on the folly of Canary Wharf, its revolving beam a constant reminder of the failed promise of free enterprise.

At least, free enterprise on a large scale.

The light didn't bother the new inhabitants of the Docklands area. People who had made their money in the boom years of the mid-eighties and now spent it on thick blinds and curtains to keep out the reminder of the slump that Canary Wharf had come to represent.

Nobody went out much at night in Docklands. The streets around the office blocks were empty, and those residents who were out on the town went by car, their feet barely touching the streets. The few pubs that remained were only busy intermittently, the long-time residents sticking to their homes in the run-down council blocks and the solitary pleasures of television: it was cheap, and there wasn't much spare money for them.

Benny Grazione had been one of those people. Now he was one of the others they despised. One of the others that he despised.

He looked out over Docklands from the large French window that opened onto a terrace five floors from the pavement. It was a nice apartment, he considered, but so it should be for the amount of bread it had cost.

In the distance he could see the irregular pattern of light

decorating the side of a council block on the Isle of Dogs. Benny, whose grandfather was an Italian prisoner of war who opted to stay in Britain after the war, and whose father had been a gambler disowned by the prosperous market gardener the patriarch had become, had been brought up in a block like that one. The lifts had never worked, and he remembered the taste of fear for a teenager walking down the stairwells. Around every corner there could be one of the teenage gangs, waiting to beat the crap out of you because you were in a rival gang – or even because you weren't in a gang at all. For the old it was even worse. They weren't in a fit state to run or fight, and it was easy for them to be robbed.

Benny had never considered their fear: he was too busy conquering his own. Besides, without the old people there would have been no easy pickings for him to begin his own career.

Benny was a bright boy: his father had always said that he would either end up rich or behind bars. The old man should know: he was in Brixton after bungling a raid on a bookmaker's office. He had no gun, just a cucumber wrapped in silver foil and carried in a plastic bag in an attempt to make it look like a disguised shotgun.

Benny despised his father's stupidity. If he'd come to him, Benny could have got him a gun.

For a price, of course.

He tired of looking at the lights over on the island. They reminded him too much of how far he'd come. He didn't want to be reminded. He was only twenty-three, and how many guys his age had their own plush apartment? Not mortgaged, but actually paid for? Of course, the severe price drops due to the recession were responsible for his being able to pay cash, but what did that matter?

It was his. Benny Grazione was respectable. And as such, he was entitled to all the things that a respectable man can have. This included the little stockbroker in his bed. She was from the floor below, and Benny had watched her come in and out for three weeks before contriving an introduction. From there on, he relied on his native charm. He'd scored, and was happy. He didn't know that she looked on him as a bit of rough, something to toy with. He would have been angry, and hit her. But then again, he was looking at her in a similar manner.

Benny adjusted the lapels of his jacket, making sure there were no creases. The phone call had said to be ready at half-past eleven.

He pulled the drawstring hanging down the frame of the window. The blinds snapped shut. In the same instant his mind stopped dwelling on his roots and snapped into the present. He walked briskly to the bathroom and splashed cold water on his face, drying it with a towel before slicking back his hair with a palmful of gel. His hair was short, black, and clung to his scalp like a skullcap. He grinned at himself in the mirror before walking out of the bathroom and into the bedroom.

On his way to the bathroom he had chosen to ignore the blonde, tousled head on the pillow. Now, the woman moaned slightly in her sleep, and turned. Her shape under the silk sheet was enticing. He felt himself stir as he watched her. Then he looked at the clock by the side of the bed. Twenty past.

He ignored the urge to climb under the sheet and take her while she was asleep. Instead, he picked her cream Armani suit from where she had carefully laid it over a chair, and threw it onto the bed. It landed on her, making her jolt awake.

"Wha–" she sat upright, her eyes unfocused, looking around the room. They seemed to focus as they reached him. "Benny, what –"

"Get dressed," he said shortly, taking her white blouse off a hanger and throwing it in her face. "I've got business. You've got five minutes."

She muttered to herself. He ignored it, and walked out of the room – though not before pausing in the doorway to watch as she slid from under the sheet and into a sitting position on the edge of the bed, trying to wake up properly. She was still wearing her stockings, and her pubic hair was matted from their lovemaking. Her breasts were small and pert, and her hair fell over one eye in a sweep.

He grinned again. It was about as friendly as a jar of acid. He thought about having her back soon: she'd come. They loved the way he treated them.

He mixed himself a rum and Coke while she dressed, constantly checking his gold Rolex. The minutes seemed to crawl by.

Eventually she emerged from the bedroom. She was wearing her skirt and blouse, with the jacket draped over one shoulder. She ran the fingers of her free hand through her long hair, pulling it back and scowling at him.

"There's no need to be so bloody rude, Benny," she said with the hint of a whine.

"Business is business, and you wouldn't want to be here when it's done," he said. He strode over to an old fashioned bureau in the corner of the room. Keeping the glass in one hand, he pulled open a drawer, extracted a small white plastic envelope full of powder and tossed it over to her.

"Little present for you, babe. Sort of apology."

She caught it with her free hand. Her face lit up. "Thanks, Benny. That's really nice of you."

She walked to the door with a smile on her face. As she opened it and made to step into the hall, he called to her:

"Tina. . .the next time you pay, okay?" He smiled his barracuda best as she scowled again. "Business is business, babe."

She slammed the door behind her, and Benny laughed softly to himself. There was more than one way to screw a woman.

He looked at his watch. Eleven twenty-nine. He slipped a CD from its case, and the room was filled with the soft sounds of sweet soul music. From experience, he knew that it calmed couriers down, and made them less twitchy. A nice relaxed atmosphere. If there was one thing he really hated, it was twitchy couriers.

There was a long mirror against one wall, and Benny pouted and preened in front of it, adjusting his cuffs and the crease of his trousers. The suit wasn't particularly expensive, but it was the first one he had bought with proceeds. He thought of it as his lucky suit, and liked to wear it when he was dealing with people for the first time. Besides, he'd never found quite that shade of powder blue anywhere else.

The doorbell chimed. Benny looked at his watch. Right on time.

He walked over to the door calmly and leisurely, not wanting to give a bad impression. It was best to start off on the right foot with these people. Appearances were everything.

He opened the door with a smile fixed in place. It took only a fraction of a second for him to register that the men standing outside were wearing ski masks. He didn't think about why this should be. Instead, he tried to slam the door in their faces.

But they had the element of surprise. A foot and a shoulder were in place before Benny could throw his weight against the door, and he was thrown backwards onto the thick pile carpet. Things blurred around him, and when he was able to focus properly he was staring up at four men in leather jackets and ski masks.

Benny tried to throw himself forward onto his feet, like he'd seen Jackie Chan and Bruce Lee do it in the kung-fu movies he watched. But Benny wasn't as fit as he thought, and he floundered until a savage kick from one of the masked men took the breath from his lungs and made his ribs ache every time he tried to inhale.

"Don't be clever, son," said his attacker in a weary tone. "You're softer than you think, and we're not. Alright?" He reached down and pulled Benny to his feet. Benny tried to aim a punch at the man's stomach, but all he received for his efforts was a fist in the face. He felt his nose split, and blood filled his mouth.

"Bit of a bleedin' comedian, ain't he?" said one of the other masked men.

Benny was limp. His whole aura of cool and hard credibility had been shattered by two blows. And now he was frightened.

"Who the fuck are you?" he bubbled through the blood that still flowed down his face. "Tong? Mafia? Look, I'll sell out to you if the price is right. I'm too young to want any wars, man."

"That's the trouble with today's youth," said the first masked man, obviously the leader. "No fuckin' guts." He hit him again, this time in the stomach. Benny's already unsteady legs gave way under him and he collapsed onto the floor, retching. "Let's sort this out quick, before the spineless little git makes me puke," he added in a weary tone.

Two of the others took hold of Benny and dragged him into the bedroom. They ripped the sheet from the bed.

"Well, well, we have been a busy boy," one of them said sardonically as he noticed the fresh stains on the sheets.

"Shows he must have balls," laughed the other, shortly.

They threw Benny on the bed. A third man came in, carrying a hold-all, from which he produced a length of rope. They tied Benny's hands to the headboard. The knotted ropes pulled tight and bit into his flesh. He winced as the fresh pain penetrated his foggy brain.

"Does that hurt, then? Poor little sod," said one of the men in a mocking baby tone, patting Benny on the cheek. The last blow was a stinging slap. "Wait 'til we've finished with you."

Benny lost control of himself and urinated on his lucky suit. It wasn't the pain, but the note of promise that he feared. Benny knew he was going to die.

The man who had initially hit him, and was obviously the leader, had stood in the doorway watching Benny being bound to the bed. He disappeared into the lounge for a few moments, and the sound of the CD grew louder — much louder. Benny had done this to other people so often: it was to drown out his cries for help, or of pain.

The masked man came back into the room, and took off his mask.

"Look on my face, sunshine. It's the last one you're ever going to see, I'll tell you that much. But before I've finished with you, you're going to tell me all I want to know."

Benny mustered his courage and spat in the man's face. There was no change in his expression: he calmly wiped off the spittle and turned away. Then Benny felt as though the fires of hell itself were in his guts as the man swiftly turned and grabbed Benny's testicles through the thin material of his suit. He had them fully in the palm of his hand, and he twisted savagely. Then he let them relax slightly before twisting again. This way the pain was forever renewed.

"Don't fuck me around, Benny. You tell me what I want to know and you'll die quickly. Hold out on me and I'll make you wish you'd never been born. Got that?" He gave one last twist to emphasise his point.

Benny screamed. It was meant to be a "yes", but came out as an incoherent sound of fear and pain.

The man let Benny's testicles hang loose and throbbing. He stood upright, and started to pace the room. Like his three companions, he was over six feet tall, and powerfully built, with a protruding gut that gave lie to his strength. His face was hard, close cropped mousey hair receding at the temples, and a moustache with a few flecks of grey.

"Look," rasped Benny through his pain and fear, "what do you want from me? I don't know anything. I'm just –"

"You're just one of the biggest men around here." The tone was soft, but with a weary edge. "Now don't try and be clever. We just want everything you know about your gang. I don't give a shit about the others. . .They'll get visitors soon enough."

"If it's a takeover, then I'll let you have the territory, everything. Just let me go, man, just let me go."

Benny looked up at the masked men, who stood impassively watching him. There was a blank malevolence about their eyes, a lack of judgement in any direction. The leader sneered down at Benny. In his face there was only contempt.

"Christ, you're fuckin' pathetic. When I joined the force there were real villains. Hard bastards who could take what you're getting without flinching. You had to admire them, back then. They were real hard men. You knew where you stood, then."

He spat on the floor, a dismissive gesture. There could be no deals. Yet there was one thing that Benny's pain-fogged brain managed to pick out.

"The force? You're police?" The words came in painful rasps of breath. He couldn't even construct sentences as the pain spread to the stretched and taut muscles of his arms, like flames licking along to his wrists.

The man leant over him. "Of course we're the fuckin' police. You think the chinks or the mob would act like this? They'd try and buy you off first, rather than dirty their hands. Only some of us don't want them, and we don't want you. So we've decided to pick your lot off, as a sort of warning. Alright by you?"

Benny started to cry. "Anything, man, anything. . ."

The next twenty minutes were the longest of his life. While the CD player repeated the sweet soul sounds, Benny told them everything he could about the small gang he headed. He gave names, addresses, and associates. He told them how his operation worked, and where the next distribution to dealers would take place. Benny had the whole of the drug market around docklands sewn up nicely: from the crack smokers in the deserted underground garages that underpinned the tower blocks, through the neurotic housewives whose doctors had pangs of conscience about putting them on tranquillisers and no longer repeated the prescription, all the way up to the upwardly mobile like Tina who craved a little something extra to lighten their jaded existence.

Rub out Benny, and you rub out most of the subculture and black economy around this stretch of the river.

Finally, Benny had nothing more to say. He lay back, panting for breath, and hoping that his death would come quickly. Every fibre of his body ached, and he knew that he was on the verge of passing out.

Without a word, the moustachioed man turned to the masked man with the hold-all. Almost with grim ceremony, the masked man produced a butcher's axe and handed it to his superior. With an equally grim pleasure he turned back to Benny, whose eyes widened at the sight of its dull blade.

"Hands first, I think," said the moustachioed man, looking at his colleagues. They nodded.

Benny screamed. "You said quick, you said quick." His breath was too short to hurl insults at his attacker.

The man shrugged. "I lied, Benny."

He moved forward, and Benny's hysterical screams rose up to compete with the music as the man took a short swing at Benny's left wrist. The hand was severed almost completely through, hanging only by a shred of tendon. A second blow corrected this error.

Benny was almost surprised by the fact that, despite the intense pain, he was still conscious. He prayed for the black relief of oblivion as one of the masked men came forward carrying a small blowtorch, with which he cauterised the spurting wound. A stench of burning flesh and blood filled the room. Benny arched his back from the bed, legs thrashing. It was too much pain for unconsciousness.

"Now the other one," said the moustachioed man, as he moved around the bed. This time the blow was stronger, and the hand fell off with the initial stroke. The cauterisation was swift, and Benny no longer knew who he was, or where: the pain had driven him beyond the bounds of sanity. He knew nothing of past or future, only the now of pain.

"I think that settles him," said the moustachioed man quietly. "Someone shut the little bleeder up, eh?"

He walked out of the stinking room, and waited until he heard the silenced pistol shot before turning the blaring CD player down to a more normal volume.

"Giving me a fuckin' headache," he muttered.

That was how Benny Grazione died.

CHAPTER THREE

"This is going to be nasty. . .very nasty."

Errol Ross took a long draw on the foaming pint in front of him. He put it back on the counter and wiped the froth from his top lip.

"You were right, Jack. The beer here really is crap."

He looked slyly at his partner, and smiled. Jack Goldman stifled a laugh as he drank from his own glass.

They were in the Blind Beggar, the pub in Plaistow from where Benny Grazione had run his gang. Every Friday was the same: in the small back room, with drinks and food provided gratis by the terrified landlord, Benny had received information and takings from the week's work. In return, he had issued orders for the coming week: who was to deliver, who to sell, and who to sort out those who had, in some way, crossed him.

And now it was Sunday, half-past two, and Benny lay on a slab like the remains of the Sunday joint. The first thing Goldman and Ross had to do was to establish how long he had been dead: at this stage, the doctor still refused to commit himself.

"I hate police doctors," said Errol, leaning against the bar and eyeing up the few straggling customers.

"Why?" Jack asked as he tried to catch the barmaid's eye.

"Because they're idiots," Errol replied calmly.

"All of them?"

Errol shrugged: "Ninety-nine per cent of people are, so why should police doctors be any different?"

The barmaid came over.

"Tell Arnie we want to see him," said Jack. The barmaid was thirty-ish, with a heavily lacquered long coiffure and thick make-up to hide her bad skin.

"Who shall I say?" she said in a flat, deadpan voice.

Errol and Jack looked at each other: it was obvious she had them tagged as policemen. There was always a chance that Arnie would be "out", and over the back fence as soon as he knew they were after him. He wouldn't need a reason: anyone who had Benny's gang in his back rooms would be over the fence before a police officer could even say "hello". Errol nodded almost imperceptibly, and Jack made to leave.

"You can tell him Ross is here to see him – call me mister Ross," he said, accentuating the word "mister".

The barmaid sneered. "Who d'you think you are then, Sidney bleedin' Poitier?" She smiled, pleased at her joke, and looked around at the sparse clientele for an approving laugh. She got nothing. They were keeping their heads down: most of them had form, and those that didn't were ripe for it. She turned back to Errol. He looked at her impassively.

"Who?"

***

She let the phone ring five times before putting it down. Every day she had rung, and every day she had got no answer. Part of her wondered if he was trying to avoid her, and part of her didn't care. That part of her just wanted some more nose candy.

"Bastard," she muttered venomously at the silent phone.

She strode around the lounge of her apartment. The furnishings were sparse but expensive: sofa in white leather, fine art print on each wall – only one per wall, to "improve appreciation" the designer told her – and a glass-topped coffee table. One black metal bookcase stood in one corner, and in the other was her home computer terminal on a small desk.

The sun shone weakly through the large French window, and she looked out at the tower blocks over the river. She hated the scenery, and wished that it could all be pulled down, redeveloped into blocks like the one she lived in. The one on which she was paying the huge mortgage.

Right now she didn't care about that. She felt jerky, strained: in need of some relaxation. She thought about the way Benny was hung, and imagined licking cocaine off the tip of his prick. She ran her tongue over her lips to moisten them, and felt herself get wet with excitement. He was supposed to be a quick screw for the hell of it, just a bit of rough. But he was good, and there was an element of danger about him that put him above the morons she met at work – men whose only excitement was in guessing when their first ulcer would come.

She made up her mind: striding across the room, she flung open her front door and went to the elevator. If he was holding out on her, she had ways of persuading him.

***

"It's like this, Arnie. We just want to find out when Benny died." Jack leant over the table in the upstairs living room. It was a tacky shrine to cheap foreign holidays with sun, sea and sex. Arnie Shawcross was an ex-soldier gone to seed, put in the Blind Beggar by the brewery in the vain hope that he was hard enough to stop the Friday and Saturday night fights that had turned it into a pub manager's graveyard. The last manager ended up in hospital with half a billiard cue and most of a pint beer glass rammed up his back passage for daring to try and step into a fight. Arnie had stopped the fights alright, but not in a way the brewery would approve of: he let Benny and his gang move in and take over. Anyone who fought on a Friday and Saturday would feel the steel of Benny's boys.

Arnie said nothing. The expression on his florid face was blank. Three hours after opening time and he'd already helped himself to far too much of the goods. It was hard for him to focus on the fact that Benny was dead. With no leader, the gang would probably factionalise. Arnie would have to make choices and hope he made the right ones. Even then, there would be those who came back for revenge: the men who Benny's boys had punished for fighting in the pub, for attracting unwanted attention.

Arnie was a worried man.

"Arnie? Are you listening?" Jack waved a hand in front of his face. There was no response at first. Then Arnie looked up with a start, suddenly jerked back to the present.

"Sorry? You say something, mister Goldman?"

Jack sighed and turned away. "What can you do with someone like this?" he asked the empty air. Errol grinned from the doorway, but said nothing. He liked to watch Jack work on his own.

In a blur of movement, Arnie found himself hauled to his feet and flung against the old iron fireplace, which his wife had pleaded with him to have opened up again in the days before she'd decided to leave. He felt the black leaded metal dig into his back, biting under the edge of his ribs.

"I have had a very bad day, so far," said Jack through gritted teeth, holding the big man against the metal, pushing harder. "My granddad is dying, and all I have to do is chase after some sleazebag's killers. Now, while on the one hand you could say it was a public service to get rid of scum like Benny, on the other hand you can't have people going around topping others just like that. It could all get out of hand. So could I, unless you start actually talking to me. Is that perfectly clear?" He released his grip, and Arnie stumbled forward, falling against the table.

He dragged himself up and into his chair. When he began to speak it was in a carefully precise manner: the manner of the drunk who wants to appear sober.

"Two meetings. Two meetings he's missed. The rest of 'em thought the first one was some woman – he's been shagging some yuppie bit he was chasing after. But two – " he shook his head "– two is something wrong. They're worried. Talking about the mafia and the triads, and all that crap. Could be he walked under a bus, even. They've started getting narky with each other already. I just kept me 'ead down, mister Goldman. I don't want trouble here, and Benny kept it quiet for me. I'm in shit now he's gone."

"Why? What do you know?"

Arnie looked up at Jack and laughed shortly. "Know? I don't know nothing. Never wanted to. It ain't knowing anything, it's just being here, innit?" His eyes looked into the distance, contemplating horrors to come. "All those bastards his boys beat on for fighting here. They'll be back. And there's whoever wins the battle for control, I'll have to pick the right one, won't I?"

"It's a hard life, Arnie," said Jack, patting him on the shoulder. He looked at Errol, his eyes full of contempt for the seated man. "Let's go and look for a few of Benny's little helpers."

Errol held the door open as Jack left the room. He was about to follow when he noticed Arnie beckoning him back.

"Mister Ross, one thing. . ."

"What's that?" Errol leant over the table, establishing eye contact.

"It's not just Benny who's gone missing. Some of the other lads haven't been around."

"Is that unusual?"

"Could be."

Errol nodded decisively. "Thanks Arnie. I'll bear that in mind."

"Any chance of getting some help? Y'know, a bit of protection if there's trouble?"

Errol grinned coldly. "I wouldn't bet on it, Arnie. I wouldn't even consider it a possibility." He made to leave.

As he reached the door, Errol turned back.

"Are you screwing that barmaid, Arnie?"

"Why?" His eyes searched Errol for some trick in the question.

Errol shrugged. "No reason. I just hope she screws better than she jokes."

He shut the door without seeing Arnie's puzzled expression.

***

"My gran used to tell me that the wages of sin weren't very nice. I don't think she ever met anyone like Benny."

Jack turned off his car engine in the courtyard of the plush apartment block. He looked up at the building through the windshield. For a moment he was silent.

"I don't know what we'll find here, but I've just got this feeling it's going to be a really shitty afternoon."

"What do you mean 'going to be', boy? It already is," Errol replied as he got out of the car. He straightened his raincoat, shaking out the creases, and looked down at the cuffs of his trousers. At least they weren't stained, although they looked dishevelled. "You know what my granny always used to say to me?" he asked as Jack locked the car.

"Don't screw white women?"

Errol's face cracked into a grin. "Yeah, she used to say that, too. But most of all she said don't let accountants puke on your suits, 'cause it really ruins the material. Let's get this over and done with."

He walked up to the security door, and pushed on it. It refused to budge.

"Poxy security measures. What these dam' people got that they think others want so bad?" He kicked at the door, which protested with a creak and a resounding clang.

Jack pressed every bell-push on the intercom system. There seemed to be no-one home in the entire block. So he tried again, this time holding the bell-pushes down for about ten seconds a time. Eventually, one begrudging resident accepted his explanation of being a police officer and released the door lock. It was unlikely that he really believed Jack, but probably only wanted to be left in peace.

Benny's apartment was on the fifth floor, and the lift was small and dimly lit. For such an expensive block, Ross expected more luxury and said so; Goldman sardonically put it down to the new asceticism in design.

When they emerged on the fifth floor, the corridor was long and winding, leading around a bend. The actual apartments were obviously large, as the bland teak front doors were spread wide apart. Harsh strip lighting lit the cream corridor walls and the plum red carpet on the floor.

"Looks like a bad hotel," said Errol.

"But an expensive one."

As they progressed down the corridor, they could hear a repetitive beating, the tattoo of someone pounding on a door. They could also hear a woman's voice in low tones – too low to make out what was being said.

They rounded the corner to find a slim blonde in jeans and a silk blouse beating on Benny's door.

"This could be very interesting," remarked Errol as they approached. The woman heard their footfalls, and turned to them.

"Are you friends of Benny's?" she asked. Jack noted that her tone was a mix of petulance and genuine concern. He also noticed that she had fine bones, and that her nipples were erect

31

and straining through the silk.

"You couldn't really say that, although we would like to find out what happened to him."

"I haven't seen him for over a week, and I suppose I'm a bit worried."

Errol raised an eyebrow. "Suppose? Only one thing to do then, isn't there?"

He moved her out of the way, stood face on to the door and raised his foot.

"You can't do that," she said with alarm.

"Too late," murmured Jack as Errol's foot crashed against the lock. The door creaked. While they watched, Ross repeated the kick half a dozen times. With each kick the wood splintered more, until the door burst open, leaving the locks in place. The blonde looked at Jack questioningly.

"He was the hardest penalty taker in the league until he had to give up due to injury. Goalkeeper's that is, not his." He left her standing and followed Errol into the flat.

The main room looked untidy but not wrecked. The electricity was off: Errol tried the light switch, as the blinds were still drawn. He looked quizzically at Jack, who indicated the CD player and amplifier. The CD was fine, but the amplifier looked as though it had shorted out. There were small burn marks on the display.

Jack wrinkled his nose. "Must have been done here."

"What must have been done?" asked the blonde, who had followed them in. "Look, who are you, and what's that frigging awful smell?" Her nose wrinkled. Jack found it attractive, despite the fact that his attention should be elsewhere. "It smells like bad meat."

Jack nodded. "When I was a kid I used to watch old horror movies, and they'd always go on about the smell of the charnel house. It was years before I knew what a charnel house was."

Errol had put his handkerchief over his face to try to block the stench. "Bedroom?" he muffled.

"Got to be." Jack led the way over to the bedroom door. It was closed. Errol was at his shoulder. Jack put his hand on the door handle, but stopped when it was halfway depressed. "It's going to stink in there."

Errol nodded. He turned to the blonde. "Listen, don't follow us sweetheart. But hang around, we'll want to talk to you."

Confusion made her angrier. She stood with her hands on her hips, challenging them. "I'll be fucked if I do what you two say. Just what is going on here?" She sounded like she was used to being answered, and quickly.

"Soon," murmured Jack, his attention focused on the door.

He opened it slowly, but still the stench of decay hit them hard, its underlying sweetness making his stomach turn. The room was in semi-darkness, curtains drawn across the small window. No use trying the light switch.

Jack stepped into the room and allowed his eyes to adjust to the gloom while Errol carefully picked his way to the window, unwilling to disturb anything. There were swarms of flies gathered about two objects on each side of the bed, and the mattress was covered in urine and blood, with some other dark stains not immediately identifiable.

"They must have done it here," said Jack quietly, surveying the rest of the room. There were things smashed: the clock, a bedside lamp. The chair over which the girl had draped her suit less than a fortnight before was broken, one leg lying on the floor, with blood smeared on it. His eyes returned to the bed. "Poor bastard must have crapped himself."

Errol pulled back the curtains. The window was open just a crack: enough to let in the flies, but not to let out the stink.

"Smells like they roasted him. Must have cauterised the wrists to stop him bleeding to death." He paused, gulping down the beginnings of vomit stirring in his gullet. "That's just sadistic," he said jerkily.

Jack nodded. He was staring at what Errol could now plainly see in the weak sunlight. The flies were clustered around the remains of Benny's hands.

There was a sharp gasp and stifled sob from behind them. Both men turned as one to find the blonde in the doorway. She collapsed to her knees, heaving and vomiting.

Jack rushed over to her. "We'd better get her out of here, then call the lab boys," he said, glad of the excuse she gave them to leave.

CHAPTER FOUR

Errol elected to wait for the arrival of the pathology team and scene of crime officers. He put the receiver of the phone gently back into its cradle, and screwed up the handkerchief he had used to stop his fingerprints getting on the handset.

"They'll be here shortly," he said in a flat tone.

"How long is that?" asked Jack, with one eye still on the blonde woman. She was sitting on the edge of Benny's plush sofa, sobbing into her hands.

Errol shrugged, sniffed, and rubbed his eyes. "Christ alone knows. Be here shortly, what the fuck does that mean anyway?"

Jack looked at him closely. He'd worked with Errol for a couple of years, and during that time they had seen some gruesome sights. Many worse than this. Yet he had never seen Errol with his cool so obviously disturbed.

"Look man, what's the matter?" he murmured in an undertone. He watched intently as Errol appeared to ignore him for several seconds before looking him in the eye.

"Hmm?" Errol's tone was distracted. Jack stayed silent, letting his intent gaze do all the work. Finally, Errol cracked a slight smile. "Okay, okay, I'll let you into a little secret. It's the poxy smell."

"Smell?" Jack gave him a look that veered between amazement and amusement. "You're having me on."

"No shit. I know we've seen worse, but that's always been in the open air. The flesh doesn't reek unless you get up close. But in here. . ." he gulped heavily, ". . .in here it's like the pit of Hell. Anyway," he continued, quickly changing the subject, "what are we going to do about blondie over there?" He gestured at the weeping woman.

"You question her, take her down to her flat. I'll wait here," said Jack. They still spoke in undertones, not wanting her to hear.

"No, I'll stay here and wait. Maybe try and open these damn' windows. They're the problem. I can live with the severed hands if I can get rid of the stench. Besides," he added, cracking a grin, "you don't get the chance to go out with many women these days. She might fancy you."

"Never shag white women, eh?" Jack laughed quietly. "Okay, whatever you say."

He turned to the woman on the sofa. She was still sobbing, with an intermittent, dry racking sound punctuating the tears.

"Come along, miss – " he paused, waiting for her to say something. She didn't even look up. He exchanged weary glances with Errol before going over and taking her arm, half guiding and half pulling her to her feet.

As they walked to the door, she dragged her arm away from Jack's grasp. He looked back at Errol, who was watching with a sardonic raised eyebrow. Jack shrugged.

As they left Benny's apartment, Errol turned his attention to the windows and began to fiddle with the locks, cursing quietly to himself.

Jack and the woman took the elevator down one floor in total silence. She looked away, concentrating on wiping her eyes and studying the bland decor of the elevator. Anything other than look directly at him. As the doors opened, Jack strode out first, and from the corner of his eye he caught her stealing a glance at him. She was trying to size him up, but why he wasn't sure.

He waited for her to lead the way to her own apartment. It was four doors down on the right, and he was surprised at the size of the key ring she produced from her pocket. Surprised because, despite himself, he had been admiring her body, and the tight fit of her obviously well-made clothes. Her jeans were designer, and it looked like she had nothing on underneath. She was certainly naked under the blouse.

Jack followed her into the apartment. To him it looked sparse and unfriendly; but he had to keep the customer happy.

"Nice place you've got here," he said. He was met with

heavy silence. She went into what he presumed was the bedroom. He heard the clatter of drawers and cupboards, and the hiss of a tap. She was changing her clothes and washing her face: he listened with minute attention to detail as he stood with his face away from the door, staring out of the French windows and across the river. Occasionally he checked his watch.

It took her four and a half minutes. He heard the door close softly, and turned round to see her move across to another door. She wore older, cheaper jeans that were frayed at the cuff, and a Hard Rock Cafe T-shirt. As she opened the door he could see a hob and a fridge-freezer.

"Any chance of a cup of tea?"

For the first time she smiled, then spoke. "I was doing one for myself, so I suppose you'd better have one too."

***

Errol had finally managed to get the windows open. A cool breeze blew off the river and carried the distant sounds of life. He felt his stomach ease as the smell of decayed flesh was blown out onto the London air. He poked around aimlessly while he waited for the SOC and forensic teams to arrive. Until they had had a good look around, he didn't want to disturb anything. At the same time, he felt that to do nothing would be an appalling waste of an opportunity.

A survey of the entire flat led him to deduce that Benny had been killed in the bedroom, and that an initial struggle had taken place in the lounge. The kitchen seemed untouched. He looked over to the bedroom, and gritted his teeth. The bathroom? Only one way to find out.

He strode quickly through the bedroom, trying to ignore the flies that buzzed over the remains of Benny's hands. Jack had covered them with a couple of plastic bags, but the flies still bounced off the plastic, hoping to get at what lay beneath. Errol found himself watching them despite his better intentions, and tore his gaze away in disgust. He hurried into the bathroom.

There seemed to be no sign of any disturbance here. Using his handkerchief again, Errol gingerly opened the doors of the bathroom cabinet. The usual array of male toiletries, with some extremely expensive aftershave, the smell of which filled the cabinet. Errol nodded approval.

"You might have been a villainous fucker, Benny, but you did know a good scent when it hit you." He closed the cabinet and looked around the room. There was a bath, a separate shower unit, a washbasin, and a toilet. Under a cursory examination the shower and washbasin looked clean. The bath was another matter. There were minute stains on the sides that may have been blood, and a couple of splashes by the overflow outlet that looked even more promising.

Errol stood up straight, and studied the toilet.

"Now if I was you, Benny, which God forbid I would ever be, where would I hide my stash?" He thought out loud, talking to nothing more than the hands in the bedroom. "I'm a nice Italian boy from the island, and I've got no class – sorry Benny, but flash is never class. So I'd be used to hiding things where no-one would look. Or where I think no-one would look. But I'd get all my ideas from *The Godfather* and crappy cop shows on TV. And the bigger I got, the more entrenched my ideas. . . they got me this far, right?"

Errol looked at the cistern mounted on the wall.

"You wouldn't be that stupid, would you, Benny? I dunno, maybe you would in your own home."

He bent over the cistern. It was plastic, with a screw holding the lid in place. The head on the screw had a broad channel. Errol felt in his pockets for a large coin, pulling out a handful of change. He sorted through it, coming up with the hexagonal edges of a fifty pence piece.

"Perfect," he said, pocketing the rest of the change. Using the coin as a screwdriver, he unscrewed the black plastic bolt screw. It yielded easily, and after a few turns he was able to pocket the coin and delicately use his covered fingers to remove the screw. He placed it on the floor, and removed the cistern lid.

"You were a very stupid boy, Benny," he said as he pulled a heavy-duty clear plastic bag from the bottom of the cistern, tutting angrily as his shirt cuff got damp. The bag was full of a white powder.

"No prizes for guessing what this might be," he said

sarcastically. "And no prizes for guessing what blondie might know about it."

***

The blonde laughed, and rose from the sofa. "More tea, Jack?"

Goldman nodded, and watched as she went into the kitchen. Gaining her confidence hadn't been as difficult as he had at first thought. A few stupid jokes and the ice had been broken. He discovered that her name was Christina Walham-Price, and she was a stockbroker with a small city firm. Benny had been an occasional date, her "bit of rough", and she was knocking on his door because he was supposed to ring her in the week and hadn't. Tina wasn't used to being ignored, and thought he was dropping her. "If there's any dropping to be done, sweetie, I'm the one who's going to do it," she told him. She didn't know what Benny did, and hadn't wanted to pry.

"Let's face it, he wasn't another broker, right? And what I don't know won't hurt me."

On the face of it she was everything Jack disliked: she was the kind of yuppie who was ruining the old London he loved, she was socially divorced from anything he knew and liked, and worst of all she was unashamed about screwing criminals. Yet despite this, there was something about her that attracted him. Jack hadn't thought about women for some time. Not since the divorce: that, the slow decline in his grandfather, and the pressure of work had been more than enough of a distraction. But Tina was having an effect on him.

He was sure she was eyeing him up because she fancied him. He shifted on the sofa, easing the pressure on a part of his anatomy that was springing to life.

"Chrissakes, son, she might be a suspect," he muttered to himself.

"You say something?" Tina put the delicate bone china cup and saucer down on the carpet beside him.

"Just wondering how Errol's doing."

"Who?"

"My partner – the guy we left upstairs."

"Oh." Her face darkened as she remembered what she had seen. She sat down opposite Jack. "Look, I really don't know anything about what went on up there, y'know. Benny and me just had a nice time now and again. That's all it really was, y'know? A few nights out and a few nights in. There's nothing I can tell you."

"Okay, that's fair enough." Jack looked down at his cup. The thought of Tina and Benny in the throes of coitus made his chest knot up. And it didn't make his next question any easier. He asked it without looking at her. "We know that Benny went missing about a fortnight ago. But we don't know when exactly. Not yet. Have you, in the last . . . I mean, did you. . ."

"Have I fucked him in the last two weeks?" Her voice was flat and calm. "No, sweetie. The last time was – oh, fifteen days ago. No, sixteen. It was a Friday night. He told me to. . . well, he made me leave early. Said he had some business."

"Did you see anyone on your way out?"

She shook her head, and was about to add to this when there was a sharp rap at the door. She looked around, distracted.

"That'll be Errol," Jack said as he rose to his feet. He was glad that she had been cut short, and at the same time irritated with himself.

When he opened the door, Errol indicated with his eyes that he wanted a private word. Jack stepped out into the hall and pulled the door shut behind him.

"What gives?" he asked.

"I had a little snoop around before the socco and forensic teams arrived. They were not happy, and gave me grief. 'You should know better', and all that crap. They wouldn't know proper policing if it hit them in the mouth."

"Spare me the lecture, man. What did you find?"

"Benny's stash. Nose candy."

"Where?"

Errol snorted. "In the fucking cistern."

"Jesus Christ on a bike." Jack slapped his forehead in exaggerated exasperation. "What a dumb schmuck. If he carried on like that all the time, it's a miracle we never caught him."

"Maybe there were other reasons. You know the stories. Look at Anderson. Early retirement my black ass. It was only the rolled-up trouser boys that kept him out of court."

"Tush, tush. You know the masons are a fine, upstanding bunch of men. . . sometimes. I take your point, though. Anything else?"

"There were some stains around the bath. Blood, probably. If Benny kept any paperwork it wasn't at home. Not much to go on, is it? What about blondie?"

"She doesn't know much. Make that nothing," he added hurriedly.

Errol eyed him suspiciously. "What gives, Jack?"

"I dunno what you mean."

"I mean that you're just a bit too certain about her. Especially after only a few minutes' questioning."

"It's been more like half-an-hour, actually," said Jack.

"Don't bullshit me, man." Jack had turned his face away, but Errol grasped him by the shoulder and swung him back. His eyes burned into Jack. "I know I said you hadn't been out with many women lately, but I was just joking, Jack. I didn't expect you to try and pull."

Jack cracked a grin. "More like the other way round. I swear she's eyeing me up."

"So Jack walks bent double, eh?" Errol punched him on the arm. "Look, I've got to talk to her."

"Why?"

"Think about it. Benny has nose candy. She's screwing Benny. What's the betting Benny spices up their lovelife with a quick toot?"

"Okay. But she ties me up in knots, man. You're going to have to ask her."

Errol shook his head sadly. "I'm going to have to get you out more at nights, Jack."

He pushed open the door, and Jack followed him into the room. Tina was still seated on the sofa. It didn't seem as though she had moved while they were outside, but Errol assumed that she had at least tried to listen. He adopted his best distant-but-friendly manner.

"My name is Ross, madam. I'm Jack's partner, and there's something I must ask you. Were you aware that Benny Grazione was a drug user?"

She shook her head. Errol fixed her with a hard stare,

searching for any sign that may betray her apparent calm.

"So he never used drugs in front of you?"

She shook her head again. "Would you like some tea, mister Ross?"

"Uh, yeah, sure." Errol was temporarily disarmed by the manner in which she seemed to be totally unfazed by his questions. When she was in the kitchen, he said to Jack: "What's her game, then? She must have known."

"Would you admit that you used coke in front of two old bill?" Jack asked with a wry grin.

"Good point," nodded Errol. "Ah, thank you," he continued in a louder voice as Tina re-entered the room and handed him a cup.

She sat down opposite and folded her hands in her lap. "Okay. . ." she paused, trying to weigh her words. Jack and Errol exchanged glances. "If I tell you guys something, will it get me in shit?"

"Depends what it is," Errol said cagily.

She nodded. "I did know about Benny's habit. It was coke, right?" She continued without waiting for confirmation. "I know it was because he gave me some last time I saw him. I've used it before, but I don't make a habit of it. I wanted some more, that's why I was knocking at his door today."

"Why are you telling us this?" Jack asked.

She looked him in the eye. "Because I want things to be above board. I don't want to hide anything. I don't know what Benny did, and I didn't want to know. I just screwed the guy, and last time he gave me some coke –"

"'Bout the only damn' time in his life Benny gave anyone anything," Errol muttered.

She fixed him with an icy glare. There was an equally cold edge to her voice when she continued. "I'm telling you this because I don't want trouble. I figure that the only way I can keep out of this is by telling you the truth from the beginning."

She told Errol the same story she had told Jack, with the addition of Benny's little habit. Errol took notes, and thanked her for her frankness.

It was only later, when they had finished with the forensic and SOC teams, and were searching Benny's flat, that Errol voiced his concern.

"There's something about that woman that I don't trust."

"Like what?"

"I dunno, there's just something that sets off the little bells at the back of my mind."

Jack put down the pile of bills, chequebooks and miscellania that he had taken from a drawer. "I think she's on the level."

"That's because you want Benny's sloppy seconds, man."

"No way. . ." Jack turned back to the papers, aware that Errol was still studying him.

Aware that Errol was right.

CHAPTER FIVE

Monday was a bright morning. Jack Goldman lay awake in his bed and watched the sun rise through the dusty patterned curtains. His wife had put them up before leaving and he'd never got around to changing them. They were thin, and the encroaching dawn lit the room with a pale light.

Jack reached over to the bedside table and groped for a packet of cigarettes. It was an instinctive thing: he'd given them up about a year before, but always did this when he had to call on the relatives of a murder victim. And that's what Benny Grazione was, scumbag criminal or not.

He sighed as his hands found nothing. Maybe he should get up and make some tea or coffee. Maybe take a shower.

He stayed where he was, staring out of the window, watching the sky light up through the crack in the curtains. He hadn't slept well. Tina had haunted his dreams, chasing him with an axe. He wondered idly if that was what they had used on Benny's hands, or if it had been a chainsaw – perhaps a butcher's cleaver? He doubted if they'd be able to tell now, considering the condition of the corpse and its hands.

Jack hadn't been sleeping well of late: he felt like everything was getting on top of him. He was no longer in control of his life. Everyone around him seemed to be slipping away in some way, and the life he was leading seemed to have no relation to the one he had led just a few months before.

Jack felt on the edge, in danger of slipping over the precipice. But into what?

He sighed and dragged himself out of bed, casting a glance at the digital alarm clock. Six twenty-three. He doubted if he would see Benny's family before ten. Plenty of time to shape up.

Jack pulled the curtains back, letting the light flood into the room.

"Sometimes I hate this job," he said quietly. There was no one there to listen, after all.

***

"Good morning, good morning, good morning, my sweet, sweet child. Do you think you could do your Uncle Errol a little favour?"

Errol Ross, in an immaculate dark navy suit, grasped WPC Wendy Coles around the waist and swung her off her feet.

"Put me down, you stupid sod," she squealed. Two of Plaistow's finest stuck their heads around the door of her little office and laughed. She dismissed them with a few well-chosen words.

"Such language towards one's fellow officers," tutted Errol as he put her down. "Now then, this little favour –"

"Won't be so little, will it?" The small, blonde collator fixed him with a hard stare.

"Now did I say that?" Errol was all mock innocence.

Wendy turned back to her files and card index. Trays and drawers of cards ran around the room, detailing every villain and suspect around the area covered by Plaistow, cross-indexed with those whose residence spilled into other parts of east London but were prone to offending not so close to home.

"Errol Ross, the hard man of Plaistow division, does not come in and swing collators off their feet – male or female – unless he's after something that would take him too long a time and too much effort. Am I right?" She turned back to him, her stare still steady.

"Can't I say hello to my favourite WPC before I ask her something?"

She laughed despite herself: "No, you can't. Your favourite WPC, indeed. What are you after, Errol?"

Errol became serious. "Benny Grazione."

She winced. "Nasty way to go. Someone really didn't like him. Not that I'm surprised." Without even looking, her hand reached out for the relevant drawer, and Benny's card was withdrawn. She gave it a cursory glance. "It's more a question of what he didn't do than what he did. Could be any one of a number of people got it in for him."

"That's very true. But what I really want to follow up is something Arnie Shawcross said yesterday. He told me that a few of Benny's gang hadn't been around. Benny might have been a little shit, but he ran a tight ship. Always knew where his boys were. They wouldn't just go walkabout."

"You don't seriously think there's been a gang war going down?"

Errol shrugged noncommittally.

"But we would have heard about it, surely?"

"Maybe not. It's only been the last couple of weeks, maybe three at the most. With Benny missing, things have got a little slack, right? No action, anyway. . ." He trailed off, leaving her to make her own conclusions.

"Okay," she said slowly, "so what do you want from me?"

Errol grinned broadly. "The names of Benny's gang cross-referenced with any bodies that have turned up. If they were minor gang men then we may not have caught on to what's going down. And any unidentified bodies, as well."

"Is that all?"

He grinned again. "I'm not asking too much, am I? Besides," he leaned forward and tickled her under the chin, "I might take you out and show you a good time. If you're really good. . ."

Wendy laughed. "Errol Ross and little me? What was it your granny used to say? Something like never screw –"

"– white women," he finished in a weary tone. "Jack bloody Goldman. I wish I'd never told him."

***

Ross was finished in the station by a quarter past nine. He had agreed to pick Jack up and travel with him to see Grazione's mother. He drove the short distance from the station to Jack's house, pulled up and sounded his horn three times. He stayed in the car, engine ticking over.

There was no sign of a response from the house. Errol tapped impatiently on the steering wheel, and sounded the horn again. There was still no response.

"Once more, Jack, then I'm out of here," he muttered under his breath. He was about to bang down on the horn when the front door opened, and Jack shuffled out.

"Jesus, you look terrible," said Errol as Jack slid into the car without even a greeting.

"I feel it," Jack snapped. He knew Errol was right: he was unshaven, his eyes were dark-ringed and bloodshot, and he was dishevelled. A quick run under the shower had failed to liven him up, and his still wet hair was straightened from its natural curl, slicked back to his head.

"Man, I think Benny's mob won't know who the corpse is when we turn up," Errol said as he turned out of Jack's street and onto Bow Road.

"I haven't been sleeping well lately," grumbled Jack. "I can't help it. I've got a lot on my mind."

"As long as you can concentrate on what we need to do right now. . ."

"Yeah, it's okay. Stop here, will you?" Jack vaguely gestured about fifty yards ahead.

Errol indicated, slowed and pulled in, to be greeted by a barrage of honking from cars behind.

"If you weren't up my arse, you wouldn't have to do that," he said, making a mental note of the licence plates of the two cars that had honked. He had a good memory for numbers, and in his temper he vowed to run them through the computer when they got back to the station. Just in case there was anything he could get them on.

Jack got out of the car and disappeared into a newsagent, returning moments later with a pack of cigarettes.

"I thought you'd given up," Errol said quietly as his partner settled back into his seat.

"So I'm starting again. Arrest me," said Jack with ill humour.

Errol shrugged, and pulled out into the traffic without another word.

They maintained an uneasy silence for the rest of the journey. Errol wanted to ask Jack what was going on in his head: they'd been together as a team for a long time. About four years, he supposed. Maybe not long by most people's standards, but longer than he would have thought anyone could put up with him. He'd seen Jack go through mental turmoil when his wife first left him, and he'd been with him the day that Jack had heard about his grandfather's terminal illness. But he'd never seen him like this: so low and demoralised. At every junction and every red light he stole a glance at Jack, who sat brooding and chain-smoking. In the fifteen minutes it took them to reach the Isle of Dogs in the morning traffic he had smoked half the packet.

They pulled up outside the concrete jungle that was Sorensen House, home to the Graziones. Errol breathed in the relatively clean air as he got out of the car, then sniffed the lapel of his suit.

"If I have to put this in for dry cleaning, I'm making you pay half, okay?"

"Sure, sure," muttered Jack, slamming the car door. He looked up at the twenty-three story tower block. "Sorensen House. Nice Aryan name."

"So what are Benny's family doing here?" asked Errol with a caustic glance at the graffiti that littered the walls. The British National Party, the National Front, and the slogan "wogs and pakis out" appeared to be favourite.

Jack and Errol walked across the litter-strewn pavement, past abandoned shopping trolleys that were mating by the kerb, and entered the block. The safety glass in the door had been kicked out, the entry-phone system installed by the council in the late seventies was reduced to a burnt out hole in the wall, and a collection of used condoms and needles had settled near the elevators.

"Nice place, man. Real nice," Errol murmured as he pressed the call button. They stood waiting for the lift, but there was no sign of life. Not even the grinding of distant machinery.

"Fuck it." Jack kicked at the metal doors. "How can people live in shit like this?"

Errol decided not to answer, and followed Jack up into the dark stairwell.

"What floor are they on again?" Jack asked.

"Nineteenth," Errol replied.

"Shit, I was really hoping I'd remembered it wrong…"

They climbed the stairs in silence, breathing heavily as they reached the tenth floor. The doorways onto the corridors of

47

each floor all looked the same. They were scarred by fire and knife gouges, coloured by pen and spray paint proclaiming the ascendancy of different gangs.

It was on the twelfth floor that they came across the gang currently at the top of the tree. Jack rounded the corner to find the landing occupied by six teenage boys, all of whom should have been in school. There was the suffocating smell of glue coming from a plastic bag lying on the floor. The kids were glassy eyed, and strung across Jack's path.

"Out of the way," he growled.

"You what?" slurred the biggest kid. He looked about fifteen. "Who you fink you fuckin' are, then?"

He squared up to Jack, who was in no mood to be impressed.

"Just move, son," he said wearily.

"Yeah, sure. When you've said please, and paid me to pass." The movement was imperceptible, but suddenly a Stanley knife appeared in the boy's hand. The vicious - blade gleamed dully in the dim light of the stairwell. Jack noticed that the other kids had lined up behind their leader.

Errol turned the corner behind Jack. He took the situation in at a glance, muscles tensing ready to spring if necessary.

"Yo, man, look at the spade," laughed one of the kids. He pointed at Errol's suit. "Nice threads. Don't come cheap. Maybe we'll let you get away without it getting cut."

"Oh, you are so hard and I'm so scared," said Errol with as much sarcasm as he could muster. He was stuck behind Jack, so his partner would have to take the brunt of the first attack, no matter what.

But Jack wasn't about to wait: he was ready to take the initiative. Swearing under his breath he rocked forward on the balls of his feet and grabbed the kid with the knife. His hands held bunches of filthy shellsuit material as he pulled the kid off balance. His knee came up to meet the kid's groin, and the knife clattered on the concrete stairs.

Errol was past Jack in a flash, and crashed his fist into the face of the next kid as he was about to thrust a flicknife at Jack. The kid crumpled, screaming as blood spurted from his split nose and lips. Errol didn't wear his silver rings entirely for decoration.

The other four wavered slightly, unsure if they wanted to overwhelm the intruders or take a beating.

Jack picked up the Stanley knife and hauled the leader to his feet by the strip of hair on his otherwise shaven head.

He held the tip of the knife to the kid's cheek.

"Right, which one of you bastards is next?"

They fell back against the wall. Jack walked slowly past them, still dragging their leader, who was whimpering about his hair. Errol followed with a nervous glance. Not at the gang, but at Jack: he was close to being out of control.

When they were a few stairs up, Jack threw the kid back down to the landing. He held up the knife.

"I'm going to hang on to this, okay? And you'd better not be here when I come back."

He continued up the stairs without looking back. Errol glanced behind: the kids retreated through the door onto the twelfth floor, like insects scuttling back to their nest.

They arrived at the nineteenth floor with no further interruptions, and passed through the scarred door into the corridor. It was dark, all the lightbulbs that were supposed to light the passage having been broken or stolen. From behind every paper-thin front door they could hear signs of life: blaring TVs, crying babies, the arguments of those forced to live in boxes.

Errol shook his head sadly. "Makes me sad to hear people living like this, man."

Jack laughed shortly. "Don't waste your sympathy. Most of them wouldn't know any better. That's the only thing you can say about Benny – at least he got out."

"What number are they?"

"Seven one three. Never forget that…"

They walked down the corridor, past the rows of identical doors, until they came to 713. Jack pounded on the door. They waited. Through the door they could hear the TV, and the sounds of someone moving about.

"Who lives here?" Jack asked.

"His mum. Maybe one of his brothers. One's in Parkhurst for armed robbery – same as the old man. He's still in the

Scrubs. If not the youngest boy, then just his mum."

"Right." Jack nodded. "Well, got to give the old girl time to open the door, right?"

They waited patiently. The shuffling stopped. The TV still blared. Jack and Errol exchanged glances. The black man raised an eyebrow and nodded. Jack started to hammer on the door again.

"C'mon, open the fucking thing," he yelled. "Police. If you don't open up then we'll kick the fucker down."

"Temper, temper," said Errol.

But Jack's tactics worked: the door opened, and a stringy youth of about nineteen in a T-shirt and cut-off jeans greeted them.

"What do you want?" he sneered.

"We've come to see your mummy, little boy," growled Errol, "so drop the attitude and tell her we're here."

"Like I don't know it from the noise you make? Let them in, Frankie."

The voice came from inside the flat, where the volume of the TV decreased. Without a word, Frankie turned his back on them and slouched back into the lounge. Jack and Errol followed.

The dingy room had yellow and red wallpaper with gigantic flowers drooping sadly towards the windows, as if towards the only source of light. The TV flickered in the corner, its images illuminating the junk and cardboard boxes that surrounded the few items of furniture. Errol took in the boxes with a sweeping glance: videos, stereo hi-fi separates, the odd small microwave.

On the TV, Richard and Judy interviewed an animated minor celebrity, ignored by Mona Grazione. The matriarch of the family sat in an old leather armchair, dressed entirely in black, with an incongruous pair of red fluffy house-slippers on her feet.

"I haven't had a visit from the Bill in a long time, boys. Make yourselves at home." She gestured towards a long leather sofa that lay against one wall. It was covered in knitted blankets and old newspapers and magazines. Errol cleared a space and sat down gingerly. Frankie laughed.

"What's so funny?" asked Errol through gritted teeth, dusting off his suit.

"You," replied the youth simply.

"Frankie," snapped the old woman, "bugger off and do something useful."

Frankie scowled at this dismissal and slouched off into another room. Jack waited until he had gone before speaking.

"Quite a little warehouse you've got going here, ma. All his own work?"

Mona smiled. "You know what things are like these days, Mister Goldman. Work is hard to come by, and a boy must do what he can to get by."

"Like your old man?"

"He's a good husband, but. . ." she gestured helplessly. "The same is true of my Angelo."

"Your Angelo is no angel," said Errol in a tone as dark as his mood. "Three building societies and two shot cashiers will attest to that. He was damn' lucky one of them didn't die."

"An occupational hazard," she shrugged.

"For who?"

"For both of them." She picked up the remote control and switched off the TV. The minor celebrity vanished to a dot, and the room grew darker. It was harder for Errol or Jack to pick out her face in the gloom.

"You haven't come here to talk about anyone other than my Benny. You have to get the bastards who did it." There was a catch in her voice. For a second Jack almost felt sorry for her.

For a second.

"So that's how you know who were are," said Errol. "You've been expecting us, then?"

The old woman nodded, barely perceptible in the gloom. Her chair was back to the window, and the few rays of light that penetrated the room left her in inscrutable shadow.

"Let's get one thing straight," Errol continued. "Benny was a little shit, but we don't like anyone being knocked off like that. Not on our manor. There's enough to cope with as it is, without some kind of gang war."

There was a pause as Mona gathered herself before speaking.

"A war is what you will have. Not from Benny's boys; those idiots will fall apart without a strong leader like my Benny. It's the Chinese, and the cosa nostra you have to worry about. One of them – or both – was behind this."

Jack and Errol exchanged glances. Both were thinking the same thing: an alliance between two gangs who were vying for the same piece of territory was, to say the least, unlikely. But it wasn't the first time that either the triads or the mafia had been mentioned in the same breath as this area.

"How do you know?" Jack asked quietly.

There was another long pause. Then she said: "It's the darkness. It descends on all of us, to pay us back for our sins. God will forgive us for what we have done in this life, but first we must be punished and atone. I pray that Benny has been forgiven."

"What a lot of sanctimonious balls," Errol spat as they left Mona Grazione with her prayers and her electrical warehouse.

"Maybe. Maybe not." They walked out onto the landing of the nineteenth floor, and looked out of the broken window set into the stairwell. "My grandad used to tell me about the dark. It's something the Jesuits instil in you at an early age. The darkness is something that will engulf us all. He's started talking about it now his end's near."

"I always thought you were Jewish," Errol said quietly.

Jack shook his head. "My dad was. My mum's a good old fashioned Catholic, like her mother before her. I hate the whole fucking lot of them."

"But the darkness?"

"I think my grandad was right about that. It's real. Palpable. Look at that lot out there." He pointed out through the jagged edges of broken glass at the people going about their business in the concrete wastelands of the island. "That's the darkness."

They walked down the stairs in silence. Jack brooded on the dark. Errol thought about how little he knew him.

Neither of them realised that the gang on the twelfth floor were still hiding away.

***

"Hello loverboy, I've got something for you." Wendy Coles sat on the edge of Errol's desk, brandishing a file. She crossed her legs and her skirt rode up, revealing an expanse of black nylon-covered thigh. Errol raised an eyebrow.

"It looks nice enough from here," he said wryly, "but I think I'm probably more interested in what's in there." He took the file from her.

Wendy slid off the desk with a dismissive "tut".

"You shouldn't lead a girl on if you're not going to deliver."

Errol grinned slyly. "If I did, you'd run a mile. You know what they say about us coloured folk."

"You're so sharp you'll cut yourself, Errol Ross," she snapped back, smiling all the while. She turned to Jack, who was seated at the opposite desk, with his feet crossed on a pile of incoming paperwork. "You should keep this partner of yours in order, Jack."

"Eh?" Jack pulled the earplugs from his ears, and the sounds of Motown filtered tinnily into the air.

"I said you should keep him in order." She pointed at Errol. "And you should pay more attention to the job."

Jack pulled his feet off the desk, depositing half of the paper onto the floor, and sat forward. "Why? What have you found in there?"

Wendy took the file from Errol's hands and opened it, licking the tips of her fingers to turn the pages with greater speed.

"Five bodies in the last month fished out of the Thames in this stretch. That's up on the average – especially for bodies that show signs of torture before death. Three of them are so far unidentified, but two are extremely interesting."

She paused for effect.

"No dramatics, Wend, please," Jack whined.

"No sense of occasion," she said sadly, before continuing. "One was Dean Arthur, Benny Grazione's second-in-command. He wasn't missing any limbs or appendages, but he did have several broken ribs and a nasty burn that took off half his face. It was only his fingerprints that identified him."

"Actual cause of death?" asked Jack.

"Single bullet wound through the centre of the head."

"Sounds familiar," said Errol heavily. "So that's Benny and his number two out of action. What about the other stiff with a

53

name? One of Benny's boys?"

She shook her head. "No. This will interest you. . .he was Courtney Gold."

Jack and Errol sucked in their breath as one. Courtney Gold was a legend on the manor: the only rival to Benny Grazione in the local gang stakes, he ran a mob who were modelled on the Yardies and were suspected of having links with them too.

"I thought he went back to the Caribbean about a month ago," mused Errol. "At least, that was the word on the streets."

"They're hardly going to admit they'd lost him, are they?" Wendy said pointedly. Jack nodded.

"At least we know that it's not just Benny's gang that are under attack. Could be old Ma Grazione was right."

Errol snorted. "I'd rather drink her piss than agree with her."

"But you might just be doing that." Jack turned to Wendy, his interest now fully awakened. "What about the three unidentified stiffs? Why don't we know who they are?"

She looked at the file and smiled grimly. "You're going to like this: they had no fingerprints, and the faces were pretty badly chewed up. I suppose dental work might turn something up eventually, but at the moment. . ." She tailed off with a shrug.

Jack sat back in his chair, blew out his cheeks, and slapped his legs loudly. "Right then, let's go," he said with an absurd gusto as he stood up.

"Go? Where, for God's sakes?" Errol cast a questioning glance at Wendy Coles. She shrugged and gestured her incomprehension.

Jack lent over his partner and tapped him on the shoulder. "We're going to pay a little visit. I hope you haven't had any lunch yet."

"You know I haven't, I've been with you all – oh shit, you're not serious, are you?" Suddenly it dawned on Errol what Jack meant.

Jack smiled. The first time all day. He should be worried when the only thing to make him smile was a visit to the morgue.

"Have fun, boys," Wendy trilled after them.

***

It was cold and bright, and stank of disinfectant and formaldehyde.

"Y'know, I think it's the smell of these places rather than the bodies that turn my stomach," mused Errol as they waited for the attendant to open the first of the three metal drawers they had asked to inspect.

"What turns my stomach is the fact that I'm actually enjoying this," whispered Jack as the attendant turned his back on them. He was a thin, middle-aged man with greasy hair, who looked as though he would be more at home in one of the drawers than among the living.

"You mean you're getting your jollies out of looking at dead bodies?" Errol raised a quizzical eyebrow.

Jack barely stifled a laugh. It would have seemed inappropriate here of all places.

"No, I don't mean that. I mean that I'm actually looking forward to a gang war of some kind. Like it's a distraction, or something. Like it's going to keep my mind off other things. I feel like a real sicko."

Errol didn't answer immediately. He watched the attendant pull out the drawer and pull back the shroud. He shivered, and not just because of the low room temperature. As he moved towards the body, he said in an undertone: "You want to talk about this later, I'm ready. But right now. . ."

All three men stood over the corpse, looking down. It was the body of a half-Chinese, half-black man, aged about thirty, with good musculature and close cropped hair. It was hard to tell if he had been handsome, as his face was missing, raw flesh and pulped bone replacing features. His chest had a lateral scar from the autopsy.

"Any ideas?" whispered Jack.

"Yeah." Errol tried to whisper too, but it caught in his throat, and he had to cough before speaking again in a more regular tone. "Yeah. See that tattoo?" He indicated a dragon on the man's left arm. "That's Tommy Lee Cheung. I'd know that arm anywhere. Best left hook in the whole of Limehouse. Bastard decked me with it one night when I was PC, down at the George."

"I didn't know Tommy was out of circulation."

Errol nodded. "He's been allegedly legit for the past year and a half. Inherited his old man's takeaway on the Mile End Road. Rumour has it that his mum added soul food to the menu."

Jack smiled wryly. "Nice little front, wasn't it? I reckon he was still working for Courtney. Must have been."

"Unless it was an old score?"

Jack shrugged. "Possible. What about the others?" he continued in a louder voice.

The attendant pulled out two more drawers and folded back the shrouds. Without a word, he returned to his small desk in the corner of the room and started to read *Penthouse*.

"Jeez, some people are weird," murmured Errol with a backward glance as he stepped forward to look at the second corpse.

"Part of the job," Jack replied. "Recognise him?"

The remark was partly ironic. The corpse was of a caucasian man in his late thirties or early forties. He had no tattoos or distinguishing marks. His fingertips had been severed, but he still had most of his face. However, the amount of time the body had spent in the Thames had distorted the flesh until it bore only a passing resemblance to humanity.

"No idea who he is, but it's got to be the same people behind it, right?"

Jack nodded agreement. "Poor bastard was such a no-mark that even when someone took the trouble to get rid of him he wasn't recognised."

They moved on to the last corpse. Another caucasian, but younger. Again, the fingertips were missing, and the face distorted. Again, they failed to recognise him.

They left without a word. The attendant didn't even look up.

When they were outside, Errol took a deep lungful of air. "Man, that feels good. Whoever is behind this, they're thorough. You've got to give them that."

"What do you mean?" Jack lit a cigarette and drew heavily on it.

"They're going for big boys and little boys. I'd lay you better odds than any bookie that the two John Does are part of Benny's gang, or Courtney's. They started with the little fish, and then got the sharks."

"Does this mean it's over?"

Errol stared hard at Jack, brow furrowed. "Aw, come on. You know better than that."

Jack knew what he meant: whoever was behind the killings would want to stop the gangs reforming and regrouping. If necessary, they would go on until every last member was dead.

They hardly exchanged a word on the way back to the station. Errol was still puzzling over Jack's earlier comments about looking forward to a gang war. Jack was thinking about that, too. Finally, he decided to speak.

"Look, when I said I was looking forward to a gang war, I didn't actually mean looking forward. . ." he emphasised the last two words heavily. "I just mean that, with my grandad dying and the wife being such a bitch over letting him see the boy. . .well, I guess I was looking at it as something to occupy my mind."

Errol pulled into the station yard. He parked, switched off the engine and sat in silence for a second. Jack watched intently, wondering what his partner would say.

"This is going to sound real dumb, but maybe you should take a break. A week off, or something. Put in for some compassionate leave. Just until you get this thing with your wife sorted." It suddenly struck Errol that, for all he believed he cared about Jack, he couldn't remember the name of his wife. He also realised how crass he sounded.

"Maybe I will," said Jack quietly.

As they went into the station, the duty sergeant stopped them. "The boss wants to see you, and quick. So you'd better iron out the stories about where you've been this afternoon." He walked off laughing. He tried to spend as much time in the local pub as possible, and thought all policemen did the same.

Jack and Errol exchanged glances, and went up the third floor, where Detective Superintendent McAllister's office was. He had been their superior for a year, following his transfer from west London. He hated them, and they weren't exactly fond of him, either. It was a meeting neither of them relished.

Errol rapped on the door. "Come", bellowed a voice from

inside. They exchanged glances again, and Errol unconsciously straightened his tie.

Jack opened the door on a stocky man in his early to mid-forties with a pronounced gut and close cropped, receding mousey hair. His thin moustache was flecked with grey.

His eyes were hard and unblinking as he demanded: "Right, you two. What the fuck are you doing about this scumbag Grazione?"

CHAPTER SIX

Wednesday night, half-past ten. The back room of the Blind Beggar was filled with the smell of stale cigarette smoke, stale beer and sweat. Six men sat clustered around a small, round table in the centre of the room, surrounded by a blueish haze. A single light, powered by a low wattage bulb, shone dully upon the table.

The monthly meeting of the Plaistow Avengers was in session. It was a name McAllister had given them in jest at the beginning of their short career. It was a name they all took seriously now.

"I spoke to Ross and Goldman on Monday," McAllister growled in an undertone. They all spoke in undertones here. You could never be too sure.

"What do they know about us?" The speaker was George Cann, twenty years in the force and, like McAllister, sick of the way that the bigger criminals could evade justice. It was his discussions over a few shorts with McAllister that had started the Avengers.

"They don't know shit," laughed McAllister. "They reckon it's the fuckin' mafia or the tong. Stupid bastards."

"But they could find out." Cann drained his glass. "We'll have to be ready to deal with 'em."

"Hang on, that's not part of our brief." Laurence James, detective sergeant on the CID and a handy man with a butcher's cleaver, raised his objection. "I thought we were going after scum?"

McAllister spat dismissively on the floor. "Goldman's a fuckin' kike, and he's on the edge of a breakdown. Worried about his poor old grandad." He adopted a mocking tone. "Worried about his poor little son." His voice switched back to an edge as hard as his eyes. "Don't worry about him. He'll be off the force in a week or two. I know that Ross is asking him to take compassionate leave."

"How the hell do you know that?" said James.

McAllister tapped the side of his nose. "I've got my sources, son, don't you worry."

Cann laughed harshly and turned to James. "You know that tasty blonde bit? Coles, her name is." James nodded. Cann laughed again and winked at McAllister. "Well, guess who's knocking her off?"

The laughter around the table was hard and nasty, interrupted by a knock at the door.

"Who's that?" barked McAllister. Five pairs of hands delved deep for hidden weapons. Only McAllister kept his hands on the table.

"It's only me, Mister McAllister. I've got your order." Arnie Shawcross's deep northern tones were tremulous and hesitant.

"Well bring it in, you little fart," laughed McAllister, cracking a huge grin at the rest of the group, who had relaxed at the sound of Arnie's voice.

Shawcross opened the door and carried the tray laden with glasses to the table. He nervously placed it between McAllister and Cann, stepped back a pace and cleared his throat. McAllister picked up a pint glass and said wearily: "What is it, Arnie?"

"I j - just wanted to say, Mister McAllister, that I'm really chu- really pleased, like, that you're having your little meetings here. It's helped to keep trouble down out front, like, and –"

"You haven't been telling people, have you Arnie?" McAllister's voice was little more than a whisper, but carried more menace than the loudest shout.

"No, of course not Mister McAllister. But word gets around, don't it?" Arnie swallowed hard, felt the sweat gather on his forehead. Benny Grazione may have been a hard man, but he liked people to know about his Saturday meetings. McAllister was different. He might be the filth, but he was far more dangerous than Benny could ever have been. "I don't know what you're doing here, do I?" he continued after an ominous silence. "And I don't want to know, do I?"

McAllister turned around in his seat and fixed his gaze on Arnie. The sweating barman noticed that this steady gaze was matched by every man around the table. His guts ran molten with dread, and he feared he would lose control of his bowels.

"I believe you, Arnie." McAllister's voice was little above a whisper, and Arnie had to strain to hear it. "But you watch what gets said. Tell me. You hear?" Arnie nodded. "Good. Now piss off and let us get on with it."

He turned back to the table, and Arnie Shawcross scuttled out of the room in relief.

"What the fuck were we talking about before that little shite came in?" asked McAllister.

"Goldman and Ross," Cann answered, still paring down his nails with the knife. "You were saying you can put Goldman out of action soon."

"Yeah," McAllister nodded. "He's not the problem. It's Ross."

"Fuckin' nigger," muttered one of the group, who had so far stayed silent. "I dunno why they let 'em in."

"I don't want none of that shit," snapped McAllister. "I don't like Ross because he's too clever. Far too clever. Given the right circumstances I would've asked him to join us. But he's too straight. He hasn't got a clue about Grazione because he's not thinking straight. Goldman is worrying him. They care about each other, like we were all supposed to do at one time. But he's a good copper. When Goldman's gone, it may not take him long to pick up the thread."

"So how do we stop him?" asked James.

"I say we ice the fuckin' nigger," muttered the silent man. Barry Winston was also a paid-up member of the British National Party, but he kept this quiet. He had volunteered to kill Courtney Gold.

McAllister shook his head. "No, we can't do that. It'd be too conspicuous. Kill a sleaze and no-one cares. Kill a copper and we get prime-time TV. Especially if he's black." He paused, gnawing his bottom lip in thought. "Leave him with me. Remember that I'm his superior. I'll put him on something else."

"Yeah, you could always put me on the murder," smiled James. "I still don't know why you put them on it in the first place."

"Wasn't me, was it?" snapped McAllister. "I was off sick when Benny's body was found. Anyway, you're on the Gold case. If I tied them together. . ." He shrugged, leaving them to draw their own conclusions.

"Look, I don't wanna step out of line," said Winston, "but I thought we came here to talk about rubbing out some more scum."

McAllister nodded. "We did. Let's get to work."

***

Sunday night. A week since the recovery of Benny Grazione's body. Time for another addition to the slaughter.

The Wang-Ho Chinese restaurant was in Marple Street, just off the Bow Road. It had first been established in the early fifties, and had been a family-run business for more than forty years. Until late last year, when a Hong Kong Chinese had arrived in the area, and made the Hong family an offer they couldn't refuse. It wasn't the money that swayed David Hong's decision, although that in itself was a tidy sum. Rather it was the way in which his seven year-old daughter went missing for a few hours after school. She turned up at eight o'clock in the evening, deposited on his doorstep by a Chinese in a Mercedes. She told her parents that she'd had a wonderful time, and that this man had picked her up, claiming to know her father, and had taken her to McDonalds, then on to see a Disney movie before dropping her home.

She had thoroughly enjoyed herself. But the message was implicit.

David Hong sold up to the Hong Kong Chinese a few days later.

The nominal owner was never seen on the premises, and the takeaway continued to operate much as before. With one exception. Above the shop, where Hong and his family had lived, there were no tenants. Instead there an office with a reinforced safe, and a small laboratory in which incoming shipments of drugs were tested for their purity.

The Triads were small in this area of London, but were

always looking for chances to expand. They had heard about the deaths of Benny and Courtney, and had looked on them as gifts from the Gods. The opinion from on high was that the mafia must be behind it, but if they were quick they could jump in and fill the trade gap first.

Over the past three days, the activity in the upstairs rooms of the Wang-Ho had increased. There were men sleeping on the floors, and the labs were working overtime on new shipments. With Benny and Courtney gone, the drugs market in this corner of London was wide open. Coke, hash, smack, crack, E. . .the punters were out there, waiting for new supplies. And the Chinese wanted to be first on the block.

The takeaway downstairs had been shut since Wednesday, a "closed due to family bereavement" notice hanging lop-sided in the window.

The six men in bomber jackets and ski-masks left their van around the corner in Hope Crescent. It made the more observant of them smile, as hope was something the Chinese would soon be short of.

McAllister checked his watch. Quarter to twelve. The streetlights bled a faint yellow light on the group. Most of the lighting in the street had been broken and not repaired. There were deep pools of shadow. Cann noted them: the cover of darkness may be useful.

James shrugged his shoulders and coughed quietly. "How many do you reckon there are in there?"

"Dunno. Used to be two in the shop, one in the kitchen, and four upstairs. Probably more now." Cann looked hard at James. "Your bottle going then, son?"

James shook his head. "Just trying to work out the odds."

"Well don't. Just do it. That's what we've got these for." Cann unzipped his jacket and pulled out the stem of an Uzi.

McAllister gestured, and they split into two groups of three, as per their pre-arranged plan. Cann, James and Winston went to the back of the shop, with McAllister and the other two members of the group – Simon Day and Peter Fitch – taking the front. Day and Fitch were, like Winston, uniformed constables who had seen more than enough.

McAllister knocked on the door of the shop. Inside was

dark, faintly illuminated by the light filtering through from the kitchens. There was no response to his first knock, so he bunched his fist and banged harder. The glass shook in the door frame.

A figure appeared, silhouetted in the kitchen doorway. "Can't you read? We're shut," it shouted in a barely accented voice.

"Open up, I wanna eat," McAllister replied in slurred tones. Day and Fitch stood to one side, out of sight.

A faint query in Chinese came from the kitchen.

"Alright, it's only a poxy drunk," the silhouette replied in English. "I'll get rid of him."

The silhouette moved away from the door. As the faint light started to flow from behind him, McAllister could see that he was relatively young. Say, early thirties. Quite muscular. Most importantly, he had a meat cleaver in his left hand.

"Open the fuckin' shop. I'm hungry," McAllister whined. He banged on the door again.

"If you don't piss off, I'll chop your fuckin' hand off," snarled the Chinese. He slid the bolt on the door, turned the key which had been left in the lock, and twisted the knob on the mortice lock.

McAllister quietly slid down the zipper on his jacket and reached inside for the Uzi.

The Chinese opened the door and brandished the cleaver. "If you don't shut up and fuck off I'm gonna –"

He was cut short with a look of shock as McAllister drew the Uzi from out of his jacket and gently squeezed the trigger.

**

Cann, Winston and James slipped quietly up the small and squalid alleyway that ran from the middle of Hope Crescent, parallel with the back of Marple Street. There were discarded and split plastic bags overflowing with rubbish. Rats scuttled quietly in the shadows. The alleyway ran past the rear gardens of Hope Crescent, then took in back entries to both Marple Street and Kitchener Road. The backs of Marple Street were to the left. Cann counted them as they moved down the alleyway. Nine along, they came to the rear of the Wang-Ho takeaway. A wall climbed seven feet into the air, with a small wooden door set in it. Cann, who was six foot two, reached up to test the top of the wall. It had broken glass set in concrete to deter burglars. Any other time, in his role as policeman, he would have applauded this. Now he cursed under his breath.

"Try the door," mumbled Winston. "I know what they're like 'round here. Forget the bleedin' obvious."

Cann gave him a dismissive look, but James reached out and turned the handle on the door. It yielded to his slight pressure, and the door opened with a slight squeak of rusty hinges.

"Told you," said Winston as he checked the catch on his Uzi. "Fuckin' dumb chinks."

They moved in through the door, stealthy and silent. There was little obvious movement in the downstairs back, but the barred windows above were lit. There were no curtains, and James counted six separate figures moving across his field of vision. One of the windows was open, and the chatter of voices mixed with the cracked tones of a badly tuned radio drifted down to them.

"Shit. Six up there at least. What about the downstairs?"

Winston shrugged. "Doesn't matter, does it? We've got these." He unzipped and pulled out his Uzi, patting it with loving care. In the half-light of the yard, his teeth shone white in a vulpine grin.

Cann drew his own Uzi. They were part of a haul taken from Courtney Gold's gang six months before. Cann always found it amusing that Gold was finished off by men carrying his own weapons. Balancing the Uzi in the crook of his arm, he drew out a Smith & Wesson .38 snub nosed pistol from a side pocket. He drew back the catch with a quiet click. The gun was a favourite, bought on an American holiday fifteen years before and smuggled past customs.

"Wait for the signal," he whispered, "and watch for any of 'em that come out for a piss."

The three men stood in the shadows, counting off the seconds.

It seemed like an eternity before they heard the staccato chatter of McAllister's machine pistol.

"Now," hissed Cann. The three men moved forward as one.

***

In the half-light of the shop front the Chinese villain's face registered shock, fear and pain in one split second, strongly enough for it to be visible to McAllister over the top of the chattering the Uzi. The rounds split his body across the chest, running ragged gashes that splattered dark, almost black blood across the shiny tiling of the floor. He fell back, the cleaver flying out of his hand and hitting the mirrored wall, shattering the glass.

McAllister roared as he ran into the shop, Day and Fitch close behind, alert for signs of movement. There was the sound of gunfire from the kitchen, exploding in the enclosed space, and the screams of the dying.

Cann, Winston and James had burst through the back door at the first chatter of McAllister's Uzi. There were three Chinese in the kitchen, their attention distracted momentarily by the events in the shop front. As the flimsy wooden back door was kicked in, one of them spun around. He reached for a gleaming sharp kitchen knife that hung on the wall. Before his hand was even halfway to the knife rack, Cann had shot him with the Smith & Wesson. A well-aimed slug made a neat hole in his forehead, the exit wound splattering blood, brain and bone splinters over his colleagues.

The two remaining Chinese were torn between the front and back. Frozen for just a split second, it was enough for Winston to click back the catch on his machine pistol and spray across them. They jerked in the hail of bullets, looks of shock frozen on dying faces.

"Clear out back," yelled Cann as they moved towards the front of the shop.

"Clear out front," returned McAllister. It was a way of covering themselves: the last thing they wanted to do was kill their own.

McAllister and Cann faced each other at the end of a short passage. The stairs to the upper floor led off. The two group leaders looked at each other, breathing heavily. Cann grinned under his mask – McAllister could tell by his eyes, which had a spark of blood lust insanity.

There were the small sounds of cautious movement from upstairs. The Chinese up there weren't going to risk coming down, and planned to entrench themselves. There was no way that any of the Avengers could take the stairs without being cut down. So far they hadn't encountered any gunfire, but that was only because the element of surprise had been on their side.

Fitch whispered urgently in McAllister's ear. "What the fuck are we going to do now? We can't hang around here for too long. The local nick's only six minutes by car, and someone's bound to have reported the shooting."

McAllister nodded curtly. Fitch was on the staff of the Mile End police station, so if he said six minutes he was being precise. Under the ski mask, McAllister chewed on his bottom lip. He didn't want to rush the stairs: that was a certain way of getting some of his men killed or injured.

"Look in the kitchen," mouthed Fitch, pulling off his mask. He gestured emphatically towards the kitchen, the mask waving in his fist. McAllister knitted his brow. The kitchen?

He watched as the three men opposite stared at each other in confusion. Winston went back and stood in the kitchen, behind the dead bodies. He stood in the spreading pool of blood. He was pointing aimlessly at different items, hoping by luck to catch onto Fitch's meaning. On the other side of the stairway, Fitch was violently shaking his head, mouthing "no, no", and getting more and more agitated.

Finally he had had enough: taking a risk that made McAllister suck in his breath, Fitch took two steps back before launching himself across the gap between the two groups. Automatic fire raked the space a split-second after he crossed it. He landed in an undignified heap at Cann's feet.

"What the fuck do you think you're doing, taking chances like that?" hissed Cann.

Fitch gave him a withering stare. "We've got three minutes by my reckoning and you're arguing about chances? The longer we're here, the longer the odds on getting out."

He pushed past Cann and strode over the bodies, into the kitchen.

"What are you going on about?" whined Winston, confused and angry. Fitch pushed him out of the way, and without a word opened a metal cupboard door. There was a huge drum of cooking oil.

"Get it yet?" His voice was hard and sarcastic. He heaved the drum across the floor, kicking the lifeless bodies out of his way as he pushed the drum through into the passage.

He unscrewed the large metal stopper on the drum, and tilted it. Viscous vegetable oil glooped out with a deep-throated gulp, covering the carpet at the foot of the stairs. It soaked in, spreading across the carpet and darkening it. The dark stain spread rapidly.

"Matches," he snapped. They all fumbled in their pockets, their heavily gloved hands awkward and clumsy now. Fitch pulled on his ski mask.

McAllister tossed a lighter across the gap. Cann caught it and knelt down, flicking the lighter until a small blue flame sparked into life. He fiddled hurriedly with the lighter, hoping that it was adjustable. It was: the flame grew longer. Cann touched it to the carpet, and the oil began to burn. Slowly at first, but quickly increasing in temperature as the burning oil heated more and more of its own slick. Fitch pushed the drum across to the middle of the gap. Bullets whistled down, puncturing the soft metal. More oil leaked out.

"Now go," yelled McAllister.

The two groups split, Fitch going with Cann's group out through the kitchen and into the yard. There were more lights on in the houses than before, and the men ran with their heads down, chests thumping and breath coming hard.

McAllister and Day ran back through the front of the shop, jumping over the dead body of the meat cleaver wielder, and out through the still-open door.

Out front, nothing seemed to have changed. It was if they hadn't been noticed. McAllister knew this wasn't the case when his ears caught the distant sound of a siren, coming ever closer.

He wanted to shout at Day to move it, but found he was concentrating too hard on keeping his own breath for running. His feet pounded hard on the pavement. Day passed him as they turned the corner. Cann had already started up the van, the back doors open. He could see Fitch and Winston in the back, waiting. Day leapt into the open gap, landing sprawling at the feet of James, who sat just behind Cann.

The siren was getting louder. Cann gunned the engine. McAllister felt as though his lungs were about to burst, and swore to God that he would start working out if he was going to do any more of this. He heaved his bulk towards the back of the van, and Winston and Fitch grasped him by the arms, hauling him in.

"Go go go," yelled Winston, pulling the doors shut with a loud crash.

Cann got into gear. The tyres squealed in protest as the van shot away from the roadside, heading into the maze of back streets and away from the direction of the siren.

Back in the takeaway, the Chinese were attempting to negotiate the stairwell. Thick black smoke poured up from the oil and burning carpet fibres, choking them as they tried to get down the stairs. The one in front slipped, unable to see where he was treading. He cried out as he fell down the six or seven remaining stairs, then the cry turned to a scream as the flames licked at him, setting fire to his clothes and blistering his skin.

The others turned and scrambled back to the top. By now, the smoke had drifted up to lend a haze to the entire upstairs. The last Chinese looked down to see the flames begin to spread up the staircase. He thought about the laboratory. With the increase of business, there were more and more chemicals being stored there. The shop would go off like a bomb if the fire spread that far.

Panic seized him, and he pushed his way through to the back room. The window was open, and he was able to suck in some clean air. He pulled at the bars, hoping that they had been in so long that the mortar holding them in place was ready to crumble. But it was still solid, holding the security bars firmly in place. He looked longingly at the kitchen roof, a few feet below, jutting out from the body of the building. It would have been an easy method of escape.

He began to cough heavily, hawking up globs of phlegm as the smoke reached his lungs.

The other Chinese were trying to climb out of the front window. They could get a foothold on the shop sign, but it was still a twenty foot drop from there to the pavement. Not too difficult at the best of times – but this was hardly the best of times. The front of the shop was pouring smoke. The glass in the windows cracked in the heat, and flames began to catch around the outside of the window frames. They had to jump clear of that, and then try to get away.

Sirens seemed to converge from all points of East London. Two police cars and a fire engine, with an ambulance on its way as the police relayed the information that there may be casualties.

One of the Chinese jumped, pushing himself away from the front of the building rather than dropping straight. He proscribed an uneven arc in the air, and hit the pavement awkwardly. He screamed as he felt the bones in his leg grind and mesh together, fracturing and crumbling. A policeman in uniform rushed towards him. The Chinese pulled himself to his feet and tried to hobble away. He only got a couple of yards before the puzzled officer grabbed hold of him, and tried to make him lie still. "You mustn't move, you've been hurt," he kept repeating in a bewildered voice.

Up at the windows, the other Chinese watched what seemed to be an arrest with resignation. They couldn't see much as the smoke grew thicker, lining their lungs and making them cough. It was intensely hot as well, and some of them cast anxious glances at the lab equipment.

The agreement was unspoken: they knew that to try to get out would lead to detention. It would be assumed that they had spoken to the police, and they would soon be dead men. The alternative was to roast or be blown to pieces when the lab equipment went up.

They all checked their guns. As one man, they held the guns to their heads. Some favoured the temple, others put the barrel in their mouth.

Outside, the volley of gunfire made the firemen and police officers look up at the top floor of the shop.

Forty-five seconds later, the roof was lifted off the building by a massive explosion.

***

Marvin Gaye was talking about sexual healing. Errol Ross was hoping to do more than talk.

He moved closer to Denise, laying his head on her shoulder. The video image of Marvin flickered on the screen, moving his hips and singing directly at the camera with those sad and tortured eyes. Denise moved down on the sofa, sliding until she was almost horizontal. She lifted her legs up and entwined them around Errol's body.

"What are you after, boy?" she whispered in his ear.

"If you don't know me by now," he replied, quoting one of her favourite songs at her.

She chuckled deep in her throat, a mellifluous bubbling that always turned him on. "Boy, you are so predictable." She leant over and kissed him, her tongue gently probing into his mouth.

Errol had lived with Denise for three years. Sometimes they talked about getting married, but more to please their families than themselves. She was a beauty technician, which she defined as "hair, nails, and smiles", and worked in the West End at a high class salon. It always tickled Errol that they met when her credit card was stolen and used in a card fraud. "Your beauty arrested me, so I arrested you," he told her. It was a pathetic joke, but it was theirs alone. No-one at the station really knew about her: Errol had seen how the job got on top of some wives, and how it could break up relationships. He tried to leave as much as possible at work. He didn't mind her talking about her work, though. After all, "how much stress is there in filing nails?"

Denise wanted him to leave the force. Her brother had a security firm that handled concerts and festivals. Errol always turned her down: somehow, catching criminals seemed more noble to him than beating up on drunk punters. But he never told her this: her brother was the apple of his family's eye because he had got on. Not many black men ran their own company, especially in East London.

Errol felt out of place among them: streetwise and used to oppression, they expected him to sympathise. But Errol couldn't honestly say that he'd had a hard time of it. His father had been a civil servant who transferred to the British civil service from the Jamaican High Commission when Errol was young. He was brought up in Orpington, in the heart of Kentish commuterland, and had attended a private school.

From there to university, then to police college. It was only then that he began to feel the edge of prejudice. It was a shock. Even now he couldn't understand why everyone, even Denise's family, expected him to wear a back-to-front baseball cap and talk in slang all the time. It just wasn't him. He had his cultural roots, but they had little to do with current street culture.

None of this mattered when they were here alone, though. He returned her passion with an equal fervour, and ran his hand up her thigh, stroking the bare flesh as her skirt rode up around her waist. She reached down to stroke his bulge, making him want her more and more.

"Let's go to bed, sweetheart," she whispered. He disentangled himself and lifted her off the sofa. "Oooh, I love it when you're masterful," she giggled.

He was halfway across the room when the phone went.

"No, not now," he wailed.

"Ignore it, baby," she whispered, tracing the line of his lips with her fingertip.

Errol cast an anguished glance at the phone. "I hate ringing phones. They really wind me up."

"Leave it." She kissed him again. For a second he went weak at the knees and nearly dropped her.

He carried her into the bedroom and laid her on the bed. She lay back, inviting him to undress her. He began to undress himself. Quickly.

But there was a phone by the bed, and it kept on ringing. The incessant repetitive tones drove through his forehead like a nail being hammered in. He undressed more and more slowly. Finally he was naked. He knelt down on the bed, sliding over Denise, rubbing himself against the material of her skirt and blouse. She reached down and felt his manhood.

She sighed. "You're gonna have to answer that phone, baby."

Errol looked down at his rapidly deflating member. "Aw, shit," he said. "I'm sorry, I'm so, so sorry." He gave her a pleading look. She pursed her lips, refusing to respond.

Errol reached across and lifted the receiver.

"Whoever this is, it'd better be good."

"Errol? Where the hell have you been?" It was Jack Goldman's voice. Errol was thrown: he hadn't expected to see Jack until tomorrow morning.

"Jack? What's the matter?"

"Don't talk, just listen. Meet me at Marple Street as soon as you can."

"Where? I've never heard of the place. . . what's this all about, Jack?"

"Never mind that. Just get here, and quickly."

"It's Sunday night, man. I'm not back on duty until tomorrow morning." He looked across at Denise. She sighed and turned away. Errol rubbed his forehead, tried to get his thoughts in order. "Okay. Look, tell me what it's all about, and I'll –"

"Just get here, for Chrissakes, Errol. This is big, and it's nasty. We've got to be in on this."

Errol sighed. "Okay, Jack, I'll be there. Where the hell is Marple Street?"

"It's just off the Mile End Road, near Queen Mary College."

"Near Queen – but that's right off our patch, Jack. We can't go blundering in there."

"Just get here," Jack snapped. The line went dead.

Errol dressed as quickly as possible, all the time apologising to Denise. She ignored him for the most part, her only contribution to the conversation being a diatribe about how he thought more of the job than he did of her. It was an accusation that he had heard levelled against almost every copper he had ever known. Up until now he had managed to avoid it coming his way.

She didn't say goodbye to him. He lived on the top floor of a converted Victorian house, and as he ran down the stairs he tried to put the worry out of his mind: it was the first real challenge to their relationship. A week or two before, he would have told Jack to get lost, wait until tomorrow. But there was something about the tone of Jack's voice that had worried him. Almost a manic excitement. Jack was on the edge. This may be something or nothing: either way, he had to check it out.

It took him less than fifteen minutes to reach Marple Street, including a short stop at the side of the Mile End Road to look it up on the A-Z street map he kept in the glove compartment. Not that Marple Street would have been hard to find: he knew when he was near by the sound of sirens, and the number of ambulances and police cars that were converging on the area.

He parked the car on the corner of Mile End Road, and fought his way through the crowd of bystanders and police gathered around the end of the road. He was surprised at being let through the cordon so easily: he was even greeted by some spotty uniform constable that he'd never seen before. Obviously, tales of Errol Ross were legion around East London's nicks. He wasn't sure if this was a good thing. He made his way down to what appeared to be the heart of the action.

"Holy shit," he whispered as he walked down the street. His eyes were drawn to the carnage surrounding the still smouldering takeaway. Body bags lay on the pavement, ready to be loaded. In the chaos he counted nine, maybe ten bodies.

Jack appeared at his shoulder from out of nowhere.

"I think our lads have just stepped up operations. And they definitely ain't the Chinese. . ."

CHAPTER SEVEN

"But guv, you can't just –"

"I can do what I like, Goldman. I'm your bloody boss, remember?"

"But –"

"No buts, Goldman, no comeback."

Jack pushed his hair back from his face, the tingling in his scalp making him concentrate on what seemed to be a falling-apart world. He leant forward over McAllister's desk.

"You can't take me off it, guv. Not now. I know things have been rough at home, but I can work through that."

McAllister swivelled around in his chair. When he was facing the wall, he said: "Your grandad. He's a paddy, ain't he?"

Jack and Errol exchanged puzzled glances behind his back.

"Yeah, he's Irish," Jack replied suspiciously. "What about it?"

McAllister completed the full 360 degree turn and faced them once again. "Nothing really," he said blandly. "I just wondered why he's a paddy and you're a yiddle."

It was no question, but rather a straightforward insult. Errol rolled his eyes towards the ceiling. Please, he thought, don't let him start saying anything about blacks. I swear to God I'll lay one on him if he does.

He cast a glance over at Jack, who looked both puzzled and annoyed.

If he doesn't first, he inwardly added.

McAllister sat back in his chair, a contented smile on his face. The spring in the swivel section creaked under his bulk.

"At least that's bleedin' shut you up," he said in a satisfied tone. "Now you listen to me, Goldman. Your behaviour in the last week has been erratic. Where were you when they dragged Grazione out of the river? What's all this bollocks about a gang war you're going around spouting, frightening the natives –"

Ross felt he had to interject. "Uh, it was old woman Grazione – the mother of the deceased – who suggested that, sir. We were merely following up on her statement."

He tried to keep his temper under control, to not let it show. If there was one thing McAllister hated more than the Jack's petulant displays of temper, it was the kind of cold arrogance and contempt, with just the vaguest hint of sarcasm, that Errol could put into his voice.

It worked.

"Don't give me that balls," yelled McAllister, rising from his chair with a swiftness that was surprising in one so large. His face was inches from Ross's, and Errol could feel his foetid whiskey breath as he fixed his eyes on a point over McAllister's shoulder. "Jackie-boy here is out there in a bleedin' funeral home feeling sorry for himself and having wet dreams about gang wars, and all you can do is tag along and hold his bleedin' hand to try and get him out of trouble. Well it ain't good enough, son, it just ain't good enough."

He sat down again, shooting his cuffs and smoothing the lapels of his suit, trying to regain a degree of composure. Jack and Errol again exchanged glances. There was suspicion in Jack's gaze that made Errol turn away.

"Now then," McAllister continued in a calmer tone, "if you really want to know what's happening, Goldman, it's this. Your friend and buddy-buddy here came to me and said you needed some leave 'cause you were too fuckin' fried to work properly." From the corner of his eye, Errol could see Jack giving him the kind of stare you don't want from friends: a mix of confusion and hate. McAllister ploughed on: "I reckon you need the time off. After last night, there's going to be ten shades of shit hitting the fan regarding these killings. Some clever bugger in the press is going to tie it all up in some way. I don't reckon they're connected. What did a low-life like Grazione have to do with the bloody Tong, or Triads, or whichever bunch those Chinese were? Now there's a thought for all your conspiracy theories, Goldman. It's the Tong and Triads against each other."

"I thought they were all the same these days," said Jack sullenly.

"If that's your idea of humour, you need a break, son," McAllister said acidly. Then he softened his tone. "I think you're getting fixated on a line of inquiry that's leading nowhere, and you need a break. Even your partner thinks you need one."

McAllister gestured at Ross, who felt as though he might throw up. McAllister ranting and raving with xenophobic venom was one thing: Errol could cope with that. What was worse was the false chumminess and concern that now oozed out of every word. Any minute now, thought Errol, he's going to get up and clap Jack on the shoulder, tell him he's got his best interests at heart.

McAllister stood up, and reached out to lay his hand on Jack's shoulder. Goldman looked at it as though it were some kind of insect.

McAllister took his hand away, coughed to cover his embarrassment. His new tone was conciliatory. "Look, Jack. You've been under a lot of strain. Just take a couple of days, sort a few things out. As for you Ross," he turned his attention to Errol, "I think you should leave the Grazione job to someone else. There's been too much muddy water stirred up already. It needs someone who's coming in fresh."

"I would have thought that any investigation carried out so far would be of value in continuing –"

"Shut it, Ross. You're a good copper, but don't push it." There was an underlying edge to McAllister's tone that gave Errol due warning.

McAllister sat down again and turned his attention to the files and papers on his desk. Jack and Errol walked out in silence. In the corridor, business carried on as usual, with uniforms and plainclothes carrying papers and files, tea and biscuits, to different offices. A low level of conversation throughout the upper floors carried a burble around the building, broken only by the shrilling of telephones. Jack shot Errol a look of pure venom. Errol shrugged. He was about to speak, but Jack didn't want to hear. He turned on his heel and walked down the corridor towards the office they shared with Laurence James and DS Lorna Dobson.

Errol counted ten before following.

Goldman was rifling through the drawers of his desk, pulling out cassettes and half-eaten bars of chocolate, a legacy of the brief period when he had given up smoking. He looked up when Errol entered the room, but said nothing. He had a look on his face that screamed betrayal. Errol wanted to talk to him about his reasons for seeing McAllister, but felt unable to as they weren't alone. Lorna was on the phone, talking to a jeweller by the snatches of conversation he could pick up, and James was pretending to read a file. Errol could feel his eyes flickering up from the page to watch them.

I never did like that honky bastard, he thought.

Jack swept the bars of chocolate into a metal waste bin that was already full of screwed up reports and half-typed documents. He put the cassettes into a plastic carrier bag, where they clanked together in a jumble of cases. From one of the drawers he pulled out a battered paperback, which he tossed at Errol. Ross caught it and looked at the cover. *Power Play*, by Robert Sidleman. "One man, caught between the mafia and the police. The only way out is to die," ran the blurb. Errol looked up from the book. Jack was sitting on the edge of the desk, regarding Errol with a sad, faraway look in his eye.

"Is that what you think?" he asked, gesturing at the book.

"That you've been reading too much of this?"

Jack nodded. "Is that what you've been telling that fat prick? That I'm fucking cracking-up or something?"

Errol shook his head sadly. "No, Jack, it's not like that. You know it isn't."

Jack snorted, shook his head. "No, I suppose not." He sounded resigned, a man at the end of a too-short tether. He'd gone beyond anger and into acceptance. "Maybe you're right. I do need to sort a few things out. I suppose I could do with the time. But I still don't understand why you've got to be taken off Benny's killing. I mean –"

He was silenced by a gesture from Errol, indicating James,

who was obviously listening. Lorna had also finished her phone call, and was replacing the receiver.

"What's the sudden silence, lads?" she asked with a smile. "You don't think I'm eavesdropping, do you?"

Errol smiled at the mousey DS, who was tougher than she looked. "It's not you I'm worried about," he said.

"If you want a bit of privacy, I'm going anyway." She turned her attention to James. "We've got work to do, my old darling. Kominsky's in Wapping have bought some of that blagged gear from Hatton Garden. I think we should pay the old man a visit."

Jack laughed. Maurice Kominsky was nearly eighty, had been a jeweller all his life, and wouldn't know the meaning of the word "straight" even if presented with a plumb-line.

James sighed heavily, and laboriously rose from his chair, slipping on his jacket, while Lorna pulled on her coat and grabbed her handbag.

"Come on, you lazy sod," she said. "We don't want Morry to do a runner before we get there, do we?"

Jack and Errol waited while she ushered James out of the office, closing the door behind her with a wink.

"I don't know how she works with that gobshite," snarled Jack in a low tone when the door had clicked shut. "There's something about him that I just don't trust."

"He's a good copper," said Errol, hitching the knees of his immaculate suit and seating himself in Lorna's chair, putting his feet on her desk. "He gets results."

"Then why don't you trust him, either?"

Errol shrugged and smiled. "I couldn't really say. I think that perhaps he's a little too much like McAllister for my liking."

Jack grimaced. "That's a terrible thought."

"Yeah, it is," returned Errol. "That's why I was starting to worry about you. They've got this driven quality, an obssessiveness that's just totally out of order. Get results, sure – but at what cost? That's what you were getting like."

Jack said nothing. He couldn't look at Errol. He knew that Ross was right, knew that he'd been using that obssessive quality as a cover for his own personal problems.

"Jack?" Errol waited for Goldman to look up. "You know I'm just telling it how it is, right?"

Jack nodded. "It was convenient, yeah? It kept my mind off the things that were really bugging me. I know you were doing the right thing going to McAllister."

"Friends again?"

Jack smiled. "There is one thing that bothers me, though," he continued.

Errol nodded. "I know what you're going to say. Why has he taken me off Benny's murder?"

"Exactly. And even if they're not connected, why the hell isn't he concerned that Benny, Courtney Gold, about half their fucking gangs, and a bunch of Chinese with a drugs lab over their takeaway get wiped out in a few square miles within weeks of each other? Okay, so it may not be a war yet. . . It ain't just me, is it?"

Errol shook his head. "No, it isn't just you. Last night was just a bit too much. If there was nothing big going down before, there sure as hell will be now."

***

Gold Wharf House lay five minutes' walk due east of Canary Wharf, on the Isle of Dogs. It wasn't as tall as the latter building, and it didn't have a beacon that flashed constantly around the whole of East London from a pyramid roof. In short, it didn't have what might be called a high profile. But that suited the tenants just fine. It was one of the only blocks on the island to be fully occupied, a full list of company name-plates filling the floor indicators in the foyer. Smoked glass that could be rendered almost one-way by subtle use of lighting, and cold, sterile, white marble stretched to the elevators, with an ostentatious security guard and attendant cameras accompanying the pretty young receptionist in a cobalt blue suit who sat at the switchboard and desk. Only one guard and only one receptionist. But then again, there was little in the way of traffic in and out of the foyer. Most of the visitors were known by sight, and had to contend with a locked entry-phone door before getting as far as the desk. Most of those who weren't recognised didn't get past the door.

It was an easy life for the receptionist and guard. The entry-phone and bullet-proof smoked glass did most of their work for them, and there was little need for the AK47 and .357 magnum that lay behind the desk, under the receptionist's copy of *Homes and Gardens*.

Monday morning, however, was a little different from other mornings. There had been a steady stream of visitors to the double doors of Gold Wharf House, most of them not recognised by the guard or receptionist. They were kept impatiently waiting while the receptionist rang the third floor ("Quine, MacKay and Potter. Chartered Brokers"), patched the security camera through, and awaited confirmation of identity. Their tempers were not improved when they were searched by the security guard in a small room behind reception, with the receptionist cradling the AK47 casually in the crook of her arm. The temporarily empty reception was hidden from outside view at a flick of the lighting switch.

By mid-day, the receptionist had admitted fifteen men and three women. All had been searched by the security guard, and a motley collection of guns, knives, mace canisters, and two rice flails lay bundled in a corner of the small room. The receptionist was getting cramp from carrying the AK47 casually enough to not frighten the visitors too much, but also tightly enough to whip into action if necessary.

At 12.03 a call came from the third floor, informing her that all the expected guests had arrived. Anyone else who turned up was not expected and under no circumstances to be admitted. There were to be no calls put through. The receptionist put down the receiver and told the guard. He stretched, cracking his knuckles, and wondered if – seeing as they were to be undisturbed for a while – there was any chance of a quick tumble with the receptionist in the small back room. Then he remembered the way she had dealt with that ponce Grazione when he had tried to call on Mr. Quine of Quine. MacKay and Potter. She had damn near broken the man's arm.

That reminded him of something. He wandered over to where the receptionist was leafing through *Homes and Gardens*, dreaming of a country cottage away from the grime of the city.

He cleared his throat. "Uh, Shirley?"

"What." It was a statement rather than a question. Her dream had been interrupted, and she wasn't interested in talking.

"I've been thinking –"

"Don't. It isn't advisable if you work here." From anyone else it would have been a feeble one-liner. From behind those slate-grey eyes it had a hard nugget of truth.

"Yeah, I appreciate that, but. . ." She was looking at him again. In that way. Her finishing school voice and icy manners always reduced him to an inarticulate wreck. Which he wasn't. That was what had got him into the organisation, rather than hanging out with losers and small-timers like Benny Grazione and Courtney Gold. They were the boys he'd grown up with. . . and grown out of.

"Out with it," she sighed. "It's probably irrelevant, anyway."

He took a deep breath. "I was just wondering why there was no-one here from Benny's gang. Or Courtney's."

She raised an ironic eyebrow. "What gangs? They don't exist without their nursemaids. And they're gone. No real organisational ability there."

"Yeah. But if this is about last night, then they've been shafted as well. Before all this, I mean. Maybe they'll know something? I mean, we thought it was the chinks, right? And it obviously wasn't, yeah?"

"Think?" She raised that eyebrow again, and made him feel like a stupid child being scolded by a teacher. "I don't think anything. I'm not paid for that. Neither are you. Leave that to Mr. Quine. It's his department."

***

"These things are regrettable, but not of our doing." Quine stood with his back to the long, polished oak table, staring out of the floor to ceiling glass wall that overlooked the murky Thames. On the far side of the river he could see converted warehouses, council estates, the remnants of light industry: London in flux. The processes of change that gave his organisation such useful openings for business.

Behind him there was an uncomfortable shuffling among the hardwood chairs. The mumble of Cantonese and Mandarin dialects reached his ears. He didn't understand the language, but could sense the confusion. He smiled to himself. Quine was prepared to stand with his back to them all day, until one of them spoke. To turn around would be to yield psychological advantage: he was on his own turf and he wouldn't give in.

Finally, an accented voice came from behind him. "When you say 'not of our doing', are you trying to abnegate responsibility for what has occurred?"

Quine turned towards the table with a wry smile on his face. "'Abnegate'? I'm not even sure that I know what that means, Mister Lao. If you may allow me to speak plainly, what I'm saying is this: we didn't do it. Yes, we knew you had a lab there and were keeping some of your men domiciled on the premises. But we had no reason to attack them. That part of the Mile End Road is yours. Surely our agreement says –"

"If you will pardon me," interjected David Lao, his voice on the surface full of deference and politeness, but carrying a steely and diamond-hard undertone, "our agreement does not, at this moment, mean a thing. It has been breached, surely?"

It was couched as a question, but the meaning was clear. Quine pursed his lips and paused for a moment, considering his answer. Lao's stare pierced through him, and as he looked along the table he could see that the seven Chinese ranged along one side were all regarding him with the same look. It was unnerving, and he felt a bead of sweat start to form in the small of his back, his forehead tingling. On the other side of the table sat four representatives of his own organisation. They were just as angry: unnecessary trouble made their jobs all the more difficult, and there were quotas to meet.

Quine walked across to the table, pulled out the chair at the head, and sat down. He felt eighteen pairs of eyes follow him every inch of the way, making his movements seem slow and sluggish. Once seated, he rested his chin on one hand, and slowly scanned the table. It was more for effect than anything else: he had no idea how he could reassure them.

"Gentlemen – and ladies," he added, acknowledging the three beautiful Eurasian women seated at the end of the table, "I appreciate that the move from Hong Kong to Britain has not been easy for you. You've had to build from scratch, whereas we've had bases here for some years. You've done remarkably well in the circumstances." He cursed himself for sounding patronising. Looking at the bland faces around the table, he found it hard to tell if anyone was offended by his ill-chosen use of words.

"I'm not a man of words, I'm a man of action. That's why I was chosen to develop this area. When I was in Vietnam –"

"You got used to killing gooks," Lao said calmly. "Looks to us like you're getting in more practice."

Quine said nothing. Inside he was fuming, but he tried to keep a cool exterior. His days in Vietnam had been spent leading combat units. He was a trained killer and leader of men. Sitting around in an Armani suit looking at sheets of paper still felt strange. The carefully contrived Ivy League and Harvard manners of Robert Quine were only a veneer that covered the man who still thought of himself as Ragin' Bull Bob of the 17th.

If Lao interrupted him one more time, then Ragin' Bull would come out on top.

"Mister Quine," said one of the women coldly, "we're used to lives being lost. In many ways that is not the point. The men can be replaced. There is, however, the matter of two point seven million dollars: the wholesale cost, of course, not retail. As I'm sure you are aware, we're not in the kind of business where we can be insured, or sue for compensation."

"I appreciate your point," Quine began, struggling to keep control of his temper, "but quite what you expect us to do about –"

"Compensation or retaliation," said Lao quietly. "It's that simple."

The four mob men on the opposite side of the table expressed their exasperation and disbelief in a series of heavy sighs, gestures, and glances at each other. Quine knew that he could not afford to lose face in front of them. Even less to lose face in front of the Triad delegation. His supposed psychological advantage was slowly slipping away with every second.

More than that, his temper had now snapped. He stood up and crashed his fist down on the table, making the glasses of whiskey and Perrier that lined the edges tinkle and shudder. Papers rustled as they moved gently under the vibration.

"Fuck it. I've tried to be nice with you yellow bastards, but you don't want nice. You've made up your fuckin' minds already, haven't ya?" His voice slipped from a cultured Harvard tone into his native Brooklyn. "You've come here to screw us for money. You don't give a shit about the dead guys apart from the loss of face. I fuckin' hate that. I care about my men. If you don't trust the men, then you don't get the job done properly. They know we treat them right. If you were pissed about that as well, then I could understand you. But the money? Jesus fuckin' Christ. . ."

He wheeled away, and walked over to the window, breathing deeply. He could hear the muttering in dialects behind him as the Chinese tried to determine his stance. He could also feel his own men staring at him.

"Look, Bob," began one of them, "what if some of our guys –"

"Our guys nothing," he screamed, wheeling around. "Our guys nothing. You saying that some of us went and –"

"Well. . ."

"Asshole. Where the fuck would that get us, eh? Where? Fuckin' nowhere, that's where." He turned to the Chinese. They were still looking impassive – inscrutable, as white tradition has it. All except for Lao, who was looking thoughtful, studying Quine carefully.

Quine decided to direct his remarks to Lao. "Listen, bub. What the hell do we gain by starting a war with you guys? Didn't we negotiate and give ground to avoid unnecessary waste? If anything, it should be you trying to muscle us out 'cause we showed some kinda weakness in letting you in. Am I fuckin' right? We've both been doing well here, and there's plenty of room for both of us to expand. Jesus, anyone would think I was fuckin' Al Capone from the way you guys are acting. I'm like you, I have to answer to someone else up the fuckin' chain. And I'm gonna have enough trouble explaining all this shit away as it is. You guys aren't the only ones to be hit, y'know?"

"You are, no doubt, referring to the small gangs on the island?" Lao's tone had changed, much to Quine's satisfaction. If not conciliatory, he was at least thinking about what was being said.

"Yeah. The greaseball kid – what was his fuckin' name?" He snapped his fingers at his own men.

"Grazione. Benny Grazione," one of them supplied.

"Yeah, right. And the spade kid."

"Ah, Mister Gold," nodded Lao. "Not the most approachable of men."

"So you tried to talk to him as well, eh?" Quine smiled, but there was little warmth in it. "So you know what these guys were like, yeah? We tried to buy them out or absorb them, and I'll lay good odds that you did as well. Am I right?" Lao nodded. "Right. So you know what little assholes they were. They deserved what was coming to them for being stupid. As a matter of fact, we thought you did them."

Lao actually smiled. "We were sure it was you. Just as we think last night was you. After all, none of your men have been killed, none of your operations broken."

One of Quine's men nodded. "Shit. You gotta admit that he's he got a point there, boss. It don't look good."

Quine silenced him with a dismissive gesture. "Bullshit he's got a point. It just means that we're next in line, that's all."

Lao gave Quine a sardonic stare. "You would say that, wouldn't you?"

There was a moment's tense silence. Quine and Lao were locked in eye contact, the others around the table watching with a mixture of awe and interest. Who would be the first to break the silence? And what would his reaction be?

Quine broke first. His shoulders began to shake, and a grin cracked on his face. He laughed: a harsh, biting sound that cawed through the silence like a wounded rook. But it was genuinely good humoured. Then Lao began to chuckle too. It was nowhere near as full blooded, but nonetheless it was amusement.

The others around the table exchanged glances – both with each other and with their supposed enemies.

Quine walked over to Lao and clapped him on the shoulder. "I like you, boy," he roared. "You're as fuckin' crazy as I used to be. To come in here and threaten us," he shook his head and chuckled, "that really takes some guts."

Lao laughed along with Quine: it was a laugh that lay half-strangled in his throat as Quine's hand on his shoulder slid under the arm, pulling the joint up and almost out of the socket as Lao's face was forced down onto the hardwood. He could smell the furniture polish, choking him. The dull pain in his shoulder flared into fire when he tried to move.

Quine pulled a small automatic from inside his jacket and placed it against Lao's head. His own men looked shocked, and the Chinese were tensed: with no weapons to hand, any attempt to rush Quine would undoubtedly result in Lao's death. Only the two women looked unconcerned by what was happening.

Lao heard the catch click off, felt the cold snubbed nose of the muzzle against the patch of skin behind his ear.

"So if it was us, what's to stop me icing you here and now? This is our building. You walked into it. No way could any of your people get out alive if I didn't want it."

"You wouldn't do that," gasped Lao between sharp, pain-laden breaths. "You do that, you start a war."

"You think I've started one already. What's to stop me?"

There was no answer.

Quine let Lao free. The Chinese slumped onto the desk for a second before slowly straightening up, massaging his shoulder and glaring at Quine with a look that would have meant instant death on his own territory. Quine clicked the catch back on and re-holstered the automatic as he stepped away.

One of the women applauded him. If it is possible to clap ironically, then this she did. The other woman – the one who had spoken before – said: "You make your point in a graphic manner, Mister Quine. I believe you are correct in saying that your men were not behind last night's outrage. This being the case, we must ask ourselves one question. . .all of us." Her gaze took in both the Chinese and Quine's men.

"Exactly," said Quine, straightening his suit. "Who the fuck is behind it?"

CHAPTER EIGHT

The Rising Sun was just around the corner from the station, and was a regular off-duty haunt of coppers who had just clocked off. Jack went straight there to drown his sorrows. He knew Errol would be round as soon as he could get away.

Back at the station, Ross was completing some last-minute paperwork before leaving when James came into the room. Errol barely glanced up, but enough to notice James take a chair and turn it around, straddling the seat and leaning his elbows on the back. He was facing Errol.

"So what's new, James? Morry confessed to a spate of serial killings in Bethnal Green? Or maybe he just shrugged and said he didn't know anything, as usual?"

James smiled. "That's what I like about you, Errol, you keep a sense of humour going."

Errol raised an eyebrow. If James was being nice to him, there was something amiss.

"You know McAllister's putting me on the Grazione killing, don't you?" James continued. Errol stiffened. James could see this, and continued hurriedly: "I reckon he thinks that because I'm on the Gold case already, I can shoot holes in the theory that they're connected."

"Who says they are?" Errol replied cautiously.

James smiled again. "Jack bloody Goldman, for one." Errol was about to mouth disagreement, but James leapt in: "Come on, Errol, it's all over the nick about him. McAllister reckons he's gone doo-lally, but I'm not so sure. He might be a bit hyper-hyper, but that doesn't mean he hasn't got good ideas. I think he may be right."

There was a silence that Errol could only construe as meaningful. Finally he said: "So what do you want me to say about it?"

James shrugged. "I dunno. I just thought that you might share his ideas, that's all. Anything you've dug up so far would be useful to me – you know that."

"Who says there is anything, Lawrence?" Errol shrugged. "I just know that Jack had some ideas they were connected. He can be close about these things sometimes. As for me –" he opened a desk drawer and swept the pile of papers inside "– I'm on holiday, and it's of no interest."

Leaving James watching open-mouthed, Errol got up, put on his overcoat, and left the office. He managed to keep a straight face until he had shut the door: then a broad grin split his features.

***

When he reached the Rising Sun, there was a pint of Guinness waiting on the table for him. Jack had already downed several, and was looking flushed. Such was his mood, however, that he didn't have the banal happiness of the slightly drunk.

"Got you a pint of the old Nigerian lager," he said as Errol slid in behind the table. "Anything interesting happen this afternoon?"

"Not yet," Errol said. For now he wanted to keep the conversation with James to himself. Jack was in the mood to storm back and confront his colleague: whatever course of action they were to take, now was not the time for that to happen. If necessary, he would lie to Jack later. . . if it became relevant.

"I wonder why I take it from that fat bastard," Jack said between mouthfuls. "I sometimes feel like I should jack it all in and do something else."

"Like what?" Errol replied, sipping on the bitter liquid. "What could you do? You're like me – a career copper who's driven by some outmoded ideal of good and evil. There isn't anything else."

Jack looked at his friend. "Fuck me, that's a bit deep for this time of day, innit? I suppose you're right, though. . . is that why it's so hard?"

Errol considered the question. "No," he said finally, "it's hard because McAllister is a conceited, prejudiced prick. He doesn't like me because I'm a nigger. A clever one. And he doesn't like you because you're a kike – worse, you're half Irish, so you're a spud and a kike at the same time. A sort of spud-u-kike." He paused while Jack spluttered laughter into his pint, then he said: "McAllister likes nice, Aryan souls like James. There's something about him that makes my skin crawl." He half thought about mentioning their earlier conversation, but decided to refrain. Instead, he said: "McAllister isn't really bothered about the Gold killing – shit, it's only another nigger dead, right? As for Grazione, he was only a wop, right? And both of them were low-life scum."

"I lay you odds that James gets the Grazione killing as well as Gold," Jack said suddenly, his face grim.

"Why?" Errol asked, wary of giving anything away.

"Because McAllister will get the result he wants: a dead end. He wants both crimes unsolved – let's face it, he'd love it if these tossers went about wiping each other out. But dammit, no-one's got the right to just kill – not just like that."

He banged his glass down on the table with a force that slopped liquid over the sides, and made the other sparse inhabitants of the bar look round.

"Easy, man, easy," Errol soothed, keeping Jack's attention until the casual observers had looked away. When he was sure that they were no longer being watched, he said: "Listen, man, maybe if James gets on the case, he'll be able to see there's a link between the two killings. Even a complete nonce like him can't miss the obvious, right?" But even as he said it, he knew it sounded hollow.

"He's McAllister's little protege, he'll see exactly what the fat man wants him to see. Another dead nigger, another dead wop, another bunch of dead chinks. With no connection. . . well pardon me, but I think it's fucking obvious. And sooner or later, people who aren't in the gangs are going to start getting hurt. So what happens to the fat man then?"

"He disclaims all responsibility and bangs on to the press and our superiors about the rise in gang crime," said Errol bitterly.

"Exactly. You know what this means, don't you?"

For a second, Errol wouldn't look at Jack: it was going

outside of all authority, of everything they had known.

"Errol. . . speak to me."

Errol turned to see Jack staring intently at him. There was nothing else he could do. "Well, I have taken a few days holiday, just to get away from the stink of the fat man. I suppose it wouldn't hurt to poke around on our own, would it?"

"Good man. I've promised to take my kid to see the old man – I'll do it tomorrow. There may not be another chance." There was a grimness in his tone that made Errol shiver. Could it really come to that?

"Okay," he said, trying to ignore his creeping sense of unease, "I'll maybe poke around a little on my own. I'll come to you tomorrow afternoon, okay?"

Jack nodded, and as Errol rose he asked: "Where are you off to now?"

"There's a few things I've got to pick up from the office. Maybe there won't be anyone much around."

He wasn't really going back, but needed some excuse to mention his conversation with James tomorrow. As he left the pub, Jack was staring morosely into his pint.

***

It was ridiculously sunny the next day, with a warmth that didn't echo the way that Jack felt. Tongue still fuzzy from the previous afternoon's drinking, and the whiskey that had followed it when he got home, Jack dressed and swilled out his mouth with mouthwash. Staring at his reflection, he wondered if his ex-wife would let him anywhere near young Danny when he looked so rough.

What the hell: that was her problem.

He set off with Sam and Dave blaring from the car stereo. But it was still only Dave, because one of the speakers refused to cough into life. If he ever heard any of their records on the radio, the presence of a second voice would take him by surprise.

He was only half an hour late, and the boy was sitting on the doorstep waiting. He ran to greet his father as Jack got out of the car, and with some effort, Jack swung the boy in the air. His ex-wife came out to see her son off, and took stock of her ex-husband with a weary eye.

"You look like shit," she whispered as Jack belted Danny into the front passenger seat.

"Feel like it, too – and all the worse for seeing you," he muttered, closing the door.

"I don't know why you come for him – especially taking him to see that old man in that awful place." She wrinkled her nose at the thought of the hospice.

Jack sighed. "They like each other. It's his great-granddad, and he's dying. Do you really want them not to see each other? For Chrissakes, this might be the last bloody time."

He cut short any possible answer by jumping in the car and turning on the ignition. He revved it to drown anything she might be saying, and pulled away.

It was a quiet journey, and short despite the traffic that clogged East London. They soon arrived in the neatly trimmed gardens of the hospice and Jack parked.

Young Danny had a toy with him: a spaceship that his mother had brought him. It was from a TV programme that he went on and on about. Jack had never seen it, and struggled to keep up with what the boy was telling him. His mind was on Errol.

The day room in the hospice was light and airy, and Danny Snr was sitting up one end, near the open French windows that looked out on the trimmed lawns and tidy flowerbeds. Only the distant roar of Hackney traffic and the soot-stained brick of the boundary wall ruined the illusion of a rural idyll.

"Da," the boy shouted, running towards the old man.

"Jayzus, look at the size of you," the old man replied, struggling to his feet and hugging the boy to him. "Christ, you'll be bigger than me, soon." He looked up at Jack, and his expression changed. He could see the haunted look in Jack's eyes. "What's the matter, boy?"

Jack shrugged. "Work. . .the darkness, I guess."

The old man seemed about to say something, but was distracted by young Danny tugging at the hem of his cardigan. The boy wanted to show him the spaceship, and soon Jack was forgotten.

Jack sat in the day room for hours, a virtual spectator at a meeting of two minds – a generation gap crossed by the joy of life he was sure could only be felt by those new to the game, and those who knew their time was running out. The old man, having little else to fill his days, knew the programme young Danny was talking about, and the pair of them played with the rocket, talking about the show enthusiastically.

Young Danny was full of school, which was all still new and exciting to him, while the old man told him of his own schooldays in Ireland, walking miles across open country to the nearest village, sometimes without any lunch or even shoes on his feet. To the boy, it was like a story from a film or TV show, and only Jack noticed the way the old man's eyes misted over when he talked about it. He had the total recall of youth and childhood that only seems to come to the very aged.

Eventually, young Danny was happily drawing on the racing pages of the paper which the old man had been studying before they arrived, and the old man turned his attention to Jack.

"So things are not so good, eh?"

"So-so," Jack replied. "What about you – any more angels?"

"No, but I swear that yer granny came back to me last night to have a go at me for seeing all of 'em. Jayzus, it must be strong stuff they're giving me."

"Does it hurt?"

"Only in here." The old man struck his chest. "Only because I know there isn't that long left, and that I won't see me laddo here growing up any more." He looked down at young Danny, engrossed in drawing a beard on a photograph of a jockey. Then he looked Jack squarely in the eye. "And because of the darkness. Sure it seems to be eating at you, boy. And that's not good. Tell me about it, son."

Reluctantly, Jack began to tell the old man about the murder of Benny Grazione, and how it seemed to tie in with the murder of Courtney Gold. As he progressed, he became more annoyed at McAllister's lack of action, and this rancour spilt over into what he was saying. When he had finished, he noticed the old man was studying him with a distant expression.

"Da?"

"Shit – it can't be happening again," the old man muttered, "not after all this time."

"What can't be happening?"

"The darkness. . . it truly is." There was a tremble in his voice. Almost as though something was communicating itself through him, young Danny left the paper, and curled up against the old man's knee. His gnarled old hand absently stroked the boy's head.

"The darkness? I don't see. . ." Jack began, but tailed off as the old man shook his head slightly, as though clearing it.

"Jack, listen to me." He spoke slowly, but there was an urgency to the tone. "Listen to me because I'm going to tell you something I've never told anyone before. Something I've always been too frightened to tell, even though it couldn't harm me now. . ." His voice trailed away. Jack knew that this was something important: his skin crawled with electricity; this was going to be something that would give him a direction – he knew it.

The old man began: "When I was a young man – not long after I'd come over to this foul country, and long before I'd met yer gran, I was working down on the docks and lodging in Silvertown. Jayzus but that was a tough place back then. You know that old saying that somewhere was so rough that the policemen would only patrol in pairs? Well it was so bad there that the police didn't patrol at all. You'd be lucky if you even saw a copper from one year's end to the next. There was one occasion when the people locked and barricaded the coppers in Silvertown nick for three days before they could get any reinforcements through – that'd be around the time of the General Strike."

"I've never heard that one," Jack said quietly, wondering if the drugs were getting to the old man. Danny could see this in his grandson's eyes, and chuckled to himself.

"It's not that muck they're pumping into me to keep me alive, y'know – of course you wouldn't know about that. You don't seriously think they'd let that get out?"

"But how come the police were so scared?"

The humour vanished from the old man's face, and it seemed to pale. "It was the gangs. . . they had them, even then.

Big lads, mostly, ex-dockers who were sick of the crappy pay and the rotten hours. They were hard, and they didn't care if they got hurt or died. That's why they could get away with it, Jack – they just didn't care. Then suddenly they all went. Three gangs, three leaders – gone in less than a month."

"How? Rounded up by the police or –"

Danny shook his head. "In a part of town where they ordinarily wouldn't go?"

"Then what happened?"

The old man was silent for a few moments, collecting his thoughts. When he began to speak, there was a faraway look in his eye, and a catch in his voice.

"I was a wild young man when I first arrived here, Jack. I'd never been away from the family before, and I used to get roaring drunk all the time. Most of my money went down the pub of a night, and often I'd roll home past closing, half-pissed. How I managed to hold down a job and drag meself up of a morning I'll never know. It was some kind of a miracle in itself.

"All that changed in one night. I was never the same again, Jack. That's where I saw the darkness, and it came over in a great wave that I thought would drown me.

"I can't even remember what day of the week it was, except that it wasn't Sunday because I'd been working all day and worked up a thirst. I was roaring drunk, as usual, and there I was on the way home in the early hours. It was cold, and God did I need to pee. You won't remember it now, but there were a terrible old row of back-to-backs along the river, with tiny little yards only big enough for a tin bath and a crappy toilet. At the very end was a scrap yard. I remember that the gate was open, and I nipped in there, intending to have a piss before getting home.

"I remember the moon was really bright, and the metal in the yard was shining, with great pools of shadow. Christ, it must be nearly sixty years, maybe more, since then, but still every detail is etched on my mind.

"There was a scuffle outside, and some muffled voices. I just knew it was trouble – could feel it. So I buttoned myself up and looked for cover. There was a piece of sheeting propped up against the wall, with an old rug against it. I managed to get myself behind the rug and under the sheeting. How the hell I did that without making a noise I'll never know, but I did. It was then that the man was pushed into the yard.

"I knew him straight away. Bob Calvert – one of the gang leaders. The other two – Charlie Timms and Harry Beale – had long since gone missing. Rumour had it that Calvert was responsible. God, but he was a hard man – and here he was, with half his ear hanging off, whimpering in the yard. I thought it was either rival gang members getting revenge, or it was whoever had done the other two. Either way, I wasn't going to stick my neck out.

"The doors to the yard shut behind the feller who had pushed Bob in. . . his face was covered, and he had an open razor. He kept slashing at Bob, knocking him down before he had a chance to get to his feet. Jayzus, there was blood everywhere. But there was no way I was going to help – not me. I was safe, God help me, and I didn't want to show meself.

"It was all over so quickly. One last cut across the throat and the blood pumped out – less power with every beat, but spraying the yard. I know I should have done something, but God help me I was half-pissed and terrified. . . what could I do?

"Eventually, the man with the razor put it away, and took the scarf from his face. He looked at Bob, and turned to go when he was sure he was dead. It was then that he was facing in my direction – God, I was sure that he could see me. The moon was full out, and it was as clear as daylight. Christ, I'll never forget that face.

"I knew who it was Jack, and I never said anything. I stayed quiet, and the body had disappeared by morning – at least, it was never found. Me? I legged it as soon as I was sure it was clear. All I did was have years of nightmares about it."

The old man was quiet, tears streaming down his cheeks. Young Danny clung to his Da, not sure what was going on, but knowing that he needed comforting. Jack was glad the boy was still too young to understand fully what the old man had just said.

"But why didn't you go to the police, if you saw who it was?" he asked quietly.

The old man reached across and grasped his grandson's hand. "But don't you see what I'm trying to tell you, Jack? I recognised the face alright. . . it was a copper. How could I go to them? That's what I mean about the darkness. . . when the right way doesn't work and you take the wrong path. . . that's the darkness, son – and it's coming back."

CHAPTER NINE

Jack was preoccupied as he dropped young Danny home. He went through the motions of kissing him goodbye, and the child didn't seem to notice anything different. But his ex-wife did. She stared at him with a look of barely concealed hate, and as the boy skipped into the house she hissed: "I don't know why you bother. Look at you – you've not even been listening to him."

Jack didn't get a chance to answer. She turned her back and stormed into the house, slamming the door behind her. It was a literal representation of the way she had been treating him for so long. He was too preoccupied to even protest, but if he had he would have asked her why she had always turned her back, even in the days before it was too late.

Perhaps not bothering to argue with her had been the trouble all along. It wasn't the hate that bothered him when he stopped to think about it, it was the lack of communication. They were strangers, and had been from the start.

For a moment it almost put out of his mind what was really worrying him: the story his grandfather had told him. What if it was happening again? After McAllister's reaction to Jack's suggestions yesterday morning, he was hardly likely to take kindly to this.

Jack manoeuvred through the busy evening traffic and arrived home to find Errol waiting for him. As he got out of his car, releasing Sam – or Dave – from the agony of singing on their own yet again, he was surprised to see Ross standing on the pavement, his fawn raincoat wrapped tight against him as the air filled with drizzling rain.

"Would you mind not standing there like a fish, with your jaw flapping loose, and let me in?" Errol inquired, striding

Oldham
Council

Oldham Library
Tel: 0161 770 8000
Email: oldham.library@oldham.gov.uk

Borrowed Items 04/11/2017 10:22
XXXX6819

Item Title	Due Date
* No doves	25/11/2017
* Bad luck	25/11/2017
A parliament of spies [text (large print)]	23/11/2017
Death of a liar [text(large print)]	23/11/2017

* Indicates items borrowed today
Thank you for using Oldham Council Libraries

www.oldham.gov.uk
Follow us on Twitter @oldhamlibraries
Like us on Facebook
@OldhamLibraryService

swiftly towards Jack's front door with a glance of distaste at the skies.

Once inside, he carefully took off his raincoat and folded it before placing it on a dining chair in Jack's sitting room. Jack watched him with amusement as he flung his own leather bomber jacket across an armchair, where it came to rest in an untidy and crumpled heap.

"Why don't you hang it up? There's hooks in the hall."

Errol winced. "Please. Do you think I really want the neck to be put out of shape by the ridiculous kind of coat hooks that a scruff like you would use?"

Jack laughed. "How to be ungracious and insulting in one breath. Got to hand it to you, son, you know how to piss people off."

Errol blew on his nails and polished them against his lapel. "Just a natural talent, I guess. Have I got something to tell you…"

"Have you?" Jack was returning from the kitchen with a couple of tumblers. He opened the glass door of a cheap mahogany-look wall unit and took out a bottle of cheaper whiskey.

"I most certainly have," said Errol as he hitched the knees of his suit and perched on the edge of a rapidly sinking armchair. Jack sat opposite him and put the tumblers on the floor, pouring an indiscriminate amount of whiskey into each. Errol picked up his tumbler and examined it. There were smears and thumb marks around the lip. He made a moue of exaggerated distaste. "Jesus, boy, hasn't anyone ever told you about what we normal civilised people call 'doing the washing-up'?"

"Not me." Jack shook his head, grinned, and gulped down some of the spirit. "Just one of nature's savages," he added through a grimace as the whiskey stung his throat and hit him in the guts. "So what's so amazing that I owe it the pleasure of this state visit?"

Errol smiled slowly. "I had a nice little chat with James yesterday afternoon. Just after I'd left you, as a matter of fact. He was in the office, and very amenable. Turns out he was thinking somewhere along the same lines as us."

"What? That the killings are connected?"

Errol nodded. "And he promised me he'd have a word with McAllister about it."

Jack sat forward on the edge of his seat. "So we're back on it? With access to the Mile End nick?"

Errol sucked his breath in through his teeth. The hissing sound told Jack all he needed to know.

"We're not back on it?"

Errol shook his head. "Not quite. When James came back he told me that McAllister is handing the Grazione killing over to him, so he can work on it in conjunction with the Gold killing. But he's not too happy about tying-in the Chinese guys with it. I don't know if it's just the thought of stepping on their toes at Mile End, or up at the Yard, or what. Or that he still thinks we're all nuts – even Laurence."

"Laurence, is it? He's a bit of a golden boy at the moment, then."

"Yeah, well. . ." Errol shrugged. "Perhaps he's done enough for me to give him the benefit of the doubt."

Jack nodded shrewdly, lips pursed as he considered how to tackle what he wanted to say next. He poured them both another generous measure of whiskey, and Errol sat back in his chair.

"What is it?" he asked. "I've known you too long to piss about, Jack. There's something else bothering you, right?"

Jack said nothing for a second. He took another sip of whiskey and rolled the tumbler in his hands. Errol sat silently and waited, knowing that Jack was composing himself.

And then he told him old Danny's story. He told him everything, from the details of the mutilations down to the implication that it was being repeated. When he finished, he drained his glass and filled it again. Errol nursed his half-empty tumbler, mulling over the tale in his mind. Finally, he said:

"Are you sure the old man's not rambling? It might have been something he read, or just out of his imagination. Those drugs they give them –"

"No. I'm certain it was the truth. He's had hallucinations on some of his medication, and it's been more surreal than this. Besides, you didn't see his eyes. They were like open pits into hell when he was telling me. That was real, Errol. Too damned real. And it may be going on again."

"Aw, c'mon. I know you want to believe him, but why does that make it what's going on now? I mean, have you heard any whispers about it?" He sat forward, intent to make his point. "C'mon, there'd be something. Someone somewhere would have picked up a whisper."

"I dunno." Jack shrugged, looked deeply into the glass before downing the remains. "I've lived in and out of the East End all my life, and I've never heard any rumours about other villains being topped by old bill. And believe me, I've heard plenty of stories about them and how they met their end. No-one took credit. You know what those sort of scum are like: they'd be boasting about it, and how they'd never get caught. Instead it's one of those great unsolved mysteries that you put down to folklore."

"So what's that got to do with now?" Errol leaned forward and re-filled his glass, drinking it down in one gulp.

"No whispers then. No whispers now. Doesn't mean it can't happen."

"In that case I'd better talk to Laurence. If he pokes his nose in too deeply –"

"No. We mustn't say a word to anyone."

"Why not?" But as soon as Errol said it, he felt a crawling in his stomach, and the certain knowledge that if Jack was correct, the only people they could trust were themselves.

***

"You want what?" McAllister sat back in chair, fingering the ends of his moustache.

"I want to take some leave, and I'm applying to take it as from this morning." Errol stood in front of McAllister's desk, trying not to look at him. He fixed his eyes on the impressionist reproduction that hung over his chief's head. Not what you'd expect from someone like McAllister: Ross would have considered him more a man for horses running through the surf, or the green gypsy woman by Tretchikoff. These thoughts did little, however, to deflect the amazement and anger of his superior.

"What the bloody hell justifies you taking leave at such

short notice?"

Ross looked down to establish eye contact. "After being taken off the Grazione murder, sir, and the suspension of my colleague Goldman –"

"Goldman is on compassionate leave," sighed McAllister.

"As you prefer." The tone of voice and raised eyebrow left no doubt as to Ross's views on this matter. He continued: "Whatever the case, I feel that I have been under a certain psychological strain. I could, of course, always go to see the police doctor, and my own GP, and get it all officially sanctioned. But that would create a tremendous amount of unnecessary paperwork. . ." He trailed off, leaving McAllister to ponder on the forms he would have to fill in if Errol proceeded in this manner.

"Okay, have it your way." McAllister said. "What else have you got on?"

"Couple of burglaries. One assault. Not too much at the moment, actually. You could easily go a couple of days without missing me."

"Don't tempt me." McAllister's tone was resigned rather than angry. He waved dismissively. "Get out, go on. Go home and shag the wife, or whoever you do shag. Get drunk, watch TV. Whatever. I'll give you five days before I expect any paperwork on them." He swivelled around in his chair, so that his back was to Errol.

Errol grinned and turned to leave. He had opened the door when McAllister spoke, his back still turned.

"Don't get dragged down by that twat Goldman. You're a good lad, Errol. You could have a bright future if you know the right people. Just think about it."

"Sure. I will."

But as he left the office, a chill rippled down his spine.

***

Jack sat in his car, three streets away from the station. Close enough for Errol to reach him in less than five minutes, and far enough away to reduce the chances of being spotted by a colleague. He slumped down in the driver's seat, eyes glued to the face of his watch. The time seemed to crawl by as he silently intoned a mantra imploring Errol to hurry up.

After what seemed like an eternity, Errol rounded the corner, walking at a brisk pace. As Jack shifted in his seat, Errol opened the door and slid in beside him.

"How did it go?" Jack asked.

"You know I was telling you how I've blown three promotions this year?" Jack nodded. "Well, make it four. He was not a very happy man. When I was a little boy, my granny used to tell me that all fat people were jolly. She'd obviously never met anyone like our friend McAllister." He turned in his seat to face Jack. "You'd better have some idea of what we're doing with this, my son."

Jack grinned. There was a vaguely wild light in his eyes that Errol found disturbing.

"Don't worry. I've got it all nicely planned out."

Before Errol had a chance to put his seatbelt on, Jack had switched on the ignition, engaged gear, and screeched out into the traffic with a protest of horns from other road users.

They drove in silence, taking the back roads from Limehouse through to the edge of the City. Around the back streets, away from the view of the commuter and the straying tourist, the hard-core East End was still second best in a competition with a rubbish dump. Empty sites readied for construction but halted by financial ruin were covered in weeds and the odd shopping trolley that signalled the presence of another tramp. Old houses and warehouse factories lay empty and boarded, their glass long since smashed by bored teenagers. Those few that were still inhabited or in some kind of use discharged disinterested human beings onto the pavements: Asian families one step away from the sweat shops that they were forced to work in, vying for space with dodgy dealing cockneys who wouldn't know a tax inspector from a hole in the road and thought "fuck" was something you said instead of a full-stop. Errol watched them with mixed emotions: anger and pity for those who were trapped by circumstances that spiralled beyond their control, and anger with contempt for those who remained to prey on the weakness of the former.

The dividing line was usually sharp: one road would be derelict and filled with post-industrial detritus, the next a homage to glass-and-concrete architecture that nestled against sand-blasted Victorian gothic. The one area on the edge of the City where this didn't occur was around Liverpool Street. The viaducts and arches left by the main-line rail terminus were filled with dark and dingy garages and "mechanical" suppliers, lit only by one dim bulb so that their activities could not be viewed from the street. Here, the empty lots and dingy buildings vied for attention with the time-and-weather-stained Victorian hives of ageing accountants, minor solicitors, and small-time brokers. This seedy grandeur bled slowly into the new magnificence of glass and stone.

This was the real City. The sharp dividing lines were an illusion. There were no real differences between the brokers who creamed a quarter of a point from their client's profits and the men in the dingy garages who sold reconditioned cars that were really two stolen vehicles welded together.

Under the arches and viaducts sat Zachariah Motors, a small concern run by Zachariah Gold, sibling of the deceased Courtney. Zak was a quiet, law-abiding man who was ten years the senior of his recently-dead brother. He was also scared of Courtney's propensity for violence, and Jack knew that the back room of the garage was used by Gold's gang members as a liaison and meeting room.

Where better to find the information he was looking for?

Even if neither he nor Errol were sure what form that information would take.

Jack pulled up outside with a squeal of brakes. He got out of the car and stood, arms resting on the roof, staring into the black hole that formed the arched doorway of the garage. Errol also got out and straightened the trousers of his slate-grey silk suit over the highly polished toes of his loafers. He shot the cuffs of his sleeves, and looked at the gaping maw with distaste. There were vague flashes of light as welding torches did their work, and a dim yellow glow of reflected brickwork at the very back of the arch. People moving about were just discernible, but whether they were looking out was impossible to say.

He turned to Jack. "Do we really have to go in there?"

"Yep."

"Well. . .couldn't you go on your own?" It was plaintive, almost painful.

Jack couldn't resist a smile. "Why on earth don't you want to go in?" He looked Errol up and down. "Or shouldn't I ask?"

Errol held up his hands in mock horror, and looked down at his expensive suit. "C'mon, man. It's so. . .so. . . well, it's just so dirty in there," he said, with a look of disgust.

"Remember you're a copper, my son. It's a dirty job, but someone's got to do it. And that's me and you."

Before Errol had an opportunity to reply, Jack was gone, headed off into the dark hole of the arch. Errol sighed and followed him, trying carefully to pick his way through the muddied and oil-filled potholes in the cobbled pavement.

Inside the garage, it took a few moments for his eyes to adjust to the dim light. Two mechanics were working on a car to the left of the entrance: one bent over the engine, head hidden behind the raised hood, the other beating a damaged wing back into some kind of shape. Zak, grey flowing through the matt black of his dreadlocks, was hidden behind a welding mask as he sweated to join two pieces of nondescript metal together. Heavy dub sounds boomed from a ghetto blaster on the floor, plugged into an overcrowded plugboard. The bass lines shook spanners on a nearby paint-spattered trestle table.

Errol felt out of place in his well-cut suit. Zak and his mechanics were in faded and greasy overalls, with the other denizens of the dark cave dressed in baggy jeans and hooded tops. They were in their early twenties, and didn't seem to have any purpose or reason to be there.

Obviously our intended targets, Errol thought.

Jack walked over to the ghetto blaster and turned it off: not by pushing a button, but by ripping the lead from the plugboard, which he held down with one foot. There was an explosion and a shower of sparks. Errol winced. There were the three mechanics and half a dozen of the others. By anyone's reckoning they were heavily outnumbered if it came to the crunch.

Zak lay down the torch, blue flame still spurting straight from the end, and removed his mask.

"Blud claat," he growled in a deep voice that mingled

confusion and anger. "Wha' you mean by coming in here and breaking up King Tubby in full flow?" He gestured at the now silent beatbox.

"Sorry Zak, but I had to get your attention somehow." Jack shrugged apologetically.

"Why don' you just tap on me shoulder and ask like anyone else?"

"That would be too easy, wouldn't it?" From the corner of his eye, Jack could see the other two mechanics were no longer engrossed in their work: instead, they stood watching his every move. One still had a panel beating hammer in his hand, the other was polishing a chromium wrench. "I know you're a good man, Zak," Jack continued, "but you've got no reason to want to talk to me – what with your brother lying on a slab."

"Don' you talk to me about that." Zak stabbed an angry finger at Jack. The huge asbestos welding gloves that covered his hands looked as heavy and effective as boxing gloves. "My brother lie on some dam' piece of stone, rotting away without a decent burial because you people haven't finished cutting up his body. But do you try and find the killers? Shh-ah," he turned away angrily with tears forming in his eyes, "when it common knowledge that the Chinese do him."

"Common, is it?" Jack could see the guys at the back of the garage shuffle and change positions. He and Errol were the real danger. Those baggy clothes could conceal any amount of guns or knives. Zak was angry, but he was a peaceful man. The others weren't.

"If it's common knowledge, then how come we don't know about it?" Errol entered the conversation. While Jack had been talking, he had manoeuvred himself around the arch so that he was behind Jack, with no-one else between him and the door. He was also within easy reach of the bench, covered in tools that had been shaken into a tangle by the heavy bass beats. One quick lunge and he had a weapon.

If it came to that.

There was an eerie silence in the garage, punctuated only by the distant rattle of trains passing over other lines. It was as though the whole of London had gone silent, waiting for someone to speak.

Errol, sick of the silence and sick with fear, decided to push the question. "I said, how come we didn't know? Obviously the music was loud, but I can't imagine that it deafened all of you."

"Babylon man," said Zak quietly, "perhaps you been working for the white man too long. Perhaps you can't see what's around you now."

There was a click from the back of the garage. Errol's hand strayed towards the bench. There was a huge pair of metal cutters, with a razor sharp blade, lying at the far end. That would be his preferred weapon, and he knew now that it would come to violence. He was sure the click had been the catch on a pistol.

"You know we're the old bill, then?" Jack asked casually, hands in the pockets of his jacket. He wanted to look as unthreatening as possible – at least until he had got the information he wanted.

"Like you don't stick out a mile," said one of the guys at the back of the hall. Heavy, cool dudes to a man, they stuck together and stayed in as much shadow as possible. Faces would be hard to recognise in this light, and that was just the way they wanted it. "I seen you, man, and the fuckin' coconut."

Errol tensed. He hated that word: black on the outside, white on the inside.

"At least we're better known round these parts than you are," Jack countered, staring into the darkness. "I can't even tell who you are, son."

"That's 'cause we all look the same to you," said another of the guys. "And to the coconut."

With a calm deliberation, holding in his temper, Errol picked up the metal cutters.

"If anyone else calls me that," he said softly but clearly, "I'm going to cut their balls off and stuff them in their mouth." He held the metal cutters up with one hand, examined them, then looked at the group clustered at the back of the garage and smiled. "Is that perfectly clear?"

Zak looked at the guys at the back, then at Jack and Errol.

"Look, I don' want no trouble in here. I just try to do me own t'ing without hurting anyone. What my brother did was his business, not mine. Like the bible says, I'm not my brother's keeper."

"Oh I wish you had been, Zak," said Jack, shaking his head sadly. "A good man like you could have stopped him beating on old ladies and robbing kids of their sweets. Him and Benny Grazione both. Now Benny, he came from a long line of scum, so you'd expect that from him. But Courtney? He had you. Why didn't you do something?"

"The boy always run wild. There was nothing I could do to stop him. When mama die, I was only fifteen, and he was twelve. I was not a man then myself, so how could I tell him?"

There was a sadness in his voice that made Errol forget for a moment that they were in a hostile environment, surrounded by people who would see them dead. For that moment he could see the tragedy of two children left alone in a city that didn't care for them because of their age or colour.

But only for a moment. There was a movement at the back of the garage that brought him back to reality. A flash of blade caught in the dim light of the bulb.

"Jack," warned Errol. His eyes indicated the back of the garage.

Jack pulled his hands from his pockets and sprung forward with a suddenness that took everyone – even Errol – by surprise. He grabbed the blue-flamed torch from where Zak had left it, and brandished it in front of his body. A quick glance over his shoulder told him that there was just open ground between himself, Errol, and the archway entrance. The two mechanics on the left were tensed, more from fright than anything else. Jack turned a few degrees towards them. Without him having to say a word, they dropped the hammer and the wrench.

"It's okay, lads. I know you're clean," Jack said. It was unnecessary, but he felt it helped him establish something: that he knew who the good guys and the bad guys were in this situation. He turned back to Zak, not sparing a glance for the group at the back, trusting Errol to keep an eye on them.

Zak was standing still, arms by his sides. His eyes were

pools of sadness and disappointment. He knew Jack from times when Goldman had been after his brother; Jack knew him too, knew he was not a man of violence.

His dignity gave Jack a pang of guilt. For a second he thought about putting the torch down.

"I'm sorry," he said simply, "I really am. But I don't trust those wankers at the back." He gestured with the torch, the blue flame barely flickering. "Get rid of them, Zak. Don't let them clutter up your life. But first tell me about Courtney. Why do you think the Chinese did it?"

"They come to him, tell him they want to take him over. He could work for them on a percentage. They could make him richer than he was, and for less work. But Courtney was a proud man, and he bow to no-one, y'know? He tell them that he's not interested. Then they tell him that he may regret it."

"Was it only the Chinese?" Errol asked, all the while keeping an eye on the guys in the shadows.

Zak shook his head. "No. The mafia come for him, too. But they were more conciliatory. They understand pride, they tell him that they give him time. One month. That month wasn't up. I don't think it was them. They understand honour, y'know?"

Jack wasn't so sure about that, but decided to let it ride. "Anyone else it could have been?"

"Like who?"

"Like the old bill?"

To Jack's surprise, Zak was almost shocked. "Babylon? They may beat a man, but they too clever to kill. Even a black man. You beat a man and he's resisting arrest. You kill him and you get everyone on your back." He shook his head. "Babylon know how to manipulate a man, they don't need to kill."

Errol smiled to himself. Despite spending his life in the City, Zak was still an innocent at heart. Errol envied him that.

He heard another click. He turned his head and caught the movement of something that was blacker than the background, blacker than the clothes the heavy cool dudes were swathed in. Black as the darkest night, black as death. . .

"Jack." He yelled and threw himself forward at the same

time. Everything seemed to run in slow motion: Errol still had the metal cutters in his hand, and they made his balance one-sided and awkward. He careered into Jack, pushing him sideways as a deafening explosion filled the small arch with noise. The smell of engine oil and hot metal was overcome with cordite and burnt powder.

They hit the floor together, Jack managing to retain a hold on the torch. It spun in his hand and the edge of the blue flame cut through the shoulder pad of Errol's suit. He felt the heat permeate to his flesh, biting into him. He screamed in Jack's ear and spun away, his hand still fixed around the metal cutters.

All hell broke loose in the garage. Errol scrambled to his feet, face contorted with pain, shoulder pad and suit smoking gently. He still held the metal cutters. Jack, too, was quickly on his feet. He kept a firm hold on the blow torch, but because of the direction he had fallen, he momentarily had his back to the group at the back of the garage. His first sight was of the two mechanics running through the arch entrance, out into the pale watery sun and down the road. It wasn't their fight.

It wasn't Zak's, either, but he wanted no-one hurt on his property. When his brother was alive, his violent mood swings had controlled his older sibling, made him fall into line with whatever Courtney wished. Now it was different. Zak had his pride, and he didn't want the remnants of the gang ruling him as his brother had.

Jack swung on his heel as he heard Zak yell "No". From the corner of his eye, he could see that Errol was looking a little groggy from his close encounter with the torch. Then his full attention was taken by the action at the rear of the garage.

The six dudes had spread out. Three of them had knives, one had a gun, and the last was making a grab for the chromium wrench. He was close enough if. . . Jack twisted the nozzle of the torch, and the concentrated blue flame spread out into a roaring jet of yellow and white, the flame ragged and wide reaching. He thrust his arm forward, and the tongue of fire touched the youth's arm as he reached for the wrench.

The boy recoiled as though flung backwards by an electric shock, the flesh on his hand and arm blistering and roasting, the skin removed by the first lick of flame. The sleeve of his wool and cotton top flared, and the flames began to spread. He fell to the ground, howling in a high pitched whine of agony, eyes rolling into his head. No way could he think about fighting – except for his life.

Jack didn't see him fall. Instead he turned to see Zak throwing his heavy frame towards the dude with the gun. He heard Zak grunting as they struggled, and could pick out a few words: "Not. . . my roof. . ."

Two of the guys with knives made for Errol. They could almost scent a degree of vulnerability. The heavy fall and the burns had dazed him, and there was a slightly glassy look in his eyes. The first of the youths dodged at him, feinting with his knife. The blade was sharp, with an upturned end that could twist deep in a wound. Errol tried to parry but missed, the metal cutters waving at thin air. The knife snicked his suit jacket, cutting a ragged tear in the silk.

The second youth made his move. His blade was a smaller flick knife, and he intended to close on the distracted Ross and drive the blade between his ribs.

Pure instinct took over: as the youth came closer, Errol drew on every reserve of strength he had to change the balance of his body, shifting his weight so that it was coming from behind the metal cutters as they arced and swung back towards his opponent. He had hold of them by one handle, and with as much power as he could muster he jerked his wrist to turn the wickedly sharp tip of the nose upwards. His momentum did the rest: the tip caught the youth in the face as he moved in, not expecting such suppleness and alertness. The razor-honed tip, where the two blades joined, carved a deep incision from his cheek up past the left-hand side of his nose, gouging at his eye before hitting the bone above the eye socket with enough impact to smash it.

The youth didn't scream. The impact was enough to knock him unconscious before his face was ripped.

Errol turned at the end of the swing. He was aware only of the fear and shock in the eyes of his other opponent who stared at his friend, lying on the floor in a widening pool of his own blood, and took flight, running past the panting Errol and out of the garage.

Three down. . .

Zak and the youth with the gun were still struggling. They careered backwards into the tool bench, knocking it over and sprawling over it onto the grimy stone floor.

Jack was half-watching them, half-watching the other dude with a knife, who was making for him. His knife proscribed circles and arcs in the air as he came towards Jack in an approximation of a crouch. Jack could see the fear in his eyes: a knife was no match for a blow torch.

"Go now, son, before I use it," Jack growled. The dude circled around him, still waving his knife. Jack stayed facing him as they circled warily. When he was past Jack the dude turned and ran, stumbling past Errol and nearly falling as he emerged into the light of day, disappearing in the same direction as the mechanics.

Jack turned his attention back to Zak, who had won his struggle, and was kneeling on the chest of his opponent. He held the youth's gun in his hand, and emptied the magazine onto the floor, bullets clattering onto the stone.

"You dam' fool yout'," he roared. "You never play them at their own game. They make the rules. They can always win. You want to end up like my brother?" He stood up, tossing the useless gun into a dark corner. He kicked the youth in the ribs. "Now get up and go." He stood back as the bewildered youth scrambled onto his feet and walked slowly from the garage, looking around nervously as though expecting to be attacked. He tried to leave with as much pride as he could muster.

"Thanks," said Jack, extinguishing the torch and laying it down.

Zak sneered. "Don't thank me. Just go and leave me in peace."

Jack turned to look at Errol, who was still clutching the metal cutters. He was looking around with a worried frown.

"What's the matter? We sorted them. No bother."

Errol shook his head. "No. Not all. There were six. I've only counted five."

"So the coconut can count as well," hissed a voice from the darkness. Out of the shadows came the final youth, who had hidden himself so well before the fight had begun. He was carrying a sawn-off Purdey shotgun. He'd stolen it himself, and was proud of owning such a prestigious weapon. He'd bored his friends with endless details on the type of shot it took, its range and accuracy. Now was his first chance to use it.

"Oh fuck," Jack whispered. The gun was pointing at him. And the extinguished torch lay at his feet.

Zak stepped forward. "Don't be stupid, boy. You don't know what that thing will do." He held out his hand. "Give it to me."

"You cunt," the boy yelled. "You should be fuckin' ashamed of yourself. You're no brother of Courtney's, man. You fuckin' want it, you have it."

"Shit," shouted Jack. He threw himself at the youth to try to deflect his shot, but while he was still in flight the gun went off with a deafening explosion.

Sawing off the end of a shotgun can give the scattershot a wider angle of fire, and increase the power of the charge if it is used in an enclosed space. But the adaptation has to be done properly.

The boy hadn't had the necessary skill. The gun backfired, throwing him backwards as the charge exploded in his face. Jack was still in mid-air when the blood and cordite hit him. He landed on his face in a pool of blood, the body of the boy thrown some four feet backwards. The remains of his head were splattered over the car that was being serviced.

When Jack got to his feet, ears still ringing, he found Zak throwing up behind the overturned bench. Errol was in the office, phoning the emergency services. He winced at Jack when he came out.

"Jesus Christ, look at the state of yourself." He looked down. "Look at the state of me. Have you got any idea how much this suit cost?"

Jack grinned. "You won't be able to afford another one, my son. By the time McAllister gets through with us we'll never be in work again. That's if we don't end up behind bars for this."

"Then I suggest we get out of here and leave Zak to explain.

The only chance we've got is to stay one step ahead of our colleagues." He looked at Jack with a gleam in his eye that spelled iron determination and will. "I figure our careers are finished even if we get to the bottom of this. It's like a fucking nightmare. We lose either way up."

"So we might as well get whoever's behind this in the first place. Right?"

Errol nodded grimly. "Right."

Errol had truly joined Jack in his war against the darkness.

CHAPTER TEN

As they drove away from the garage they could hear sirens in the distance, whining their way through the crammed City traffic to Zak's hell-hole.

"I think we might just have got away in the nick of time, as they say," Errol remarked, examining a tear in the knee of his suit. "How did I do that?"

"Probably when you pushed me over," Jack said without taking his eyes off the road. "Bloody stupid thing to do when I had a blow torch in my hand."

"I know," Errol replied, thoughtfully fingering the shoulder of his jacket. "But fuck it, the time for recriminations is past. Long since."

"So you're with me, then?"

Errol shrugged and exhaled loudly. "The way I see it, I've got no choice now. If we're going to go down, then we might as well drag the real villains with us."

"Not exactly a rosy view of the situation –"

"What do you expect? Yesterday I was just off a murder case and ready to clear up a few other offences, looking forward to a few more years without promotion. Boring, but steady. Now. . ." He threw his arms up in exasperation. "I'll be lucky to get eighteen months minimum. And just where the hell are you going, anyway?"

Jack threw the car into a tight turn, off the road and down an alleyway leading into Leadenhall market. An awesomely beautiful Victorian gothic monstrosity in red-painted wrought iron scrolling, picked out in white and gold, with small shop-cum-stall units beneath that housed anything from a newsagent to a fishmongers, at this time of day it was packed with workers taking their lunch break.

The last thing they would have expected to see was a battered Ford driven by a man covered in blood and oil, accompanied by a man in an expensive but severely damaged suit.

But that was what they got: Jack was determined to take as many short cuts as possible before the police caught up with them. The fact that the alleyways-cum-roads that criss-crossed Leadenhall were too narrow for more than one car, let alone the pedestrians, and that there were two parked delivery vans blocking what roadway there was, didn't seem to unduly bother him.

"Shit, man – watch the people," Errol yelled. He wanted to close his eyes, but couldn't: compulsion drew him to watch in horror as the pedestrians scattered in front of Jack's car when it mounted the already narrow pavement to squeeze around the parked vehicles. The wing mirrors went quickly, followed by a hideous teeth-grinding squeal as the paintwork on the right hand wing was left behind on a lump of Victorian gothic stone.

They emerged out the other end, and Jack swung the car around towards Aldgate, bumping across the pavement and onto the road amid a squeal of brakes and the massed symphony of a dozen car horns.

"I know this is probably a very stupid question," Errol began, as calmly as he could muster, "but where the hell are we headed?"

"Arnie Shawcross," Jack muttered.

Errol waited for further explanation, but none was forthcoming. "Am I to deduce something from this?"

Jack sighed. "Courtney's boys think it was the Chinese. Arnie will know what's happened to Benny's boys. We talk to them, then we talk to the Chinese, then the mob. Simple and methodical."

"Oh. Well, I'm so glad you've got a plan, Jack. I thought you were just charging at this in any old manner." Errol's voice dripped with a sarcasm that turned to thoughtfulness when he looked down at himself. "I'm not sure how much more talking I can take, though."

Jack guided the car along Tower Hill, East Smithfield, and

onto the Highway. They were soon out of the City and into the heart of the East End. He'd taken a circuitous route to throw off any attempts to follow them. It was unlikely that anyone could have been onto them that quickly, but if asked, Zak would have seen them heading west, not east.

They passed Arnie's pub at speed. Jack turned into the nearest side street and parked.

"Why not outside?" Errol asked.

"What – both go in the front and give him a chance to leg it?" Jack shook his head. "No way, Jose. You go in the front, and I'll work my way around the back. He won't be best pleased to see either of us after last week."

"Especially looking like this," Errol added wryly.

They got out of the car and parted company. Jack took the back roads until he was walking up to the pub from behind. It was on a corner, and the yard backed onto houses with shops on the right hand side. On the left, however, only an eight foot brick wall kept anyone out of the yard. It was topped with broken glass set in concrete. Jack took his jacket off and threw it up over the glass. He took three steps back, preparing to take a running jump at the wall, oblivious to the stares of passers-by. It was only then that he noticed the crimson door set in the wall.

Surely not. . .not even Arnie would leave it unlocked? But if there had been a delivery from the brewery that morning. . .

Jack tried the door. It opened at the push of a fingertip, swinging smoothly on its hinge. He grinned. Arnie deserved everything he got, just for being so dumb. Jack pulled his jacket from the wall and slipped it on before going in the back.

Errol walked around the front, painfully aware of the stares from passers-by. He cast his gaze down at the pavement and tried to pretend that he wasn't really there. His shoulder was still smarting from the burn, and muscles he didn't know he had were telling him that he should have worked out more. He could feel the draught slipping through the holes in his suit trousers, cold air wafting around his knees. When he tried, unconsciously, to straighten his jacket, one of the lapels came away in his hand.

"Three hundred pounds," he muttered in disgust. "Three

hundred pounds and they can't stitch a lapel on properly."

Errol took the material over to a waste bin and deposited it before squaring his shoulders and entering the pub.

It was quiet inside, with only three or four customers this close to opening time; but to Errol it seemed as though a hush descended when he entered the saloon bar. He could feel all eyes turn to him. At this time of day that wasn't unusual. But when you're in a ragged suit, aching, and know that your former colleagues are probably after you at this very moment, then it feels unusual.

The barmaid was gawping at him, her jaw hanging loose. Errol could see the fillings in her bottom teeth.

"Bugger me," she said finally, "look at Sidney bleedin' Poitier now."

"Very amusing," Errol said dryly, leaning on the bar. "I suppose Arnie would be out if I asked you?"

"You know Arnie, dear," she said, as noncommittally as possible.

"Don't I just," Errol muttered. He found the flap in the bar and raised it, walking past her. She watched him go without a word. When he'd passed through into the back she turned to one of the few customers in the bar – an old man sitting in the corner nursing a pint of bitter.

"One of these days I'll quit, go and work in a classier place."

The old man said nothing. He had his own views on her.

Errol paused in the dingy hall, listening. He could hear heavy breathing from behind the closed door of Arnie's sitting room. It sounded as though he was alone. From the hall he was unable to see out the back. He hoped that Jack was in position.

With a remarkable lack of drama, he reached forward and turned the doorknob, walking into the room as though expected. After Zak's garage, anything would be an anti-climax.

"Hello Arnie. Surprise, surprise. . . oh Christ, put some clothes on, man."

Arnie Shawcross was sitting in his underwear, nursing a bottle of scotch and watching schools television with the sound turned down. He turned in slow motion, senses dulled by drink.

"Wha –" The rest of the question was cut off by a smelly dressing gown thrown across him, taken from the back of a dining chair by Errol. Arnie struggled to his feet, pulling on the dressing gown.

"Jack? You there?" Errol called. He heard a muffled affirmative. "Get in here, man. He's in no fit state to run."

Errol heard the back door open, and Jack appeared in the kitchen doorway.

"Christ, look at the state of it," Jack said, catching sight of Arnie.

"You can talk," Shawcross said, taking in the condition of Jack and Errol.

"Yeah, well, we've had a close encounter with what was left of Courtney Gold's boys," Errol said quietly. He looked at Jack: how much should they tell Arnie?

Whatever they thought, they had already said more than enough.

"Oh right," said Arnie, as though a light had come on in his brain. "I didn't know you was with Mister McAllister's boys. You weren't at the meeting the other day."

"What meeting –" Errol began. He was cut short by a gesture from Jack.

"You know what it's like," Jack said slowly. "Sometimes you just miss things. I didn't know there was a meeting, to be honest with you. Did you, Errol?"

Errol shook his head. "No. No idea." He didn't know what Jack was doing, but felt there was no choice but to play along and hope it all became clear.

Arnie grinned blearily and tapped the side of his nose. "Don't worry, Mister Goldman, I won't say anything to anyone else. I know when to keep my mouth shut."

"'Course you do, my son," said Jack, ushering Arnie back into his seat. He took the bottle and filled a glass, handing it to the smiling Shawcross. "Listen, Arnie, I know you won't say anything. That's cool. But Mister McAllister – well, you know what he's like. He doesn't like other people knowing his business. You've got to promise me you'll keep schtum." He held his finger in front of his lips.

Arnie winked. "S'alright, Mister G. I know I can trust you,

now. I know I wasn't s'posed to listen at the door, but well. . . if a man can't know what's going on under his own roof." He gestured expansively, spilling the spirit over his dressing gown.

Jack refilled the glass. "That's fair enough, Arnie. But you know Mister McAllister: he can be a right bastard at times. He wouldn't like to know you'd been listening in."

Arnie frowned. "You really think so?"

Jack nodded. "Tell you what," he added with a piece of mock acting that was so bad it made Errol wince, "if you tell me what you heard, I'll be able to tell you if McAllister would be really pissed off at it."

"You'd really do that for me?" If Arnie had been a dog in Battersea Dog's Home, such a pathetic display would easily have won him a new owner. Errol, who had caught on to Jack's intentions, had to resist ruining the set-up by laughing. He stifled a giggle.

Jack looked Arnie in the eye, and nodded solemnly. "We're mates, Arnie. I'll do it just for you."

It wouldn't have won an Oscar, but it was a good enough performance to impress a drunken Arnie Shawcross. The whole story came out: how Arnie had listened at the keyhole while McAllister and Cann had planned their raid on the Triad drug lab, how he had been approached by Cann shortly after the discovery of Benny's body, with a proposition that he dare not refuse, and how he was "really glad" that someone was cleaning up the East End.

"After all, Mister G. , you blokes have your hands tied by the law, don't you?"

Jack nodded vacantly, not really listening. There was too much else to absorb.

"So you did that bastard Gold's gang, eh?" Arnie continued, pitifully keen to be part of the action. "Fucking good job, too. That nigger cunt was getting far too uppity. . .begging your pardon, Mister Ross," he added, suddenly remembering through the fog of alcohol that Errol was still leaning against the table.

"That's alright," Errol said dryly, "you can't help being a honky shithead, can you?"

Arnie laughed nervously.

"So do we need to ask what we came here for?" Errol asked, turning his attention away from Arnie, who returned to his glass.

Jack shook his head. "I think it's pretty fuckin' obvious that we know what's going down. Trouble is, we've only got the word of a drunken semi-criminal." He looked at Arnie with barely-concealed contempt. "That's going to be fuck-all good."

Errol pondered it for a moment, before saying slowly: "There's only one thing for it."

"What's that?"

Errol grinned, but there was no humour in it. "If you can't beat 'em, join 'em."

***

McAllister waded through the large numbers of scene-of-crime officers, paramedics, and uniformed men who cluttered up the pavement outside the arch. Inside, his eyes adjusting to the dim light, he could see Zak Gold sitting on a cleared workbench, talking to a uniformed constable. James was standing over a bundle of rags on the floor, pointing and gesturing to Lorna. She looked as though she was about to re-visit her lunch. As he squinted, McAllister could see that the bundle of rags was an uncovered corpse. There was no head visible. James finally finished talking and gesturing: with one last gesture he indicated for a hovering paramedic to cover the body. As he turned, he saw McAllister. He said something to Lorna, who nodded before turning away. She was obviously only too pleased to be doing something else other than looking at the deceased.

James walked briskly across the garage to the threshold, where he spoke to McAllister in hushed tones.

"Thought you'd better be here, sir. Two dead and one injured. All three members of Courtney Gold's gang."

"What's that got to do with me – I mean officially? I may have to justify being here."

James sighed heavily. "You're not going to like this at all. You see him over there?" He pointed to Zak. McAllister nodded. "That's Gold's brother."

"Then this is where the gang met?"

"Exactly. Nice bloke, really. Totally clean. I think his brother terrified him and he just did what he was told. Anyway, they still met here, trying to establish some kind of powerbase while they squabbled amongst themselves for leadership. There were half-a-dozen of them here today. Two mechanics as well. Then they get a visit from two men, asking questions."

"Do we know who these men are?"

James paused, then nodded tersely. "Only too well. It was Ross and Goldman."

"What?" McAllister's voice rose in pitch and volume. He took a deep breath to calm himself: if anyone was looking at him, he'd give them time to lose interest before continuing. "What the hell were they doing here?"

"Laying waste to it," said James with a grim smile, glancing at the mayhem around him. "Apparently the six pseudo-yardies started on them."

"And Ross and Goldman sorted them?" McAllister couldn't keep a note of admiration out of his voice.

James gave a brief laugh. "Apparently Goldman used an oxyacetylene torch to burn one of them when he made a lunge. Died on the way to hospital. He gave another one the option of doing a runner. The lad was sensible. Ross laid out one with a pair of metal cutters: he's in hospital. They reckon he'll lose an eye and have a wicked scar, but he'll live. Another one of 'em did a runner rather than face the wrath of Ross. That makes four. Number five had a gun and Zak grappled with him – wrestled the gun off him, emptied it, and sent him away with his tail between his legs."

McAllister grunted in satisfaction. "Nice work. About time he asserted himself. What about laughing boy?" He cast a glance over at the headless corpse.

James shook his head. "Thought he was top man. Had a sawn-off shotgun and tried to blow Zak away. Stupid bastard had sawn it wrong and blew his own head off."

McAllister sniffed. "Novel enough way to commit suicide." He looked around, taking in the activity surrounding them. "Okay. You take care of the official end. I'll see to Ross and

Goldman."

"What. . ."

"It's a pity – they could have been a nice addition to the team. But they've been too high profile already." He grinned maliciously. "They'll have to go, won't they?"

CHAPTER ELEVEN

Errol looked at his watch. It had stopped, the dial broken in the fight at Zak's garage. "Shit," he said, "any idea what the time is?"

Jack shrugged and, keeping one eye on the traffic, reached over to turn on the radio. Like the tape deck, it was old and didn't work properly. Errol had to decipher the inane babblings of the disc jockey through the mist and fog of static and interference.

The idiot radio pilot finally gave a time check as they arrived outside Errol's house. It was one forty two.

"Pity we missed the news," said Errol dryly, "I bet we were the lead item."

Jack laughed as he parked the car.

After leaving Arnie's, they had decided that a change of clothes and quick shower were the next items on their agenda. McAllister could wait. There would be police already on the look-out for them, some of whom were bound to be part of McAllister's little clique. Some of the police would have a description, and some would know them by sight. It was going to be hard for them to move around, especially on their own manor. Even harder, given the way they looked at the moment.

The next problem to consider was: whose house would have the more surveillance? Chances were that both their homes were being watched right now. So was returning home a viable option? As far as both could see, the answer had to be yes. If they were going to get any further they had to get changed, get cleaned up. It was a risk, but one that had to be calculated.

Jack's terraced house had an alleyway running between the bottom of his small back yard and the yard of the house opposite. This could give them a getaway route, but would also be an area that would be heavily manned.

Errol's flat was on the top floor of a three-storey house. There was no fire escape. The gardens of the houses opposite backed straight onto his garden. Once in the flat, they would be trapped.

"Ever hear the one about the rock and the hard place?" Jack asked.

Errol smiled. "I say we go back to my place."

"Why?"

"Two reasons. One, my old granny used to say that people relax when they think they've got you cornered. Two, there's no way I'm going to be seen dead, let alone arrested, in some of your clothes."

"I think you make it up about your granny. Sometimes I don't even think you had a mother. . ."

So they went to Errol's flat. And now Jack had pulled up, switched off the engine. His hand was trembling. Errol anxiously scanned the street. Usually he could spot surveillance a mile off – too many years of doing it himself had made him wise to all the tricks. There didn't appear to be anyone in sight.

"Either they're really good on this patch, or they aren't here."

"We'll assume the former – though I wouldn't be surprised if McAllister wants us to himself."

"How the hell could he pull that off?" Errol asked as he opened the car door.

Jack shrugged. "I dunno. Maybe he's put his own men onto us. I mean, we don't know how many nicks have got little McAllister clones in them, do we?"

Ross and Goldman got out of the car and walked across the pavement, trying all the while not to look too conspicuous. This was not easy, considering the condition of their clothes, and what Jack was now beginning to smell from the blood and mud that covered him. The attempt to look casual was not helped by the way in which they walked: a funny, clipped walk that verged on breaking into a trot. They got up the steps and stood uncomfortably by the front door as Errol fumbled with his keys. Jack had left the car unlocked to avoid any such fumbling on his part: besides, who'd want to steal an old wreck like that?

Errol got the door open, and they were in. Jack slammed the door behind them, and stood resting his back on it. He closed his eyes, whooped with relief, and smiled.

"Mission accomplished," he said softly. The smile turned to a frown as Errol shook his head.

"They might be up there waiting. It depends if they went to Denise."

Jack felt the world crumble: he'd been so relieved, and this reduced his hope to ashes. They had to be able to get away from here, but if Errol's girlfriend had let them in. . .

Errol led the way up the stairs at a crawl, treading softly on each step and peering cautiously around the bends in the stairwell. There was no sign of anyone or anything. When they reached the top, he put the key in his front door, and turned to Jack.

"Shit or bust. . .as my old granny never said," he whispered with a smile. He turned the key, and the door swung silently open. Inside, all was quiet. "I think we might just be. . ." He swiftly went from room to room while Jack stayed on the threshold, ready to run if necessary. Finally, Errol reappeared in the hallway. "It's okay, we're on our own."

Jack closed the door behind him with a sigh. "Thank Christ for that. I get first crack at the shower, okay?"

"Sure. I'll make some coffee and keep a look out."

Errol left Jack's steaming mug of coffee on the dining table and sat by the window in the bedroom. It looked out over the street below and afforded him a good view of the road. There was little activity beyond the occasional passer-by. As he sat and sipped the scalding liquid, Errol thought about the situation he was in: if it was up to Jack and himself to gather some kind of incriminating evidence against McAllister, then they would have to try to convince him that they were willing to join his renegade faction. This would also solve the problem of how they were going to get out of being arrested for the mayhem in Zak's garage. That was hanging heavily over them, but if they apparently joined McAllister's boys, he'd be able to cover it up in some way. These things happened.

Of course, he mused, even if they got evidence against McAllister, and could name the rest of his renegades, who would believe them? They were effectively outlawed and on the run themselves as of – he looked at the clock alarm by the bed – two hours ago.

The whole situation had got out of hand in a very short time, and it gave Errol a headache to think about it. So he tried to clear his mind while he watched the street.

He was nursing the rapidly cooling mug and staring out onto the street when he heard a discreet cough behind him. He turned with a jolt, as though wakened from a reverie. Jack was standing in the doorway, hair plastered to his head, wrapped in a towel.

"I need some clothes," he said sheepishly. "I can't put mine back on."

"Yeah, sure." Errol was glad to have something to take his mind off their problems. He opened one of the two wardrobes in the room. "This is all mine." He pointed to neatly hung suits, jeans, jackets, and shirts. Jumpers were folded neatly on little shelves. Everything was neat and pristine. Errol looked Jack up and down. "I think most of it will be too big. Can I suggest that you wear this and this –" he pulled out a black polo neck and a pair of 501s – "along with this." He tugged a wide leather belt from off of a small rack, where it neatly hung with several others. "Underwear is in the dressing table, third drawer."

Jack smiled. "You missed your vocation, old son. You should have gone into the schmutter trade, like my old man always wanted for me."

"You'd still have got into trouble," Errol replied. "Coffee's on the dining table, and keep looking out the window, man. Nothing so far, but I might just have been missing something."

Errol took his turn in the bathroom while Jack dressed and drank his coffee. When Errol returned, Jack was perched on the window ledge, looking out onto the street. His hair had started to dry already, and its curl was returning. The jeans and polo neck suited him, but he still had on his old cowboy boots, covered in filth and blood.

"You look sharp, man, sharper than ever," Errol said

admiringly as he towelled himself down. "But couldn't you do anything about those?" He pointed at Jack's boots.

Jack looked down. "I think they go with the outfit, man."

"Not when they're covered in shit like that."

"Maybe not, but you're a different size to me, aren't you?"

Errol conceded the point and dressed himself similarly to Jack. It was a time for functional wear. Things had been tough already, and they would probably get tougher before the day was out.

"Head up," said Jack suddenly and softly, "we've got company."

Two police cars appeared from each end of the road. They parked, and McAllister and James emerged from the back of one. They briskly jogged down the street to be met by two plainclothes officers that neither Jack nor Errol recognised. They conversed before going into the house opposite Errol's apartment.

"Shit," Errol said softly. "No wonder we didn't spot anyone."

"Time to move," said Jack, looking over Errol's shoulder. "We'll leave the car. Front is no option. What about the back?"

"I told you. The gardens back onto one another here. Unless they were in the house behind, they can't get at us from there. Come to that, we can't get out."

"Fire escape?"

Errol shook his head. "They'd have to come in the back of the house and up the stairs. If they're covering the front of the house, they could rush us really easily. We could go out the back, but –"

"But they've already thought of that," Jack said, looking out of the window. James appeared from the house opposite, and called down the street. A uniformed constable came running from one of the cars. They conversed hurriedly before mounting the steps to the front door. Even from the top floor, Jack could hear the banging. James appeared beneath the window and shouted something down the road. Another uniformed man appeared from one of the cars. He was carrying a sledgehammer.

"They're not fucking about, are they?" Jack said, biting his lip. "What's the roof like?"

Errol looked shocked. "You've got to be kidding."

Jack fixed him with a look of despair. "So what other choice do we have? Give up like naughty little boys? Shit or bust, man. Your choice."

Errol said nothing for a moment, his mind racing to find alternatives. Then it hit him: "Okay, so we haven't got a fire escape, but next door have."

"Climb across?"

Errol nodded. "Yeah. It's not going to be easy, but it'll be easier than the roof, that's for sure."

"Let's go for it," Jack said tersely.

Aware of the hammering from three floors down, they hurriedly made their way into the lounge. There were two windows, old and sashed. Errol pushed up the one on the left and looked along the narrow ledge. A drainpipe was located on the dividing line between the houses, about three feet from the window. The black-painted edge of next door's metal railed fire escape was another two feet further on. The bolts and brackets holding the drainpipe to the wall could provide some kind of foothold, but the thick yellow paint would make them slippery.

Errol looked down and gulped. He drew his head in and turned to Jack. "What do you reckon?" he asked quietly.

Jack listened intently. The thumping on the front door had a crisper edge to it: the sound of splintering wood.

"I say fuck it, I'll try first." His grin had the edge of desperation.

Jack heaved himself out onto the ledge, clutching the bottom of the raised window for support. Errol hovered, unsure of what to do.

"I'll go for the pipe," Jack hissed through gritted teeth. He shuffled along the ledge until he was holding the side of the window frame with his right hand. With the left he reached out towards the pipe. By leaning over as far as possible he was able to wrap his hand around the pipe. It felt reassuringly solid. Now for his foot. . . breathing deeply three times to steady himself, Jack tensed every muscle in his body and threw himself out towards the pipe. The muscles in his left arm ripped and burned with agony as his whole weight was carried by them. The corroded underside of the pipe, unpainted and ragged with years of paint drips from where the brush could just about reach, bit into his fingers.

Errol sucked in his breath and held it. He looked down. Three storeys was a long way. The front door was yielding, if the splintering noises were anything to go by.

Jack swung in the air, left foot scrabbling for the bracket, right leg hanging free. He brought his right arm across and wrapped his hand around the pipe. It brought some relief to his agonising left arm. Finally his left foot gained purchase, and it was simple for him to secure a foothold for the right. . .Halfway there. He looked across at the fire escape, close enough to reach out: but did he have the strength?

Only one way he was ever going to find out. He swayed slightly on the pipe to try to build himself a little momentum. He counted to himself: one. . .two. . .three. . .

Four. He swayed towards the fire escape and flung out his left arm and leg simultaneously. With the strength of his swing he was, for one glorious second, weightless in the air, and his foot and hand gained an easy purchase on the metal construction. He let his right hand side fall free and pulled himself over, flinging his leg over the fire escape. His momentum carried him onto the platform, to collapse with a clatter.

Errol exhaled slowly: he didn't know who was more relieved, himself or Jack.

Jack pulled himself to his feet. "Come on," he hissed. "Get going, you lazy git."

Errol began to climb onto the window sill, then paused, looking down. It was a hell of a long way.

The front door crashed open, and he could hear the muffled, bellowing voice of James at the foot of the stairs.

This was no time to drop any bottle that he possessed. Drawing in a deep breath, Errol positioned himself to reach out for the pipe. He was a bigger man than Jack: taller, so that his reach was slightly longer, yet heavier. Would he have the strength to carry his own weight, he wondered?

There was really only one way to find out: he reached out and grasped the pipe, throwing his leg after his arm before he even had time to think about it. He pulled himself out, grasping for the pipe with his right hand, feet scrabbling for the brackets. It was easier than he thought. He paused for a second to get his breath back.

"Don't fuck around, we haven't got the time," Jack hissed, holding out his hand. "Come on, for Christ's sakes."

Errol mentally called Jack every impatient son of a bitch he could think of, but decided to save his breath for the task ahead. He swayed a couple of times before throwing out his left arm and leg. He clutched at the railings of the escape, and pulled his body over. Jack grabbed him, taking a great handful of jumper from his back and pulling. They collapsed on the fire escape in a breathless noisy heap.

"Let's get out of here," panted Jack, scrambling to his feet. He was halfway down the fire escape before Errol was up and following.

They were dimly aware of a din coming from Errol's flat. James and the uniforms must be close to breaking down the front door. Jack and Errol took the steps two or three at a time, swinging over the iron hand rails rather than rounding the landings. They were exhausted by the time they reached the garden below.

Jack paused, looked up and down the row of neat gardens with their wooden fences. "Which way?" he said between gasps.

Errol pointed to one end of the row. "Down there," he rasped between breaths. "Dead end. Brick wall. Out onto street."

Jack nodded briefly, saving his breath. They set off over the gardens, mounting the six foot wooden fences and clambering over them like they were on an assault course. They took them neck and neck, the desire to stay free spurring them on when every muscle screamed for rest.

James looked out of the window and saw Jack and Errol five – no, six – houses down, taking the gardens in three or four strides before flinging themselves at the fences. He cursed them under his breath before looking across at the fire escape.

There was no way he was going to try that, not even for McAllister.

He took out his radio and pressed the transmit button. "They're out the back, boss. Heading over the fences like fucking greyhounds. Going for –" He paused, and turned to the uniform behind him. "What's the name of that road at the bottom?"

"What road's that, guv?" the constable replied, unable to see out of the window beyond James's head.

"That fucking end, stupid," James yelled, staring out of the window and pointing.

Errol was perched on top of the brick wall, helping Jack to climb up.

"Oh fuck it, they're away," James yelled into his radio.

Jack swung his leg over the wall and steadied himself. "Thanks," he grunted. "I'm nearly done for."

"Let's just get down," Errol gasped, lowering himself into the street. Jack followed.

They stood on the pavement, panting heavily and trying to get their breath back. Jack's ribs felt like they would explode, his heart hammering against the bones. Errol rasped the air painfully into his lungs, phlegm gathering in his throat and choking him. He felt like he might just puke. Yet all the while they stood there, both men were only too well aware that they would have to get away quickly. James must have seen which way they were headed, and McAllister and the uniforms were still in cars. It would take only a minute or two for them to screech around the corner and take them into custody.

Jack straightened up, sucking in breath noisily. He clapped his hand on Errol's shoulder. "So far, so good," he rasped. "Where the hell do we go now?"

"I dunno," Errol barked, coughing as he spoke, hawking up the phlegm that choked him. "Anywhere."

Jack laughed through the pain. "Oh yeah, really fuckin' decisive."

Errol began to laugh, alternating a dry whoop with the spasms of coughing. He stopped when he noticed a car glide around the corner. It wasn't a police car, but it was moving at a slow pace. Errol's instinct took over. He nudged Jack in the ribs.

"What the fuck –" Jack yelped in pain.

"Company," Errol whispered, pointing at the car.

"McAllister?"

Before Errol could answer, the car pulled smoothly into the curb. It was a jet black Mercedes with smoked glass windows and an aura of menace. The back door opened, and a tall, muscular man in an Armani suit got out.

"What the –?" Errol began.

"Don't say a word," the stranger said quietly. "Just get in the car. Or do you want to get arrested?"

"I think we'll take a rain check and our own chances," Jack wheezed between the spasms of pain.

"I don't think so," the stranger said softly. A long barrelled .44 Colt replica appeared in his hand.

"Hey, I'm not arguing," said Errol, holding up his hands. He moved forward and into the back of the car, looking up and down the street. How come there's no police when you need them?

Jack stood crouched against the wall, still breathing heavily. He shook his head. "No way. Not until you tell me who the hell you are."

The stranger grinned and clicked back the hammer of the gun. "I don't need two of you."

Errol peered out from the inside of the car. "Jack, don't screw around. Better a live prisoner than a corpse. Right?"

Jack paused. In the distance he could hear the gunning of engines and the starting up of a wailing siren. James must have shifted his portly frame down the stairs and out to McAllister.

"Okay, I'll come."

He climbed into the back of the car, followed by the stranger, who slid the gun back into his holster. He closed the door behind him and settled into his seat.

"Kill the engine," he said softly. The driver – overweight and sweating in a cheap suit – switched off the ignition and took the key out, placing it on the dash. "Keep quiet and still," the stranger continued, "they won't be able to see in."

The police cars roared around the corner, sirens blazing. They sped past the black Mercedes, turning the corner at the end of the road, disappearing from view.

They sat in silence in the back of the car until the sirens had faded away into the distance.

"Okay," the stranger eventually said. "Start the car and take us home."

The driver took the key from the dash, switched on the engine, and moved off, turning in a circle to head back down the road where Errol lived. As they passed, Errol looked out at the battered and broken front door, hanging off its hinges in pieces. He winced: if he ever got out of this alive then he was sure that he'd be stuck for the bill.

Jack turned to the stranger. "I don't suppose you've got a bar in a flash motor like this, have you?"

The stranger grinned. "Don't worry about it. You can have a drink when we get there."

"Get where?"

The stranger wagged a finger: "Just you wait and see."

***

Gold Wharf House was as imposing and quiet as ever. The mid-afternoon sun glinted on the glass frontage, making it hard to see the receptionist and the security guard sitting at their respective desks, looking bored. It was getting towards the end of their shift, and both were keen to leave.

The Mercedes pulled up with a soft purr in front of the main entrance. The stranger got out of the back, ushering Errol and Jack towards the doors. The security man came forward and opened them.

Jack looked back at the stranger. "I've never heard of anyone getting in here without using the intercom before."

"Man, I've never heard of anyone getting in here even with the intercom," Errol added. He walked past the security guard and into the glistening white marble lobby. "Way cool decor," he nodded approvingly.

The stranger followed them in, chuckling as the door closed behind him. "So glad you approve, Mister Ross."

"That's okay," said Errol with a dismissive wave. "I don't care what the fuckin' mob think."

"Careful what you say," snarled the guard, stepping in front of Ross. "Shall I deck him, Mister Quine?" he said to the stranger.

Jack leant back on the receptionist's desk, tickling her under the chin. "What's a nice girl like you doing in a cess-pit like this?"

She smiled icily. "Earning more money than you'll ever see."

Jack laughed, and walked over to Quine. "So you're Bob Quine, are you? The mysterious 'mad dog' we've heard so much about down the nick."

Quine smiled. It was like the smile of a shark. "That's me, Mister Goldman." He walked over to the elevator and pressed the button. "You've got an attitude problem, but that's okay by me. I like you guys."

"Ah, but do you really know us?" said Errol, joining him at the doors of the elevator.

"Oh yes, I know a lot about you," said Quine. "You two are the solution to our little problem."

The elevator doors opened with a ping. Quine stepped in. Jack and Errol exchanged glances before following. What was going on?

"You're just so macho, Clint," the receptionist said to the guard with withering sarcasm, making Errol laugh as the doors closed on the lobby.

The elevator ascended in silence. Quine didn't look at them, preferring to stare straight ahead at the double doors. Jack and Errol exchanged glances again, both curious and worried.

With a ping, the elevator stopped its smooth ride, and the doors slid silently open. Quine stepped out onto a polished floor of black marble shot through with white. The walls were similarly decorated, with expensive abstracts framed and lit at intervals. Jack and Errol followed him, itching to find out what was going down.

The corridors on this upper floor were curved, winding in a circle around the building. They had no idea what floor they were on, as there had been no indicator in the elevator. From the length of time it took and the way the acceleration had jellied his bowels, Errol assumed that they were at least twelve floors up. Jack was looking for a window, but could see only a procession of closed doors.

135

They walked on in silence. The trip began to assume a faintly ludicrous air. Snatched from the jaws of arrest by a man they knew to be the head of the Mafia's London arm, brought to a building they knew to be the headquarters of the mob, and led around a winding corridor on a mission to who knew what. . .

"Did you ever read *Alice In Wonderland* when you were a kid?" Errol whispered.

"Funny you should say that," Jack returned in low tones, "I bought it for the nipper a few months back. Why?"

"This is like the beginning, where she followed the white rabbit. Only we're the rabbits, and one of us is black."

Jack chuckled. They were going to need a sense of humour if they were to get out of this building alive.

Finally, they came to an imposing set of oak double-doors. Quine stopped, waiting for them to catch up. He still said nothing. When Ross and Goldman stood with him, he twisted the handles and flung them open.

The Chinese and the Mafia men were seated as on the previous morning. They all turned at the sound. At the far end of the table, nearest the window overlooking the river, David Lao stood up.

"These are the men?" His voice carried a note of confusion. Quine nodded. Lao looked at his colleagues in bemusement, then back at Quine. "These are the men who wiped out the remains of Gold's gang?" Again, Quine nodded.

"Uh, look you guys," Jack said hesitantly, "I don't know what this is all about, but I think you should know that we're still serving officers, and could arrest the lot of you." He smiled. Errol looked at him as though he were mad.

The mob men began to laugh. A slow ripple of chuckling spread from them around the table. Even the normally stoic Chinese were seen to giggle. The laughter continued for some seconds before dying out.

Errol was reminded of all the Kafka stories he had read as a student. The sense of surreality and paranoia.

They were being deliberately obtuse, and Jack was fencing with them. Time for things to stop.

Errol drew a deep breath. "Okay, let's stop all the bullshit. I don't know how you found out about this morning – I'd guess that you monitor police frequencies – but you know that Jack here is on leave, and so am I as from about ten this morning. If we tried to arrest you, we'd probably end up at the bottom of the river, but I think we can safely assume that my friend here was trying to break the ice." He shot a glance at Jack, who grinned. Errol continued: "We thought that you were behind the killings of Grazione and Gold, and some of their men. That was until the little affair on Sunday night."

Lao nodded. "We came to see Mister Quine, here. As his people were the only factor in the equation not to be affected by a loss of personnel, we assumed that he was behind the killings."

"That's reasonable, but totally wrong," said Jack.

"This I now know," Lao muttered reflectively, rubbing at the side of his neck.

"Exactly. Mind if we sit down?" Without waiting for an answer, Jack seated himself next to one of the Eurasian women. She looked at him as though he were an insect. "I love you, too, sweetheart," he said sweetly. Errol sat opposite Jack, on the Mafia side of the table.

Quine smiled and walked to the head of the table, where he seated himself. "Go on, please," he said with a magnanimous wave of the hand.

"We know who's behind all the murders. And it isn't either of you." Errol indicated each side of the table. "That doesn't mean that we have to like being here."

"So you're going to let yourself get arrested? Left to the tender mercies of your own men?" Quine shrugged, and imperiously waved his arm. "There's the door. Just go right now."

Jack and Errol exchanged glances. Neither man moved.

"Okay," Quine continued. "Let's get down to business. It's your guys, right?"

"Yeah." Jack shook his head. Being a copper was still important to him, and having to admit all this to a bunch of criminals was hurting. "Our boss – a fat bastard called McAllister – is behind it all. I think a guy called Laurence James is in it –"

"Think?" Lao snapped. "Don't you know?"

"So what the fuck do you know?" Errol returned. "Just listen."

"Thanks." Jack continued: "Apart from McAllister and James, who we're not a hundred percent sure about, we don't know who else is involved. We can't go to the police and turn ourselves in, so to speak, because we might end up in the back of a car with two of McAllister's little soldiers."

"And you'd never be seen again, right?" asked Quine. Jack nodded. Quine laughed. "You've got to hand it to this guy McAllister. He's really organised himself."

"Yes, very noble, I'm sure," said Errol with heavy irony. "By your standards this may be admirable, but it puts us in a ridiculous position. Who do we approach? And what hard evidence do we have?"

Lao pondered the point for a moment, before saying: "Given that you feel uncomfortable being in the same room with us, I suppose a temporary alliance is out of the question?"

Jack's only reply was a wide grin.

"On the other hand, a little discreet protection in the shadows could benefit you," Quine added.

"What do you mean?" Errol shifted uncomfortably in his chair.

"Well, as I see it your only option is to try to join this bunch of vigilantes. You certainly have the credentials after this morning's display." Quine gave a short laugh. "Infiltrate and gain the evidence. Blow it apart, right?"

Jack shifted in his chair, looking uneasy. "Well, actually, we had thought that ..."

Errol stayed him with a hand. He turned to Quine and Lao. The others had been silent, and he fingered these two as the spokesmen. "Look," he began, slowly and with a bare grasp on his temper, "you know what we're going to do. You're one jump ahead of us in this. You tell us what chance we've got of getting away with it?"

Lao smiled. "On a long-term basis, none. But there is a way."

"So, if you're so clever, you tell us what it is."

Lao's smile grew broader. "If you really want to know, it

can be easily arranged."

CHAPTER TWELVE

"You fuckhead. You total moron. I ought to take you out the back and put you out of your fucking misery."

McAllister was turning from red to purple in the back of the car as it roared around the streets of East London in a zig-zag pattern, trying to cover as much ground as possible and also cope with myriad one-way systems. James sat next to him, flinching under the full force of McAllister's wrath.

"Covered about two miles, guv," said the driver without turning. He took another corner with a screech of burning rubber, siren disharmoniously clashing.

"Okay," McAllister yelled. Then, calming down, he added: "Sorry. Not your fault, son. It's this idiot here." He jerked a thumb the driver couldn't see at James. "Get on the blower to the other car, okay?"

The driver called through to his opposite number, and handed the radio over his shoulder to McAllister, who snatched the receiver.

"'Allo," he bellowed. "Fitch? Any sign?"

Fitch's voice crackled over the static. "Not a poxy whisper, guv. Wherever they are, they ain't here."

"Alright. . ." he paused for a moment, trying to collect his thoughts. "Right, get back to your nick. Leave it to me. I know those wankers, they'll crawl out of the woodwork soon enough. 'Specially that yid Goldman. He can't help sniffing after trouble, like a dog after a bitch on heat. They'll be around soon enough, and we'll be ready for them."

He signed off and handed the receiver to the driver, who had slowed to the speed limit, sensing that a chase was off.

"That it, then, guv?" he asked as he put the receiver back. "Anything else you want?"

McAllister shook his head. "Not now. You've done a good job, son. What did you say your name was?"

"Rudge, sir. Work out of Mile End. Can I just say it's an honour, and I'd be only too glad to help in the future. We need more like you, Mister McAllister."

McAllister clapped him on the shoulder. "Good lad. I'll remember you. If I need you, Fitch'll get in touch. He's my man at Mile End. Where's the other driver from?"

"Bow Road, I think. But he don't know what this is about. He was part of the surveillance team."

"So how did you get here?" McAllister frowned. He'd assumed that all the men at Ross's had been "his" boys.

"I know Fitch, sir, and he knows I'm willing. I didn't know the story until this afternoon, though." His tone was worried. He didn't want to put a fellow officer in the mire, especially not in these circumstances.

"I came with the Bow Road boy, sir," James explained. "We've ended up in different cars in the confusion, that's all."

McAllister turned to him. "Well I'm so glad you were paying attention at some fucking point. If you were as bleedin' sharp about bashing down doors we might not be in this position."

James flinched again. It was something he was making a habit of this afternoon.

On the way back to his office, McAllister brooded in silence. Ross and Goldman were making things messy. Until today it had been easy to keep their extra-curricular activities separate from their official work. Now it was beginning to get complicated. He'd assumed that the stake-out people had been part of his cell. With James and Fitch there, he hadn't noticed the drivers. He'd assumed that they were sympathisers at the very least, people who Fitch and James had thought ripe for recruitment. The fact that this was only partially true concerned him. He couldn't have "outsiders" poking their noses in to his little cell. Secrecy was paramount.

They arrived at Limehouse station, and McAllister heaved his bulk out of the car. He stuck his head in the driver's window and got his first good look at the driver: youthful, probably only in his early twenties, with greasy hair, wide-set eyes, and a flattened nose.

"Where are you supposed to be this afternoon?" McAllister asked. It was best to check that the boy had a cover story.

"I'm actually off duty until eight tonight, sir. I did this as a favour to Fitch. He's a good bloke."

"What about the car?"

"Out of commission, sir. Supposed to be serviced tomorrow morning. I can get it back in dock in fifteen minutes."

McAllister smiled. "Good lad, Rudge. I'll remember you. Be in touch soon. Off you go."

Rudge smiled with a rather pathetic eagerness. "Okay, guv. Look forward to it." He moved into gear and drove off, leaving McAllister standing in the yard, facing James.

"Come on, stupid. We've got things to talk about."

They walked across the station yard and into the back of the building without exchanging a word. James began to mount the stairs towards McAllister's office, but his boss turned off.

"Where –"

"Just go and wait for me," growled McAllister. James shrugged and trudged up the stairs. McAllister went through a door into the canteen. It was the middle of the afternoon, and only six or seven people were in there. Two WPCs were comparing their notebooks, and a plainclothes Detective Inspector was sitting opposite, listening to their stories. A uniformed sergeant and two constables were at another table, talking football and eating distinctly unhealthy plates of fried food. McAllister exchanged nods of greeting with most of them, and with Lil, the cook who was on duty at the canteen. She had a cigarette drooping from her bottom lip, as usual, and McAllister looked from her to the plates of food, wondering how much ash was in the chip fat.

He shuddered at the thought, but immediately dismissed it from his mind. There were other matters to consider. Sitting in the far corner, nursing a mug of tea and the *Daily Mirror*, sat George Cann. An empty plate stood on the table in front of him. McAllister hurried over.

"You on duty yet, George?" he asked softly.

Cann looked up from his paper. "No. Got another –" he consulted his watch "– ten minutes before I'm due at the desk.

Why?"

"We've got a problem."

Cann raised an eyebrow, but said nothing. He knew that it didn't do to speak too openly.

"I think you know what – or who," McAllister added. "James is up in my office. Spare us five?"

Cann nodded, grunted, and got to his feet, carefully folding his paper before sliding it into a pocket on his tunic. As they walked slowly out of the canteen, he made small talk to cover anyone who was watching.

"You seeing your bit again tonight?"

McAllister shook his head. "No such luck. Bit of business has come up. She'll have to wait."

"Shame. She's a nice bit of business herself."

They left the canteen and walked up the stairs. On the first floor landing they missed Wendy Coles, on her way down from the collator's office to the canteen for a cup of tea. She did, however, bump into one of the two WPCs who had overheard McAllister and Cann.

"Shame about your boyfriend," the WPC said cattily.

Wendy looked bemused. "You what?"

"Your boyfriend, love. Mister McAllister."

"What about him?"

"Oh, hasn't he told you yet?" Her voice dripped with relish and venom. "He won't be able to make tonight. He's got a bit of business on."

Wendy adopted an aggressive stance, hands on hips. It was reflected in her voice. "Yeah? And what do you know about it?"

The WPC smiled. "I just heard him talking about it," she said with no little satisfaction. "Down in the canteen he was, with Sergeant Cann. If you don't believe me, ask Pete." She pointed out the DI who had been talking to her in the canteen. He was on his way back to his own office.

"Ask me what?" he asked, mystified. But Wendy had already turned around, and was running up the stairs towards McAllister's office. "What's that all about?" he added.

"Slag," whispered the WPC, ignoring him.

She walked off, leaving him standing on the stairs,

thoroughly confused.

"They shouldn't have 'em in the force," he muttered under his breath, shaking his head sadly.

***

McAllister poured three measures of whiskey into paper cups and sat back in his swivel chair, gently moving from side to side. He picked up one of the cups and took a sip.

"We've got to get them sorted. As soon as possible."

Cann picked up a cup too and walked over to the window. James sat forward in his chair, nursing his drink and staring into it as though it contained all the answers.

"Top 'em," said Cann softly. "That's obvious. But where and when, that's the question."

James shook his head. "I don't know. They're coppers."

McAllister sighed heavily. "I think we've had this conversation before. I tried to avoid harming them. I shifted that cunt Goldman onto sick leave, and put you on the Grazione scum's case. If Ross wasn't so devoted to that yid, then we'd be home free."

"Instead of which we're on the verge of being blown open," Cann murmured. "Listen, Larry. If Ross and Goldman are captured alive, then we all fall. They'll spill all that they know."

"But we don't know that they're on to us. They just damaged some of Courtney's boys."

Cann shrugged. "Maybe you're right. But think about what we know: they're onto something that's bigger than an inter-gang war. They're talking mob and Triads at least. That means the Yard." He turned to face James and crushed the cup in his hand. "If they get involved, then we're well and truly fucked. They're not going to be able to ignore what's going on. You think the mob or the chinks are going to be happy with the Yard poking their size tens in it? Are they hell. They'll be after us as well."

McAllister turned one hundred and eighty degrees in the chair, facing the wall. "If Ross and Goldman are brought in alive, they'll face charges over this morning's caper. They'll make a lot of noise." He swivelled back to face James. "They're dead. No option."

***

Outside the office, Wendy Coles raised her hand, prepared to knock. She was fuming, and wanted to find out what McAllister thought he was up to.

"They're dead. No option."

The words were muffled but audible through the thin door. Wendy stopped, hand half-way to the wood. Instead, she flattened her ear to the door, first checking that the corridor was empty.

***

"I still don't like it," said James sullenly. "I didn't join to kill other coppers."

Cann threw the crumpled cup across the room. "Don't fuck me around," he said quietly. His attempts to contain his anger and keep his voice low gave it a harsh, penetrating edge that made James wince. It was his day for being bawled out by his elders, if not betters.

"We've got to do it, or all go down," said McAllister simply. "You ain't married. George is. So is Day. And Fitch. Fuck knows about Winston. I've got kids to support still. It's not their fault my ex is a lazy bitch and wants me to support her for the rest of her natural. Point is, we've all got commitments. And we've come too far to blow it."

James drained his cup and crumpled it under his shoe. "Alright, I know you're right. Doesn't mean I have to approve, though."

"Good boy," said Cann, nodding approval. "Big question now is how we're going to get the bastards? I mean, where have they gone?"

"Well it ain't Goldman's house, 'cause we've got that covered," said James. "And we've got Ross's woman on side. She thinks he's flipped or something. Probably blames the job."

McAllister grunted with satisfaction. "Any sightings, come direct to me. No one moves on them without my say-so. All we can do is sit and wait."

The phone rang. McAllister frowned and looked at James. "You don't reckon –"

"God's a fucking copper if it is," Cann said wryly.

McAllister picked up the phone, then clamped his hand over the mouthpiece. His eyes were sparkling with excitement. "You're not going to credit this. It's Ross." He returned his attention to the phone. "Errol, son, what's all this about?" His tone was warm and friendly, but blatantly bogus.

"Don't screw me around." Ross's voice was tinny but still terse at the end of the phone. "You know why I'm ringing you."

"'Course I do, son. You want to turn yourself in. You're a sensible boy. Not like that Goldman. Is he with you?"

"Yeah, he's with me. And we don't want to turn ourselves in." There was a moment of static silence on the line, as though Errol had to take a deep breath before plunging himself in. "We know about you, McAllister. We know about your little games."

"I don't know what you mean, son?" He made faces at Cann and James, trying to communicate with them. They looked at each other, puzzled.

"You know exactly what I mean. You've been cleaning up the ghetto. And about time too. We did a bit of that today, and it feels good. We'd like to join your little campaign."

"Well that sounds good to me. Trouble is, you haven't been too clever about it. There's people after you. That's a lot of shit to get you out of. . . and it creates a hell of a stink."

Cann and James watched McAllister with a mix of curiosity and incomprehension, trying to work out what was going on.

"You can work that out," said Errol. "You've been smart enough to keep this whole thing going without being uncovered so far. We only tumbled you by accident."

"As a matter of interest, son, how did you find out? I'm sure you realise that this kind of thing is important for security."

"We paid a visit to Arnie Shawcross after we left Zak's garage. He thought we were with you already."

"I see." McAllister put his hand over the mouthpiece. "That wanker," he hissed. "They know about us because that little shit Shawcross told them. Pissed as a fart again, probably. He's a dead man." He uncovered the mouthpiece and returned to Errol. "So what do you want?"

"Jack and me want a meet. Tonight."

"Where?"

"Wanstead Flats. Near the London Cemetery, where the island and the pond is. You know it?"

"Yeah. I took my kids there when they were little."

"How sweet. Half eleven tonight, okay?"

"Deal." The line went dead on him. McAllister replaced the receiver.

"So?" Cann asked.

McAllister sat back. "You won't believe this," he said with a smile, "but that prat actually wants to meet us. Him and Goldman. Tonight. And in a quiet place." He laughed out loud. "Bang, bang. Fuckin' simple."

***

Wendy Coles stood back from the door, her mind racing. He hadn't said where the meeting was taking place, but he'd made the purpose of it only too clear. She shuddered at the thought of being close to him. And the things she'd told him about information that had passed through her fingers. By her reckoning, that made her partly responsible for at least a dozen deaths.

Two more tonight, unless she did something.

She walked slowly back down to her office in a daze. She sat down at her desk and tapped a pencil on a note pad. Up and down. Up and down. . . the point broke on the desk, and with it her concentration.

She had to find Jack and Errol. She couldn't let them go to their deaths. She couldn't have that on her conscience as well.

But where would she start looking?

CHAPTER THIRTEEN

Errol put the receiver down, and turned away from Quine's desk. He could feel his heart pounding, and the scent of fear lurked nastily under every breath.

"Well?" asked Lao, at his elbow.

"Didn't you hear, man?" Fear reduced Errol's voice to a husky croak.

"No. Anyway, I think we should all know." Lao looked back at the table. The silent gathering returned looks of affirmation.

"Okay," said Errol, "we meet at the arranged time, at the arranged place. And I hope that you're right there with us."

"We will be," said Quine. "In the meantime, I suggest you gentlemen get some rest."

"Where?" asked Jack. "We can't go home – either of us. And this place is about as restful as an electrode on the balls."

Quine barked a short laugh. "We don't do that sort of thing any more. Not often. But I do take your point. There should be –" he turned to one of his associates "– Lenny, what about Bow? That free?" The man nodded. Quine turned back to Jack. "We've got a safe house in Bow. We'll take you there. Don't worry about a thing."

Jack nodded. "Alright. But look, I haven't had a piss all day. I've really got to go, yeah?" He cast a glance towards Errol.

"He's not the only one," Ross quickly added. "So unless you want the seat of your car stained, then. . ."

Quine sighed. "Lenny, show them the bathroom."

Lenny rose from his seat and guided Jack and Errol to the bathroom. It was a spacious accommodation, about a hundred yards from the boardroom and just around a bend in the building. While they went in, Lenny waited outside.

Inside were two cubicles, with three stand-up urinals against the far wall. Opposite the cubicles were three sinks, with a mirror running from sink to ceiling along the width of the wall. Jack walked over to the urinals and unzipped in front of the one nearest the mirror. Errol stood next to him. This way Jack could mouth words at Errol without them being reflected in the mirror. Just in case it was a two-way affair.

"Bugged?" Jack mouthed.

Errol looked down at the urinal and nodded, barely perceptibly. "Probably," he muttered under his breath.

Both men finished and zipped, before standing in front of the mirror. Jack stuck out his tongue, examined it. He turned the cold tap on full blast, so that it splashed over him.

"Ah, shit," he exclaimed, "where's the towel?" Looking around, he spotted a roller towel hanging on the back of the door. He walked over to it, leaving the tap running. Errol also turned on a cold tap, and rinsed his hands. When he went to dry them, he left his tap running as well.

Both men now stood by the roller towel, with two cold taps running fast and their backs to the mirror. Their only worry now was that Lenny was standing on the other side of the door. They could only hope that it wasn't too thin.

"So whaddaya reckon," Jack mumbled quickly.

"Smells, man. Real bad."

"Yeah. I mean, a safe house?"

"Right. They're not going to take us there and let us live, right?"

"Right. We've got to do something."

"What?"

"I don't know. I'll have to think about it."

"Well don't spend too long, yeah?"

They left the towel and returned to the sinks, turning off the taps. It must have been obvious to anyone watching that they were trying to communicate secretly. Their only hope was that they hadn't been overheard.

They left the bathroom, Jack in the lead. "Alright, laughing boy," he said to Lenny with a sunny smile, "where next?"

Lenny didn't say a word, contenting himself with a grunt. He led the way down the curved corridor, away from the boardroom. Jack and Errol exchanged glances before following. They wound around the corridor for what seemed to be the whole length of the building, and probably was: they ended up in front of the elevator again.

"Where are we going, Lenny?" asked Jack. He tried to keep a cheery friendliness about his tone. Lenny grunted in reply. Maybe Jack just shouldn't have bothered. He exchanged another look with Errol, who shrugged. Whatever their fate might be, they could only – for the moment – go along with the flow.

The elevator arrived, and took them down to the reception. They stepped out into the lobby, where the receptionist and the security guard stood, AK47s cradled in their arms, flanking Quine. He was grinning broadly.

"Gentlemen," he began, his voice carrying an irritating cheeriness, "are we ready to go?"

"Do we have any choice?" Jack replied in an equally irritating tone of voice. His reply was the clatter of AK47s being raised, safety catches released.

Quine held up a hand. "Leave it. These guys are too valuable to us." The guns dropped. "This way, gentlemen," he continued, without a shift in tone. He led the way out of the building and into the back of the Mercedes. Lenny followed behind Jack and Errol. For a second, Errol thought about making a break. But it was quiet around this part of the Wharf, and running into early evening. The offices would be emptying – those that had been occupied in the first place – and there would be no-one around to see him get mown down. Unless he made a break for the river and dived in, there was no way he'd get more than a hundred yards without acting as cushion for a round of fire. And he'd never been that strong a swimmer.

Lenny sensed the momentary halt in Errol's progress, and prodded him in the back. It wasn't with his hand. Errol joined Jack and Quine in the back of the car. Lenny slammed the door behind him, walking around to the front and seating himself next to the driver.

The car purred smoothly into gear and started away from Gold Wharf House, where the receptionist and security guard put away their guns. She went back to *Homes and Gardens*, and he nursed an erection, still wondering if a tumble in the back room was even a remote possibility. Such idle musings were a thing of the past for the men in the car.

It was a short trip from the island to Bow. The car turned off the Bow Road and made its way through the early evening traffic to Old Ford, where it was held up in the snarl of traffic that gathered around Old Ford Church, a medieval relic in the middle of a twentieth century road. Quine sat silently beside Jack and Errol, ignoring them. He gazed out of the window, seemingly lost in his own thoughts. Jack had thoughts of his own: he doubted if he would see little Danny grow up, and was certain that he'd beat his grandad to the pearly gates of the great beyond. The old man was sure he'd go to hell, if it existed. Too many years of Jesuit education had convinced him that no-one was good enough to go to heaven. Jack's education had been a received mix of Jesuit creed from his grandad and grandmother, and a strange kind of agnostic Judaism from his father, a Jew who was religious only when it suited him. As a result, Jack didn't believe in anything much, except perhaps the existential slow death of the human soul. He smiled wryly to himself: surprising what crap you'll think of when you want to do anything except focus on the truth.

Whatever Quine said, he was sure that in a few, all-too-short, hours, both he and Errol would be dead. If McAllister and his boys didn't get them, then the combined forces of the Triads and the mob would.

Errol spent the entire journey thinking of only one thing: how they could get away.

And every idea drew a blank.

Finally they were out of the jammed traffic, and headed for Bromley-By-Bow. A desolate slice of the East End, decimated by roads and flyovers that led down to the Blackwall tunnel; a two-tunnel, four lane highway that took the bulk of London's traffic under the Thames, connecting the north and south of the metropolis. Most of the houses along this stretch of town were boarded up, the flats half-empty. The pubs lay derelict, either empty or deserted of custom, windows protected by thick iron mesh. The few shops were the same. All the factories, the public baths, the fire station – all deserted and in ruins, boards covering those windows which hadn't been smashed. The only operating industry was the refinery by the mouth of the tunnel, discharging vaguely sweet fumes into the air.

The Mercedes turned off a slip road, and crawled around a couple of side streets until it came to Kitchener Road, the remnant of a glorious time when the Empire had made enlightened councils spend money on council housing.

The car stuck out like a diamond in dirt: a touch of ostentation that was unwelcome in a street where only the very poor and the very old still clung on. It rolled to a halt in front of one boarded-up property.

"Gentlemen, we've arrived," Quine said with a smile.

"So I'm supposed to get excited?" said Errol, with an approximation of his old sarcasm. It was feeble, but all he could manage.

Shepherded by Lenny and the driver, Jack and Errol followed Quine into the house. He opened the padlock on the boarded-up door with a key taken from a large bunch. As they walked into the darkened room, Quine switched on the electric light.

Both Jack and Errol gasped. From the outside, it had seemed like a slum. Inside was another story altogether. The hall was carpeted simply, the walls painted apple-white. It was functional, but clean. They could see the kitchen at the end of the hall: it was spotless, with a new cooker, fridge, and washing machine. There were cupboards which, if they had looked, were full of tins.

Quine led them into the lounge. It was painted in a rich apricot – not, perhaps, too tasteful, but certainly opulent. There was a three piece suite, dining table with two chairs, and a TV and video. There was also a telephone.

"What about the other rooms?" asked Jack in amazement.

Quine smiled. "Neat, huh? There are two bedrooms and a bathroom. It's simple, but clean and kept in good maintenance. Hey, listen to me, you guys, I sound like a real estate agent, right?" He laughed and sat down in one of the armchairs, crossing his legs. "Sit down, sit down," he said, gesturing to the sofa. Jack and Errol exchanged puzzled glances before complying. The whole situation was beginning to verge on the surreal.

"I like you guys," Quine continued. "You've got guts, y'know? I feel like I can really talk to you. Most of the time I have to keep up this pretence, like I'm a real cool businessman, unfazed. That's bullshit. I'll level with ya –" he leant forward, lowering his voice so that Lenny, standing in the hall, wouldn't hear him clearly. "Most of the guys I deal with are putzes, right? The kind of guy you'd like to spit in their eye. Not you. That bit where you tried to arrest us?" He directed this to Jack. "I nearly pissed myself laughing. That's real cool, if you can keep your nerve at a time like that. So I'm gonna play it straight down the line here. The chinks, they want you dead. They want you guys iced when we deal with McAllister and his bums. Me? I'm not so keen on that idea. I wanna wire you up so that you've got the evidence to put that sonofabitch behind bars. I don't want you dead."

"My, my, how very humanitarian of you," said Errol dryly.

Quine laughed again. "Y'see what I mean? You guys crack me up. No, humanitarian ain't what it's about. It's really good business sense."

"Say what?"

"The chinks want blood. They look at it like a balance sheet. Their men die, so your men die. All very neat. But I don't see it like that. At the minute you guys in the police – if you'll pardon me – are shit useless at stopping us. But you get dead police on top of all these gangsters dying, and you get a real hot time for all of us. Now, I don't mind the chinks getting it in the neck, but I don't want us to have extra heat. That's bad news for me, 'cause I'm answerable. So I wire you guys up and put some back-up behind you so you don't get shot, then you hand the tapes over to Scotland Yard, asshole McAllister and his seven dwarves get put behind bars, and we all go back to what we were doing before. You get the Bennys and Courtneys of this world, and we make more money. Sound cool?"

"It sucks," said Errol coldly.

Quine shrugged. "Hey, I don't expect you to go along with all of it. It's against your principles, right? But at least you get to stay alive."

"That's all very well," Jack began, "but there are a few things that don't add up. I mean, we know this house is here. What's to stop us organising a raid on it when we get free?"

"Two things. First, we can move it. Put steel shutters inside any house on this or any estate round here, and it's safe. The decor and fittings – well, we're well-organised, right? That's our strong point. Tapping into the phone or electricity is easier than pissing in a pot. Second thing is that you'll never own up to being here."

"Why not?" asked Errol. But he knew the answer before Quine could say it. "No, I get it," he added, holding up his hand to silence Quine. "If we admit to having been here, then we have to admit to working with the mob and the Triads, and then all hell breaks loose. We lose our careers and you come after us. In the meantime, you could have moved all this anyway. No-win situation, right?"

Quine nodded, smiling. "That's what I like about you. You're a bright boy." He looked at his watch. "Hey, a quarter to seven. I've got a dinner date with very classy lady. You boys make the most of what's in the kitchen. I'll see you later – I'm overseeing this one myself." He smiled and winked broadly, as though trying to impart confidence to them.

He slammed the door behind him as he left. It clanged metallically. Agreeing that there was little they could do for the moment, Jack and Errol busied themselves in the kitchen. Neither had eaten all day, and now they had time to stop running and think about it, both of them were famished. While he cooked, Errol wondered about the keys to the house. It was reasonable to presume that Quine had locked them in. But did Lenny have a key? Although there was no logical reason to doubt Quine's assurances of their safety, there was still one option he'd left unspoken: wire them up, mow them all down, then leave the tapes to be discovered on the bodies. That could satisfy the criteria of both Quine and the Chinese.

They talked of these matters in low undertones while the sound of pots on the stove covered their mutterings. Lenny stayed out in the hall, just too far away to catch it all. In fact, he seemed unconcerned with listening in.

"How the fuck are we going to get out of here?" whispered

Jack in a hoarse undertone.

Errol shrugged. "Quine locked up when he left. The padlock's on the outside. Looks like we're stuck here until he gets back."

"No, there must be some other way. Think about it: if the house is locked from the outside at the front, there must be some other way of getting in and out. This isn't a place for prisoners. We just need to think about it, maybe have a look around."

Errol cast a glance out towards Lenny, who was examining his nails minutely. "So how are we going to do that without Mister Gorilla there getting some idea of what we're up to?"

Jack shrugged. "Did I say I could work everything out?"

When their meal was cooked, Errol ladled it onto two plates, and they took them into the lounge to eat; he made a point of leaving out Lenny. As they ate, Jack eyed the phone in the corner.

"I really need to call home, man. I left the answerphone on, and I need to see if there are any messages."

"Why?"

Jack looked at him, his eyes reflecting a sadness that went beyond their current predicament. "If I'm going to die, I at least want to know if my grandad got there first, y'know?"

"So use the phone," Errol said simply.

Jack picked up the receiver, and was about to dial when Lenny placed his hand gently over the cradle.

"No, son, you don't do that," he said quietly. His voice was gravelly and deep, and all the more menacing for its lack of volume.

"I'm just going to ring my answerphone," Jack replied peevishly, "not the fuckin' old bill."

"Doesn't matter," Lenny said – still in that quiet and menacing tone. "No calls."

He had been silent in coming up behind Jack. It was hard to believe that such a big man could move so swiftly and quietly. But he wasn't the only one who could move in such a way. While Lenny had been talking to Jack, Errol had crept into the kitchen. He gently picked up the saucepan in which he had cooked their meal. A simple, throw-it-in-the-pot stew was all it had been: it had, however, needed a large pot. The saucepan which stood on the work surface was large and copper-bottomed. It weighed heavily in Errol's hands. If he acted quickly, Jack could make his call and then they could search for an exit.

As he crept back into the lounge, Jack and Lenny were still arguing about the pros and cons of phoning out. Jack was trying to persuade Lenny it was purely a personal call, and if he was going to die then he wanted to know about his grandad. Lenny was stoically unconvinced, repeating a simple and unchanging mantra of "no calls, no calls".

Getting closer, Errol drew back the saucepan, holding it with both hands and readying himself for a swing at the back of Lenny's head. Then the very thing happened that he had been hoping to avoid: Jack caught sight of Errol from the corner of his eye. For the briefest of moments he hesitated in mid-sentence, his eyes drawn to the strange sight.

It was enough to make Lenny turn. Errol had no choice but to act – now. With a yell of intense concentration and effort, he swung the pan towards Lenny's head. There was a shocked look on the big gorilla's face as the copper bottom of the pan, hurled at speed, smashed into his face. His nose turned to jelly, blood spurting as the flesh split under the pressure. His front teeth – false, replaced after a fight several years before – broke free from their bridge, choking him. If he had still been conscious, he probably would have seen bright lights explode inside his head. Instead he fell like a stone, knocking the phone off the small wall unit on which it was kept. The unit, nothing more than DIY-store ply and chipboard, splintered under his weight as he fell hard.

Errol looked at Lenny, lying prone, then at the bottom of the saucepan. It was splattered with blood and mucus, and something that looked like a bone splinter slipped down through the ooze.

"I didn't think it'd be that effective," he whispered in awe. Then, snapping himself back into the present: "You make that call. We still might not get out of this. I'm going to tie this twat up tight. When he comes around he's going to want to kill me. I don't aim to be here, but my granny always did believe in safety first."

Before Jack could answer, he had left the room. While Jack called home, and gave his answerphone the code for it to play back his messages, Errol scoured the upstairs rooms for something dependable with which to secure Lenny. He found it in the bedroom which contained two single beds: there were long curtains at the windows, which were purely decorative as the windows were covered with metal plate. The curtains were looped back and tied with a thick, golden cord. Errol took the cord from one curtain: it was of a good length. He pulled at it, testing its strength: it was strong enough. He grabbed the cord from the other curtain and ran downstairs with the two lengths.

In the lounge, Jack was ignoring the prone body of Lenny. Instead, he was listening with impatience to his messages. There were a couple of routine police matters: informants wanting meets, and a message from Bow Road station relating to a robbery he'd been working on a few months back. Then there was a message from McAllister, telling him to get his ass into the station and give himself up. Sharp, but not incriminating. Smart of the fat man to assume that Jack would call his machine at some point.

But it was the last message that he really wanted to hear. After McAllister's harsh tones, and a few seconds' silence as the tape spooled on, his mother's voice came over the wire. She sounded tired and careworn, beaten down.

"Jack, it's me. You there? Pick up. . ." There was a pause, and then: "I suppose you're out working again, or getting drunk with other coppers. Well think about this. While you're out there enjoying yourself, dad is dying." Her voice broke with sobs, making Jack wince. Tears prickled the backs of his eyes. "He's going, Jack. The nuns reckon it'll all be over by the morning. He's slipped into a coma. If you hear this before tomorrow, please try and get here. God knows I never could make it up with him, but he loved you like you were his, not mine. Oh god, just try and get here. . ."

With a click, the phone went dead. After a couple of seconds of the dialling tone buzzing in his ear, the machine automatically switched off, and there was nothing but silence.

Jack sat with the phone still at his ear, tears rolling down his face. Who was he crying for? Was it for old Danny, for his mother, or was it for himself? He had no idea: his head was full of conflicting thoughts and memories. He could remember his mother arguing with his grandfather when he was young. Mostly over him. His mother couldn't accept that Jack would rather spend time with the old man than holed up in suburban hell with his family. She could never accept that he loved the East End and its decay. He loved the way the people clung on to their identity when all around them was changing. She couldn't accept that he wanted to do something that dragged him down the social ladder she had so assiduously climbed at her own mother's prompting.

In the end, his mother couldn't accept the vast chasm between the men and women in the family. Right or wrong, the women had chosen one path, and the men had stubbornly stuck to another. Ultimately, this was why he was crying. They were divided, falling into that emotional pit that his grandad called the darkness.

He realised that he was crying for himself.

When Errol came down the stairs with the cords, he found Jack still clutching the receiver, tears running down his face.

"Jack, is he –" he didn't want to finish the question.

Jack shook his head slowly. "Not yet. He's in a coma."

Errol stood uncertainly. He wanted to comfort Jack, but was torn between that and finishing the task in hand. A groan from Lenny brought him back to his senses.

"Let's get this bastard tied up," he said, almost to himself. He sunk to his knees and turned Lenny over, pulling his arms behind him. He looped the cord over Lenny's head, pulling it down to his chest. With his knee in Lenny's back, grinding him into the carpet, he pulled the cord as tight as it would go, looped over arms, chest, and around his hands. Rolls of flesh on Lenny's arm spilled over the tight cord. Errol tied several knots in the cord, until there was no longer enough to make another knot.

The shock and pain started to bring Lenny round. He moaned softly, moving his head against the carpet. He vaguely realised that something was wrong, and strained against the constraining ropes. The shock cleared his head, and he roared, kicking out in rage. The cuban heels on his shoes caught Errol a blow to the calf. Although not a particularly painful or crippling blow in itself, it caught a nerve in his leg, and deadened it. Unable to feel, or support weight, Errol found himself toppling over. There was nothing he could do: he fell sideways and crashed to the carpet.

Lenny turned himself over and thrust himself into an upright position.

"Jack, for fuck's sakes," Errol yelled, struggling to move his leaden leg and get back on balance. The shout seemed to rouse Jack from his reverie. Jumping to his feet, he took one step across the room and crashed his booted foot into Lenny's already bloody and torn face. The sharp toe of his cowboy boot ripped the skin over Lenny's eye, causing him to scream in agony. He fell backwards, once again rendered unconscious, his head hitting the carpet with such force that it bounced a few inches before settling again.

"About time, too," said Errol as he massaged his sore calf. "Now help get the bastard tied properly."

They looped the remaining cord around Lenny's legs, tying it tightly. Errol stood up, ready to leave, but Jack remained over the body.

"What are you doing?" Errol asked in bemusement.

Jack looked up and grinned, brandishing the wallet he had just extracted from Lenny's jacket pocket. "When we get out of here, we're going to need this. I mean, have you got anything on you?"

This was a good point: they'd had to escape from Errol's apartment so quickly during the afternoon that neither of them had had a chance to grab any money.

Jack left Lenny on the floor and joined Errol in the search for a way out. Both men were convinced that there must be one: but where? They started on the ground floor, trying all the shutters in the lounge and kitchen. The door was a non-starter, although Errol checked it for any hidden catches.

"McAllister was right about you," Jack said sardonically as he watched his friend meticulously search the door.

"And which particular insult would that be?"

"The one where he told me you'd be a great crime writer but

a shit copper as you had too much imagination."

Errol said nothing, just smiled.

The downstairs drew a blank. If there was nothing upstairs, then they were as good as dead.

Jack and Errol took separate bedrooms, neither of which yielded a result. Things were starting to look desperate. There was only the bathroom left.

"Doesn't look too great for us," Errol said miserably as they met on the landing.

Jack shook his head. "No. On the other hand. . ." he made a quick mental calculation on the size of the lounge. That was two rooms knocked into one. Two rooms upstairs, both of which were small. . . perhaps that was the answer. "We might be alright yet, old son," he said gleefully, punching Errol on the shoulder.

Jack went into the bathroom, and felt around the metal shutter covering the window. "If I'm right," he said while he searched, "then the bathroom and the two bedrooms are the combined length of the lounge."

"So?"

"So the kitchen's an extension, probably with a flat roof. In which case. . ." He felt a small catch at the very bottom of the shutter. It clicked at a touch, and the shutter loosened.

"In which case, this is the perfect way out," he said in triumph as he pulled the shutter up over his head. Errol took the weight of it as Jack fiddled impatiently with the catch on the window frame. There was board over the window, and it took him some seconds to push out the few nails tacking it to the wall. It fell with a clatter onto the flat roof of the kitchen, only a couple of feet below.

"Oh, very nice," Errol said admiringly. Jack looked over his shoulder and grinned again before clambering out of the window and lowering himself onto the kitchen roof. Errol followed, his muscles still protesting about the weight of the metal shutter, which he lowered gently behind him.

They climbed down from the end of the kitchen extension, using a drain pipe to aid their descent. It was now dark. Although neither man had a watch, Errol estimated the time at around nine o'clock, possibly a half hour later. Now they had to work out how to get into the road, as they were surrounded on all sides by overgrown gardens and boarded-up houses.

There were lights about three or four houses away, so they climbed over the broken fences and across the weed-strewn gardens until they reached the garden of the property. From inside they could hear the sound of a television.

"What shall we do?" Jack asked. "Go straight in and freak them out?"

Errol shrugged. "I don't see that we've got a lot of option. Let's just go for it."

They walked up the garden towards the back door, Jack in the lead. If they were lucky, it would be the home of someone elderly, who'd create no problems. If they were really unlucky, it could be a squat filled with large and hairy bikers who would hit first and ask questions later.

Luck was on their side. An old couple sat watching television; they were shocked at th sight of the intruders, and the old man protested that they had no money. Errol did his best to reassure him that they didn't want anything, and they were out of the door before the old couple had a chance to move.

Out onto the streets: they both felt happier with open ground around them. A few moments to get their bearings, and they headed in the direction of Bromley-By-Bow underground station.

"D'you think they'll call the police?" asked Errol.

"Maybe. I wouldn't blame them."

"Neither would I. But neither would I want our descriptions getting back into circulation too quickly."

Jack shrugged. "Nothing we can do about that."

They emerged into the relative civilisation of the Blackwall Tunnel Approach Road, on the far side of which lay the station.

"So what the hell do we do now?" Errol asked.

Jack looked at his friend with an expression that showed his real concerns. "I'm going to the hospice. I've got to, man. I must. After that. . ."

Errol grabbed him by the arm, stopping them both. "If you do that, there's a good chance they'll get you."

"Who?" Jack queried with a smile, "our lot, the Chinese, or the mob?" He laughed shortly. "Some choice, eh?"

Errol grinned wryly. "Put like that. . .okay, you go to the hospice. I've got a few plans of my own."

"Like what?"

Errol noticed a bus pull in at the stop across the road. It was headed back towards Hackney. "Never mind, man," he said, bolting into the road and dodging traffic. "Just make sure you get to Wanstead tonight."

"But –" Errol's sudden movement had taken Jack by surprise, and he was prevented from following by a sudden surge in the traffic. When he was able to dodge the cars, Errol was already on the bus, and it was pulling away.

"Dammit," Jack yelled into the night. Whatever stupid idea Errol had in mind, Jack had wanted to be part of it. Now he could only go his own way.

CHAPTER FOURTEEN

It took Jack forty minutes to get to the hospice. Ten minutes to wait for a bus. Twenty minutes for the bus to get to Victoria Park in Hackney, where he jumped off. Another ten minutes to hurry through the empty Hackney back streets, out into Cambridge Heath Road. Forty minutes in which to think about the old man, dying with all his family around him. All except Jack. He didn't even know if he could afford to stay that long: there was Errol to think of. Errol used to call Jack crazy, but he was just as capable of doing some idiotic things himself. The last thing Jack would ever consider was going to Wanstead that night – it was like walking into a trap set by both sides. Errol, on the other hand, was just stupid enough to do it. . .if he thought he had a plan.

Jack strode into the hospice through the entrance he'd used just a day before. The old man had enjoyed his day with young Danny; Jack was glad his ex-wife had relented. If he managed to get out of this, he'd have to explain to his son about death. Maybe.

Maybe someone else would have to explain about the death of the old man... and Jack.

They were clustered around Danny O'Day like flies around a piece of rotting meat: the whole family. Sons, daughters, in-laws, kids. Only his ex-wife and son were missing. He was glad. The stench of hypocrisy smelt worse than the decay of death and the odour of antiseptic that he'd noticed on previous visits. The other men in the ward were all asleep, either ignoring what was happening, or blissfully unaware of it. Jack's boots clattered on the floor, cutting through the low hum of whispered conversation around the bed.

Jack's mother turned around, barely acknowledging her son.

"So you decided to show your face then," she said bitterly. Initially her face was set hard and unforgiving, but it melted when she saw he was covered in dust, dirt and splashes of blood. "What on earth have you been doing?" She was now concerned and moved towards him, but he waved her away.

All the family turned to look at him. His father moved forward, opening his mouth to say something. Jack gave him a look that strangled any hypocrisy at birth: he hadn't spoken to his dad for five years, and had no intention of doing so now. The crowds of relatives parted like the Red Sea, allowing Jack to get in close to the bed. Danny lay on his back, arms outside neatly folded sheets. He looked peaceful, with his eyes closed, although his breathing was laboured. He seemed too neat, too clean: his hair had been brushed back, and there was no stubble on his cheeks, as though the nuns had shaved him ready to meet his maker.

Jack knelt beside the bed and grabbed the old man's hand, squeezing it tight, trying to say everything he'd ever felt about him in one futile gesture. There was no response: not that he'd really expected anything, but some part of him hoped for a fairy tale ending, where Danny would open his eyes and grant his blessing on them all before finally slipping away.

Instead, it would be boring and mundane. He'd lie here all night, slowly fading, while the family sat in irrelevant reverence, pausing only to bitch at each other. Had Doreen been better to Danny than Joe, or Joe better than Marie? Faces and names, that's all his relatives were to Jack. Useless.

He felt a hand on his shoulder. Turning, he saw his Uncle Joe, Danny's eldest son, looking down at him with a reverence and respect that bordered on parody. Jack shrugged him off. Joe looked like Danny but a neat, sanitised, suburban version of him.

"Don't be like that, Jack," he simpered. "At a time like this we should all be pulling together."

"You what?" hissed Jack, anger contorting his face. "You couldn't stand him, thought yourselves above him." He addressed himself to them all. "You treated him like dirt and now you gather round like fucking vultures. Except there are no pickings here, 'cause he didn't have the same twisted values as you lot. Why don't you just fuck off and leave him to die in peace?"

He turned back to Danny. The old man lay impassive and unaware of what was going on around him. Behind Jack's back there were mumblings and mutterings of discontent. He heard his father's voice begin with a cough: "Jack, there's no need –" interrupted by Joe's wife, Aileen, "I always said that boy would come to no good."

Jack leant over his grandfather, laughing to himself. "They couldn't organise a piss-up in a brewery, could they, Da?" he whispered to the old man. "Hopeless, the lot of 'em. I know what you want. I'll be off now. You remember me telling you about Errol? Crazy bastard's got himself in shit – even deeper than me, this time. I've got to go and help him. But you know I love you, you old git. I'll see you around some time, eh?" He kissed the old man softly on the cheek and rose to his feet, letting his grandfather's hand fall back on the immaculately made bed.

Jack turned and walked away. He had nothing more to say to any of them. His mother held out her hand to stay him, but he ignored her. There were things to do.

Jack left the ward and walked slowly down the long corridor towards the exit. The next time he'd see Danny, the old man would be in a wooden box. That's if Jack didn't end up in one first. But he preferred to remember him with a cigarette hanging from his mouth, nursing a pint of Guinness and studying the *Sporting Life*, wondering if he'd get a win-double at Wincanton. Not lying there, artificially clean.

The tears were running down Jack's cheeks as he reached the double doors at the end of the corridor. He didn't realise he was crying until they ran into the corners of his mouth and he tasted the salt. He paused before the doors to wipe them away. Then, with a deep breath, he walked through the entrance and out into the night.

***

The knocking on Devon Calvert's front door was loud and insistent. It went on and on, ignoring the imprecations of the householder to "shut the fuck up" as he blearily made his way down the stairs. He shook his head, trying to clear his sleep-addled brain. He was over six feet, heavily muscled, and carried a carving knife in his right hand. It always paid to be careful.

Devon opened the door. "What the hell is this all about?" he moaned. The words stuck in his throat as he saw who had been knocking. "Mister Ross – what's going down?" His eyes widened in shock. The last time Devon had seen Errol Ross, the copper had been in the witness box and Devon in the dock. The charges were drug related, and Errol had been doing his best to keep Devon out of prison. Firstly because the charges were a frame-up, and secondly because Devon was the best informer Errol had. Unfortunately, it wasn't enough, and Devon did three months. That had been about a year before, and he hadn't seen Errol since his release.

All of this ran through Errol's mind as he stood on the doorstep. "Aren't you going to invite me in, Dev?" he asked as he barged past Calvert and into the small, scruffy lounge. The air was heavy with the smell of soldering irons and ganja, pieces of circuit board scattered across the coffee table among the dirty mugs and discarded roaches.

"What. . . I mean, what. . ." Devon scratched his head with the hand that held the knife. Then he remembered he was naked. "Shit. Let me get some clothes on," he said, running up the stairs. Errol stayed in the lounge, chuckling.

When Devon returned, Errol started over: "I need your help, Dev. Could you wire me up?"

"I don't do that sort of thing any more, Mister Ross," Devon replied, casting a guilty glance over the contents of the table. "Those are out of radios'n'stuff," he added.

Errol smiled. "Don't piss about, Dev. You did the best bugging and tapping around these parts. You forget I went to court for you. I knew that Courtney had you set up, just because your prices went up."

"Up?" Devon snorted, sitting down on the ragged leather sofa and searching for something useable among the roaches. "Courtney's trouble was that he wanted me to do it for nothing. I mean, a man's got to eat, Mister Ross."

"And he never found out about. . ." Errol raised an eyebrow.

Devon looked shocked. "You know Courtney, Mister Ross.

If he knew I was your snout, I'd be dangling from fucking Tower Bridge by my bollocks. Or I would have been, if the cunt wasn't dead."

Errol sat down next to Devon. "So what are you doing now? It's a bit early for you to be in bed. Especially sleeping." He looked around for a clock. The video, if it was set right, gave him ten twelve. Just over an hour and a quarter.

"I've been working on a job," Devon said uneasily. "Nothing dodgy, honest." He could see from Errol's expression that he didn't believe him. "Well, anyway, I've been on this job, and I've been doing nights and everything, without a stop. I went to bed about six 'cause I've been at it four days without sleep, and I did this when I dropped off." He showed Errol a small solder burn on his forearm. "It's like a warning, innit?"

Errol noticed that Devon carefully avoided mentioning the nature of this little job. But now wasn't the time to rake over the coals. He wanted help, so he had to play by Devon's rules.

"I'm not interested in what you're up to, Dev. On my life. On my granny's life. I do need your help, though. I've got to be wired up."

"I thought you had geezers who did all that for you?" Devon replied suspiciously.

Errol smiled. "This is a little private job."

Realisation dawned on Devon's face. "So you're moonlighting, eh? Shit, everyone's at it these days. Why didn't you say so in the first place? 'Course I'll help you."

"How much?"

Devon shook his head and declined the notes Errol pulled from his pockets. "Call it mate's rates, Mister Ross. You owe me one now."

It was an ominous thought, to be in debt to someone like Devon; but Errol was in no position to argue. Besides, you can't pay off those type of debts when you're dead or in prison. And he was sure he'd end up with either option.

"You're on." But it wasn't without trepidation.

Devon nodded abruptly in satisfaction. "Follow me, then," he said, rising from the sofa. Errol followed him out of the room, wondering where they were headed as Devon opened the cupboard door leading under the stairs. To Errol's amazement he pulled back the carpet and opened a trap-door in the floorboards. He looked up and grinned.

"Funny what you can find in these crappy old houses, ain't it?" He climbed down a ladder into a small cellar. Errol laughed, shook his head, and followed. As he descended, a low-watt bulb suddenly illuminated the small room. It smelt of damp, and part of the wall was lined with black plastic bags, tacked to the wall with gaffer tape and half-driven nails. When Errol was at the bottom of the ladder he had to stand with his head bent, otherwise he risked knocking himself out on the joists.

Devon was sorting through a pile of junk on an old trestle table. He had soldering irons, reels of tape, small cassettes from Dictaphone machines, and in one corner a pile of DAT recorders.

"Since you're not strictly legit any more, I might as well give you the full s.p.," Devon grinned. "I've got the lot down here, enough to wire up anything from a rat to a suite of offices. And that lot over there –" he pointed at the DAT recorders "– means I can do a nice line in tape counterfeiting if it comes my way." He turned back to the bench, and began to unwind a length of thin wire. "So what's the job then, Mister Ross? Just got to wire you up, or what?"

"Just me," said Errol slowly. How much of the story should he trust Devon with? He decided not to risk too much. "There's this geezer down Wapping and Limehouse who's as bent as a nine pound note. But he's fucking clever – got me and Jack on the run for something we didn't do."

"You on the run?" Devon stopped, looking amazed. "Straight up?"

Errol nodded. "We need evidence before we can get ourselves in the clear and get him done, know what I mean?"

Devon shook his head sadly, returning to the unravelling of wires. "I'm with you on this, Mister Ross. I hate bent coppers. Wasn't it one who got me banged up?"

Errol sighed inwardly with relief. "Glad you see it like that, Dev."

"Nah, I really hate 'em," Devon continued, tinkering with a

small recorder. He stopped screwing the heads tight to emphasise a point with his screwdriver. "Point is, Mister Ross, you know where you are with coppers like you. We're on one side, you're on the other. It's a kind of understanding, right? But bent coppers?" He returned to the matter in hand. "You can't talk to 'em. For a start, they might go back and grass you up to someone like Courtney fuckin' Gold. Sod that. If I'm going to get nicked, I want to end up in nick, not in Epping Forest on the end of a knife. It's a hard old world, Mister Ross, and if people don't play by some sort of rules, then everything goes under. Am I right?"

"Right," said Errol, leaning back against the ladder. He was only half-listening. His mind was occupied with the meet: would Jack make it? He didn't fancy facing McAllister alone. And he wasn't even tooled up. "Dev, got any shooters?"

Devon looked truly shocked. "Fuck me, Mister Ross, ain't one surprise enough for a night? Have I got any shooters. . . well, I don't as a rule," he continued cautiously, "but as it happens I was looking after something for my brother-in-law. Hang on." He put the recording equipment down on the bench, and reached over to the black plastic bags. Pulling one aside, he revealed a hole in the cellar wall. Inside was another bag, tightly wrapped in tape. He took it out, and scored it open with his screwdriver. Inside was a Mauser machine pistol, the shoulder grip detached. There were two magazines of ammunition. He solemnly handed it over to Errol. "If Malcolm ever finds out this got back in circulation, let alone to someone who was old bill, I'd be dead. And I ain't joking. So look after it."

Errol took the pistol. He inserted one magazine and put the other in his back pocket. The grip and bag he dropped to the floor.

"I owe you for this, Dev," he said, breath coming hard as the adrenalin started to flow. It was becoming all too real.

"You owe me big time. Don't forget when I call it in, okay?" He waited for Errol to nod agreement. "Right then. One last thing."

"What's that?"

Devon chuckled, shaking his head. "You want this fucking

recorder fitted, don't you? After I've gone to all this bother as well."

Errol smiled. His nerves were getting the better of him. Chill out and relax: it was the only way to give himself a chance. "Okay," he said, "let's do it."

"Right. Pull it up." Devon indicated Errol's polo neck, which he stripped off. "Okay. This will hurt like hell when it comes off, but it'd take a bomb to shift it."

While Errol stood, wincing and shuddering at the cold touch of the small microphones and wires as they were trailed across his skin and attached by sticky tape which he felt pucker over his chest, Devon wove an intricate cat's cradle of wire and microphones around his body. There were four, attached to two small micro-recorders which he looped on Errol's 501s.

Devon stood back, examining his handiwork. "Yeah. That'll do nicely. You see these." He fingered the four microphones, which were at four points marking a square on Errol's chest. Errol nodded. "Well, they're the best that money can buy. They could pick up a gnat farting at a hundred yards. Even through this –" he picked up Errol's jumper and felt the wool's thickness "– you'll get good clarity up to sixty yards. Audible to eighty. Four microphones gives you a good circle of sound, allowing for anything that may get in the way while moving around, or any background noise. Two recorders will give you a copy or a back-up. The tapes will last seventy minutes, and the batteries haven't been used since I changed them a couple of weeks back." He handed Errol his jumper. "That do you, Mister Ross?"

"That –" Errol pulled the jumper over his head "– is brilliant. But there is one last thing."

Devon rolled his eyes. "What now?"

Errol grinned sheepishly. "Call me a cab, would you? I've got to get over Wanstead Flats by half eleven."

***

Jack was leaving the grounds of the hospice when he heard the squeal of brakes and screech of tyres behind him. He turned swiftly, prepared to flee: being on the run from everyone was too much for his nerves, especially at a time like this. A small, sky-blue Vauxhall Astra had pulled up a few feet from him. A street light reflected on the windscreen, rendering the occupants invisible. Jack's heart leapt into his throat as the door opened, and someone hurriedly got out.

It was with a strange mixture of relief and anti-climax that he realised it was Wendy Coles.

"Christ almighty," Jack began, voice trembling, "I wondered who it was then –"

Wendy cut him short. "Jack. Where's Errol?"

"I don't know. He –"

"What do you mean, you don't know? Where is he, you twat?" She shook Jack by the arms.

"I mean I don't know." Jack pulled himself away. "He got on a bus and said he'd meet me later." He didn't want to tell her where: he couldn't trust anybody.

"Jack, listen to me," she said, grabbing him again. "I overheard McAllister and Cann in his office. I don't know what you're supposed to be doing with them, but they're going to kill you. I've been over half of East London looking for both of you. We've got to stop Errol going. Now. Wherever it is."

Jack said nothing, his brain racing: could he trust her? She seemed genuine enough. "What does it matter to you?" he asked, buying time – and maybe hoping to learn something.

"McAllister's been fucking me for months now, using me, the bastard. I thought there was something there but. . .he just wanted information on a roundabout route. I've been thinking about it. While he's been screwing me, I've been telling him the whereabouts and activities of every villain on the island and it's surrounds. And I like you, and I like Errol." The last sentence was added as an afterthought, but Jack could see from her face that there was more to it than that.

He mentally flipped a coin: she won.

"Okay, I'll come with you," he said decisively. "What time is it now?"

Wendy looked at her watch. "Quarter to eleven."

"Right. We've got three quarters of an hour to get to Wanstead Flats."

She nodded. "No problem."

"One thing, though," Jack added, holding up a hand to stay

her. "I want to go to St Catherine's Dock first."

"What. . ." Puzzlement was writ large on her face.

"Just do it, babe." There was a steely edge to his voice that would brook no argument.

They got in Wendy's car and screeched into the night. It took her just eight minutes to reach the entrance to St Catherine's Dock. Jack opened his door and turned to her.

"Five minutes, that's all."

While Wendy kept revving the engine, making the old car tick over so that it wouldn't stall, Jack hurried down the dock, past the benches and over the beautifully restored, almost to the point of looking fake, cobbles. He stood at the brink of the water, looking over the chain railings into the Thames. The oily water flowed sluggishly beneath the dock.

For a moment, time stood still. The sound of the engine and the distant thrum of London by night died away. The twinkling of the lights from converted warehouses starred the waters, and Jack was taken back just over a week, to when he had brought Danny here for the last time. He remembered the old man hawking phlegm into the river, partly due to his illness but also to express his disgust at the way the city had changed. He had spoken of the darkness, and Jack had listened, not sure of what it really meant.

Now, as he looked over the dead water, he knew: knew that the darkness was the greed and corruption that was no longer kept at bay. Knew that it meant people like Grazione and Gold being elbowed out of position by bigger, nastier machines like those of Quine and Lao. But ultimately the darkness wasn't about them, nor was it about the likes of McAllister and James, who were no better than the people they were trying to stop.

In the end, the darkness was about the people who let it happen. The people like himself, Wendy, and Errol. The people who tried to do their best but lost direction or gave up hope. The people who let the canker of hopelessness eat into their souls until there was nothing left: no joy, no love, no hope.

Now he finally grasped what Danny O'Day had spent most of his life trying to do: fight against that one memory of seeing the police kill Bob Steele. Fight against the despair of an established order crumbling. Established in a mental sense: a sense of values and morals. Danny had spent the rest of his life wrestling with that. Jack was in a similar positon. But he could pick up the torch and run.

"Goodbye, Da," he whispered to the water. "I must be bloody thick, but I finally got the point."

He turned and ran back to the car. Wendy was watching him anxiously.

"What was all that about?" she asked tentatively as he eased into his seat.

"Tell you someday. Just drive."

She ground the car into gear and set off in the direction of Wanstead Flats. It was eleven o'clock. They had half an hour to get there, and the roads were clear.

***

The cab driver dropped his fare by the gates of the London Cemetery. On one side of the road lay a vast expanse of green and shrubbery bordered by houses. A little way back down the road lay the suburban remnants of Epping Forest known as Wanstead Flats. But the cabbie was curious.

"Tell me, squire," he said as he counted out change under the weak light of the dashboard, "what do you want to come to the cemetery for at this time of night? I mean, it's closed, ain't it?"

Errol smiled grimly and took the change. "I'm booking myself a plot."

"Fuckin' nutter," the cabbie grumbled as Errol slammed the door and walked away. The cabbie put the car into gear and turned round in the forecourt of the cemetery, accelerating out into Rabbits Road without pausing to look for other traffic.

Errol stood by the wrought iron Victorian gates, waiting for him to go. The gothic towers holding the gates in place and giving the staff an office of some kind loomed ominously in the dark night. Owls hooted and squirrels ran riot with urban foxes over the acres of old headstones and greenery that lay behind the gates. Errol had wanted to be dropped here: it was nice and memorable, should the cabbie have recognised him. It was possible that he and Jack had been featured on TV by now. At the very least there would be enquiries made of local cab firms: God alone knew how many of those he'd had to do himself in the past.

The cemetery was just far enough off the track to throw anyone, and near enough for him to walk quickly to the rendezvous. He had little idea of the time, only that it was now past eleven: the cabbie had turned up the eleven o'clock news on his car radio, and after that there had been a couple of songs and some idiotic babble on Capital FM. Say, ten past?

Errol felt the cold sweat of terror trickle down his back, forming a pool in the hollow, making his jumper stick to him. On his chest, he could feel the beads of perspiration gather on the edges of the tapes, run down the wires. It made him itch like hell.

Trembling, he began the short walk back to the rendezvous. At this time of night, the roads were virtually empty around these parts. During the day they were clogged up with funeral traffic and people making a short cut between the Romford Road and Leytonstone Green Man, from whence they could easily reach the M11 and M25. Now, only the occasional set of headlights cut through the dark.

On one side of the road were a few shops and some houses. The far side was devoted to the Flats: great expanses of flattened forest now given over to football pitches and other recreational activities. Except for the small section that Errol headed for: this was still wild, and in a grove of trees was a large pond, in the middle of which lay an overgrown island. Ducks, geese and swans placidly inhabited the pond, and the island was not quite cut off; on the side farthest from the road, a thin strip of raised, sandy soil provided a footpath. Children played there in summer.

This was where Errol was to play a totally different game.

When he reached the outcrop of trees, he prepared to cross the road.

"Jack, wherever you are now, I hope you get here," he muttered to himself, reaching under his jumper and flicking the tiny switches on the two tape recorders – one for back-up. There would be enough tape to record any meeting that was to take place this evening. Somehow he couldn't imagine it being a long, drawn-out one.

Errol started to walk across the deserted road, in small measured steps. He scanned the darkness for any signs of life. The permutations of the meeting's possibilities raced through his mind. If everyone played it straight, then McAllister would assume that he and Jack wished to join their vigilante group, it would be recorded, and Quine's men would act as security. Then he could hand over the tape to C10, Scotland Yard's internal investigation department, leaving everyone happy.

Alternatively, McAllister could try to kill them, and Quine's men could defend them. Or Quine's men could try to rub them all out in one fell swoop. Altogether, it didn't look like a particularly pretty picture for either Jack or Errol. All he could hope was that they could somehow scramble out of it in the same way that they had at Zak's garage.

Was that really less than a day ago? Probably only twelve hours if you stopped to add it up. Errol winced, feeling muscles ache from the day's activities. He was sure that he had injured himself in some way, apart from the burn on his shoulder: the adrenalin of being on the run had dulled it up until now, but the pain and fatigue slipped through his preoccupation.

Errol set foot on the rough kerbstone that separated the Flats from the road. He paused for a fraction of a second – long enough to clear his mind and steel his nerve.

He didn't get a chance.

"Hello, Errol old son. You're early. Where's that fuckin' kike?"

The whiskey-foetid breath was unmistakable. McAllister clapped his hand on Errol's shoulder, propelling him forward a stumbling step.

"Glad you made it, at any rate."

Guided by McAllister's hand, Errol stumbled through the dark foliage, away from the road and around the pond. In the dark it was hard to pick out the strip of soil linking the island to the rest of the Flats, but McAllister's aim was unerring. Errol took hesitant steps across the strip, blundering through the trees around the edge of the island. In the middle was a clearing. Five men stood like Easter Island statues in long overcoats, calm and impassive. By the dim light of the crescent moon, Errol found it hard to make out their faces.

That made the odds three to one – if Jack showed. If he got here too late, then it was six to one. Unless you counted Quine's men: but they were an unknown quantity. Christ, he wished they hadn't been so hard on Lenny. That would anger Quine, as would their escape. Right now, any ally was a good one.

"You don't know the lads, do you?" McAllister whispered in his ear.

"No." He didn't want to commit himself by saying any more.

McAllister stepped in front of Errol. "You know James, yeah? I think you know George Cann as well." Cann nodded at Errol. "This is Day, Fitch, and Winston. They work at other nicks than yours and mine. We decided we were sick of all these wankers getting away with shit 'cause they knew how to remain just outside of our grasp. There's too much of it going on, son."

Errol cleared his throat. "I'm with you there. Me and Jack both."

Cann smiled – or at least, it looked like a smile in the darkness of the night. "That was a nice job this morning. Bit stupid to do it in the light, though. And unmasked. Impetuous, wouldn't you say?"

McAllister nodded briefly. "Yeah. And we can't afford that. You I could take, but that fuckin' nutter Goldman?" He shook his head sadly. "No way. He's too out of order."

Errol stood stock still. He noticed that they were starting to fan out on either side of him. If he chose to run, there would be nowhere to go. The very reason Quine had chosen the island – its isolation and lack of cover – would be the end for him.

"I'm sorry about this, son," McAllister continued. "I don't expect you'll believe me, but I am. You're a good copper. You could have been an asset to us. But you will insist on running around with that loony kike."

"There's no other viable option, Errol. I'm really sorry. I joined up to ice villains, not good blokes like you." James spoke for the first time, his voice heavy with emotion.

"Whoa – wait up, here," Errol pleaded, looking around anxiously. With no sign of Jack, it would be okay to temporarily dump him in it and buy some time. "Who says I want to stick with Jack? He's unreliable and a bit crazy. He's my friend, but fuck it – we're talking about my life, here. Why should I go when I can get rid of him for you? Wait 'til he gets here."

"No, son." Cann spoke slowly and softly. "That won't work. Even if we could trust you over that – and I don't, 'cause I know you're too strong on mates to ever do that – then there's still the little problem of this morning. How can we explain that one away?" He took a gun from his pocket.

Errol looked around swiftly: all six men had drawn guns, and had formed into a semi-circle that now surrounded him on three sides. He had been manoeuvred so that the path to the mainland was behind them. Behind Errol were only a clump of trees and the pond. He could run, but there was nowhere to hide for any length of time.

The six men raised their guns in unison. Crazy thoughts crossed Errol's mind: it was like being in a bad gangster movie, where all the deaths were orchestrated. If this was going to be a re-run of a Sam Peckinpah movie, then he'd go down fighting.

He reached under his jumper for the butt of the Mauser, pulling it free of his waistband. He levelled the gun and pulled the trigger: a splutter of fire anticipated the first shots from McAllister's men, and cut through Winston's overcoat, carving a great gash of torn flesh across his abdomen. He looked down in shock and screamed, a strange high-pitched wail that cut through the still of night. The gun dropped from his hand as he fell backwards, twitching as he hit the ground.

It was only a fraction of a second, but it drew the attention of the others: they turned towards Winston, taking their collective eye off the target. Errol took that chance to turn and throw himself into the clump of trees. A volley of shots followed him.

He hit the ground with a muffled thump, branches pressing into his flesh, leaves and earth filling his mouth. A searing pain filled his shoulder as the earlier burn was reopened by the impact and started to weep. But there were other searing pains: one in his calf, cutting off all feeling momentarily before hitting him like a red hot needle skewering the muscle. He screamed into the ground for this and the other pain: a dull thump of heat that speared under his rib, gouging out the muscle and splintering bone. Part of his mind clung on to sense and prayed that nothing vital had been hit. Splinters from the trees showered around him where the other shots had hit, missing their target. As the initial pain died, he could feel the warm flow of blood down his leg and his torso. He tried to throw himself over onto his other side, so at least he could take another shot when they came for him.

But they didn't come. And all he could hear were the distant yells of pain and anger.

As McAllister's men fired, four figures appeared from the water around the island. They were wet through, glistening in the dark. Each held a hand gun. One of them was Quine, and another was Lao. Neither trusted the other enough to depute responsibility. They were accompanied by a mob hit man and a Triad hit man, both hand-picked for tonight's mission. They had been waiting on the edge of the island, hidden by the water, since ten o'clock. Numb from the cold, they had nonetheless kept silent for the whole meeting, biding their time.

The chatter of Errol's Mauser had been their call to action: emerging from the water, they had been hidden by the trees when McAllister's men had turned their fire on Errol. Quine, leading by his military experience, had strung his men around the edge of the clearing so that they, like McAllister's men, were in a semi-circle. Before the first volley of shots had died away, Quine had fired. In the dark, and after so many years, his aim was rusty: the shot intended for Cann's chest had caught him in the arm. He spun to the ground in shock and pain, his weapon flung from him. Lao fired high and wide, fright making him lose whatever skill he possessed. Day and Fitch dived for cover and fired back while McAllister risked his own skin to drag Cann to safety.

"Who the fuck are they? Who?" He yelled – to no-one in

particular.

James did what Errol would have expected: he took flight. He ran across the strip of soil, stumbling into the water. The stumble saved him as one of the hit men fired. The shot was off target because of his fall, and it ripped the shoulder of his overcoat with enough force to throw him into the pond.

The hit man stepped forward and took aim to finish the job. He was stopped by the twin beams of car headlights which illuminated him and temporarily blinded his sight.

CHAPTER FIFTEEN

It should have been an easy trip: from St Catherine's Dock through to Hackney, down the Eastway to Leyton, cut through to the Green Man roundabout at Leytonstone, then along to Blake Hall Road and along Aldersbrook. At the end of Aldersbrook, where it ran into Rabbits Road, lay the rendezvous.

Wendy put her foot to the floor, and sped through the Eastway, regardless of the traffic coming off the Bow flyover turn-off. Even at this time of night there was a steady stream, brought up short by her cutting across.

"Shit," Jack said, turning in his seat to watch the pile-up behind them. "Calm down for Christ's sakes – we want to get there alive."

"We want to get there in time," she said grimly, casting an eye at the clock. It was just past eleven.

They roared down the Eastway, making good time. Wendy negotiated the one-way system around Leyton with ease, and hit the Green Man roundabout. . .

And trouble.

"Oh shit. Shit, shit, shit," she yelled, emphasising each word with a thump on the steering wheel.

"Oh great." Jack couldn't believe it: the middle of the night, and some idiot in a ten-tonner had decided to spill his load across the roundabout. It was hard to tell exactly what had happened, but the lorry appeared to have jack-knifed, the doors on the container spilling open and depositing several tonnes of frozen lamb across the road. Cars were backed up around the roundabout, honking furiously.

They were on the Leytonstone High Road turn-off. They needed to get to the Bush Road turn-off, which was the next on their right. Unfortunately, the traffic flow was, being English, to the left. The road was at a standstill, and time was running out.

Jack looked around hurriedly. "The traffic ain't moving, Wend. Not at all."

"I know," she sighed. "We're stuck."

"No we ain't," he said with a manic grin. "It's only the next one on the right, y'know?"

She looked at him with a furrowed brow, not understanding. Then it hit her: "Yeah, great idea," she beamed.

Gritting her teeth, she ground the car into gear, and reversed up as far as she dare – there was another car approaching from behind. It screeched to a halt and hooted furiously. Wendy threw the car into first gear and turned out of the traffic. The oncoming side of the road was empty, as nothing could get past the roundabout. It gave Wendy the perfect opportunity to cut across, and up onto the pavement. Jack prayed that there were no pedestrians as the car flew across the flagstones and wove its way between the walkway and the cars stuck on the roundabout. Horror dawned on the panicked and frightened faces of drivers who couldn't believe that anyone was driving through them in the wrong direction and they tried to back up out of the way as Wendy skilfully manoeuvred her car between them.

She had no time to waste.

Jack shut his eyes and hoped for the best. When he opened them again, they were speeding down Bush Road to turn into Blake Hall Road and Aldersbrook. He looked at the clock: only a few minutes wasted.

"Hang on, my son," he whispered under his breath. But deep in his gut there was an uneasy feeling that something was going wrong.

Wendy drove the last mile and a half in a couple of minutes, touching seventy as she threw the car around corners.

"Where is it?" she said tersely as they hit Aldersbrook. Jack scanned the dark expanse of the Flats, the lights of faraway houses and tower blocks shining in the distance. A dark clump of shadow loomed in front of him.

"There," he yelled, "over there. Now."

With a squeal of tyres, Wendy threw the car into a turn. It bumped up the kerb and hit the rough turf and grass with a bone-jarring crash. Jack was thrown up in his seat, hitting his head on the roof. Wendy felt the steering wrenched from her grasp, and the car careered to the right. She pulled hard on the wheel, correcting the path of the vehicle.

"Fuck me," Jack yelled, "watch it, for Christ's sakes. We're not going to be much use to Errol if we're in pieces."

"Just shut up and tell me where we're going," she snapped.

Jack pointed to the clump of trees surrounding the island, and she steered towards it. There was no obvious activity, and she skewered the car around the circumference of the pond. As she almost completed the circle, the headlights illuminated James falling into the water. They also picked up an oriental assassin, levelling his gun. . .

***

The lights blinded him, and he couldn't draw a sight on a frightened and breathless James, who used the opportunity to scramble out of the pond and start running towards his car. McAllister's men had arrived in two vehicles, and James's was one of them. Behind him there was the sound of sporadic gunfire.

For a second, the assassin halted, hesitating between his options. Should he pursue James, or go and warn his companions of this new factor in the equation?

He decided on the latter, and ran back onto the island, yelling in Cantonese. With a skill possessed only by those of great training and cunning, he made his way to Lao's position without becoming a target for Day or Fitch.

"What's he fuckin' yelling about?" hissed Quine.

"People," said Lao. "Either we ice them or get out."

"I say get out," growled Quine's assistant. "This is getting stupid. We get pinned down here much longer and the place will be crawling with police."

"I say that's a good call," Quine agreed. "We know who these muthafuckers are now. We'll get them later."

"Ross and Goldman?"

"I reckon Ross bought it. Goldman I can settle later. Let's go." His tone was decisive.

Lao looked at his compatriot, who nodded his own agreement. The four men began to retreat into the water, laying down covering fire.

On the other side of the clearing, Cann – still clutching his arm – wriggled closer to McAllister. "We've got to get out of here. There are people out there – don't know who they are. But Ross is dead and we can find out who those cunts are later. I can hear a car. I just hope to God it's James."

McAllister nodded curtly, and relayed instructions to Day and Fitch: "Cover yourselves and make for the cars. This is too fuckin' hot."

Hidden in the bushes, listening to the mayhem through a haze of pain, Errol wondered what had happened to Jack.

Having watched James run, and the assassin melt back into the darkness of the island, Wendy and Jack exchanged glances.

"What the fucking hell is going on here, Jack?"

Jack's tone was grim. "I think me and Errol were about to be double-crossed. I only hope that whatever he was going to do. . ." He said no more, flinging open the car door and starting off towards the island at a crouch. Suddenly chaos descended: Jack flung himself to the ground as McAllister ran across the path from the island, supporting Cann. Day and Fitch were close behind. McAllister fired in Jack's direction. He heard the crash of breaking glass, and Wendy screaming in pain.

Jack was saved by James panicking: he spun his car across the line of fire between the vigilante group and Goldman. Yelling incomprehensibly, he flung open the car doors. Day and Fitch helped Cann into the back while McAllister heaved his bulk in beside James, who threw the car into gear and screeched off before the doors were even shut.

Jack had scrambled to his feet, and back towards Wendy's car.

"Wend, are you okay?" he yelled.

"Yeah, just about." She appeared from behind the lights, blood streaming down her face. "He got the windscreen. This is only a splinter of glass," she added, wiping some of the blood away. "What about Errol?"

"C'mon." Jack grabbed her by the hand, and they ran across

onto the island.

It was empty. In the distance, Jack could hear another car start up and drive away. "Shit. Quine," he muttered.

"Who?"

"Never mind. Where's Errol?" He looked all around. The clearing was empty. He yelled into the night: "Errol. Where the –"

"Shut up." Wendy silenced him. "Listen."

It was definitely there. A groan, coming from the undergrowth directly in front of them. They ran over.

"Oh sweet Jesus," Jack cried.

Through a haze, Errol heard Jack's voice. He smiled, and pulled up his blood-soaked jumper. "You stupid honky bastard," he slurred. "Always too late. But I got them. I got them."

Everything went black.

***

Errol could remember very little of the journey to hospital. He faded in and out of consciousness, knowing only that Jack had managed to turn up, and he had that sweet little collator Wendy Coles with him. For some reason, she too was covered in blood. Maybe it was his.

He was aware of Jack ripping the tape off his chest. It should have hurt, but he felt nothing, not even a pulling sensation on his skin. He tried to tell Jack about the set-up, and how he'd got Devon to tool him up and wire him up at the same time. But it only emerged as a few weak groans.

"Where the hell did he get that?" Wendy asked, taking her eyes off the road to look at the bloodied Mauser Jack was holding.

Jack shrugged. "Don't ask me, babe. Probably called in a few favours. The wiring looks like Dev's work – one of Errol's snouts. Maybe the toy popgun came from him." Jack shifted in his seat and slid the gun into his belt.

"What are you going to do with it?" Wendy asked suspiciously.

Jack smiled, eyes twinkling. "I've got a few ideas. Just drive."

The Green Man roundabout was still jammed solid as

Wendy turned into Bush Road. This time she didn't hesitate: she drove up onto the pavement and round the traffic, weaving her way across from Bush Road to Leytonstone High Road, to the next exit – Whipps Cross Road. She sped past the line of traffic, and out onto the clear road behind, heading for the far end, where the hospital stood.

She skidded into the turn leading to the hospital, running over the cattle grid protecting the grounds from the herds that roamed the forest. The bumps made Errol moan louder.

"Don't worry, mate. Just hang on," Jack said through gritted teeth.

Wendy drew up outside the entrance to the casualty department. Leaving the engine running, she helped Jack to gently lift Errol out of the back seat. While Jack carried him, she went ahead, opening the doors. Casualty was packed as usual, but Wendy was prepared to pull rank. She got out her warrant card and flashed it at the hapless receptionist.

"Police. There's an officer here with multiple gunshot wounds. So fuckin' move it," she barked.

In a matter of minutes, Errol was in a cubicle, doctors around him, while Jack and Wendy hovered.

"So what's the score?" asked Jack.

A male nurse turned to answer. "The wounds aren't too bad, but he's lost a lot of blood. You may just have got him here in time." He scrutinised Wendy closely. "You should get that looked at, miss. Hey, where are you going. . ."

Jack pulled Wendy out of the cubicle. "We need to talk. Now, before the old bill turn out in force."

"But what about Errol?" she asked as Jack pulled her through the reception and into the cold night air.

"Errol's in the best hands. We've got things that need sorting. Come here." He led her to her car, and picked the tape recorders out of the back seat. "Take these to Scotland Yard, now. C10 will love 'em. Tell them to get to the Blind Beggar as soon as possible."

"Arnie Shawcross's hole?" she said, her collator's brain kicking into gear.

"Right. That's where McAllister's little boys hole up. They'll probably be licking their wounds. If the local boys get here and get us tied up, we'll lose all our momentum. We've got the edge, so we've got to take it. The Yard. C10. Now," he reiterated, pressing the tape recorders into her hand. "Take the car and don't fucking stop for anything."

"What are you going to do?"

Jack grinned and tapped the bulge the Mauser made in his waistband. "Let's just say I've got a few scores to settle."

"Jack, leave them. Come with me."

"No. If they're there, then I can keep them there until you get the C10 boys to show."

"They've already damn-near killed Errol. Don't throw yourself after him."

Jack laughed shortly and grasped Wendy. He held her to him, grateful for another human being who could understand. "That's the point, babe, isn't it? It should have been me and him, but I was out to fuckin' lunch somewhere. I let him down, I let myself down, and I let the old man down."

She pulled back and gave him a puzzled look.

He laughed again. "Promise I'll explain that when we've got time. But not now. Get going, Wend. Please."

"Okay." There was a note of reluctance in her voice as she pulled away from him. She walked around her car and got in, placing the tape recorders on the seat next to her. The engine was still ticking over, and she revved it into life. "But you be careful, Jack. I don't want to buy two bunches of grapes when I come up here again."

"Or a wreath," he joked. From the look on her face, he could see that it fell flat. "Okay. I'll be careful."

She pursed her lips and nodded, saying no more as she pulled out, disappearing at the end of the casualty approach, past the wooded driveway that led out onto the Whipps Cross Road.

Jack turned away and took a deep breath, filling his lungs with the cold night air. He felt a rush of blood to the head, and lights exploded behind his eyes. More than ever, he needed to be clear headed and keep his wits about him.

From the corner of his eye, he saw the nurse who had been tending Errol come striding towards the exit doors, obviously headed for him. Whatever else Jack wanted, it wasn't to be detained here. He looked quickly around: ten yards away, a cab was dropping off an old man who needed, for whatever reason, to go to casualty. The old man was fumbling with his change.

It gave Jack the few seconds he needed to make the ten yards to the car.

"You for hire, pal?" he asked, jerking open the back door.

"No, I ain't," the cabbie said absently, watching the old man shuffling away and cursing him mentally for taking so long. The last thing he wanted was a filthy, blood splattered loony in his cab. And that was what Jack looked like.

"Let me put it another way," Jack said. "I've just hired you, okay? I've got money." He threw the remains of Lenny's wallet on the front seat.

The cab driver sighed. "Look, pal, I've got a controller who radios me where I've got jobs. You want a cab, you phone for one. That's how the system works. Alright?"

"I don't think you heard me," Jack said, pointing the muzzle of the Mauser at the cabbie's cheek. The nurse was closing on them, peering intently into the cab. "I said you're for hire, and I've hired you. Yeah?"

"Listen son, anywhere you want to go, I'll take you," the cabbie stammered nervously.

"Right. First thing is get out of here. Now."

The cabbie accelerated past the nurse, who yelled and grabbed at the door. But he was too late: the cab was out of the hospital before he had a chance to even get to a phone.

Jack sat back in the car and sighed heavily. Wendy had her part to play, but the final move was his alone.

"You know a pub called the Blind Beggar?" he asked the cabbie.

CHAPTER SIXTEEN

James felt calmer behind the wheel, more in control of the situation. He blocked out the arguments in the back seat between Day and Fitch, and Cann's whimpers of pain. He also tried to block out the brooding presence of McAllister in the seat next to him. But that wasn't so easy: the big man was seething at the ambush, and possibly even more annoyed by the grumbling in the back seat.

"Where am I taking us, guv?" James asked nervously, keeping one eye on McAllister and one on the road.

"Back to the Beggar." McAllister's tone was flat and unemotional. From experience, James knew that this was a bad sign. It was the artificial calm before the raging storm.

He changed gear and slowed down as he hit the Romford Road, turning right and heading back towards the heart of the East End. He was sure that they weren't being followed, and didn't want to attract any attention by speeding – not with George Cann bleeding all over the back seat.

James felt the sweat gather on his brow, and wondered how he'd ever got involved in this nightmare: one thing for sure, it was too late for him to back out now. He might end up like Winston.

"Guv," he began tentatively, "when they find Winston, d'you think they'll be able to trace him back to us?"

McAllister grunted. "Doubt it. So what if they fuckin' do?"

Day and Fitch were appalled. "What do you mean, 'so what'? He was our mate, we shouldn't have left him like that."

"Right, so you want us to risk getting caught with a corpse bleeding all over the upholstery – 'oh, I'm terribly sorry officer, but he just seems to have been shot several times, and by the way it's perfectly alright because we're police officers'.

Grow up, son. Winston is a dead man – or at least, he will be by now."

"That's not the point," Day protested.

"Then what is?" said Cann, through the mists of his pain. "He can't tell anyone anything. We've got to look after ourselves."

"George is right," James snapped. "We've got other things to worry about right now. Like who those bastards were that tried to top us."

The car went quiet. That was a problem no-one wanted to consider.

They arrived at the Blind Beggar at about the same time Wendy and Jack were depositing Errol at the hospital. The building was in silent darkness. James banged repeatedly on the front door while Day and Fitch helped Cann from the car. There were very few people about, and those that could be bothered to look assumed Cann was just another drunk who needed a friend's arm.

McAllister stayed in the car, silent and impassive. James kept banging. There was no response. He kicked the doors and swore loudly before turning to McAllister.

"There's no-one bloody answering," he spat. "That filthy bastard probably doesn't even clear the bar after locking-up."

"What do you expect?" sighed McAllister sadly, finally heaving his bulk from the car. "I should have chosen somewhere else. Come on, round the side."

McAllister led the way, James following close behind. Day and Fitch lagged a little way back, as they were supporting a man who was becoming more and more of a dead weight: Cann had lost a lot of blood by now, most of it soaked into his clothes and those of Day and Fitch. A small trail of blood spots marked his path from the car to the front of the pub, and then round the side.

James and McAllister waited for them to catch up. They were standing in front of the door that Jack had found unlocked earlier in the day. McAllister reached for the handle: it yielded easily.

"Arnie Shawcross," he said sadly, shaking his head. "What a tosser. He deserves everything he gets."

They entered the pub yard, James closing the door and bolting it behind them, and walked across the yard to the back door. That was also unlocked. They entered the back of the pub, McAllister leading the way. James brought up the rear. He locked the door, and dropped the key in his pocket.

The small kitchen was filthy, with grease stains on the cooker, and plates piled in the sink. A tumbler stood on the scored worktop, a cigarette butt stubbed out in a thin film of whiskey. McAllister looked at it, and grinned humourlessly.

"Not like Arnie to waste any liquor, is it?"

The closed door in front of them led into the lounge, and there were squeals and moans coming from behind it. McAllister turned to the others and grinned.

"Surely not?" James said in amazement.

Without a word, McAllister turned the door handle. The warped door swung open of its own accord. A strange sight greeted them. The blonde barmaid, face contorted with a mixture of pain and ecstasy, lay across the table, her short skirt rucked around her waist. Her tights and pants were halfway down her thighs in a bundle. Arnie stood behind her, staring blankly into the distance as he rutted like a dog, with his shirt tail hanging over his pumping buttocks, his trousers gathered around his ankles.

McAllister laughed: it was without mirth, cold and harsh. Enough to jolt Arnie back to the present. He pulled away from the woman, erection waving wildly and glistening under the electric light. The woman opened her eyes and squealed in fear and embarrassment, reaching behind to try to pull up her underclothes. Arnie stumbled over his own trousers, and fell backwards, knocking an armchair across the small room. It overturned and thudded against the wall.

"Sorry to interrupt your fun, Arnie," McAllister said with a sardonic smile, "but we've got a little problem. And we need your help." He stepped forward as Arnie stumbled to his feet.

"You always know you can rely on me, Mister McAllister," Arnie stammered. "Always willing to help."

"So you should be, you cunt," McAllister growled. "It's your fault we're in this mess." He reached out and grabbed Arnie's penis, jerking it down suddenly and with force. Arnie screamed in pain, high pitched and choked. He doubled up and sank to the floor in agony.

The barmaid, now fully dressed, ran over to comfort him. She didn't like Arnie that much, and let him screw her so that she could keep her job; even so, she hated to see him in so much pain.

"What was that for?" she asked, eyes blazing with hatred.

"Shut up, you slag," McAllister said, turning away. He directed his comments to Day and Fitch. "Take George upstairs, make him as comfortable as possible. I know this bent doctor in Aldgate." He turned to James. "You know Isaacs?" James nodded. "Then call him. Tell him I want him here now, with plasma, or blood, or whatever. Tell him exactly what happened to George."

"Is that wise?"

"I've got stuff on him and his schoolgirl patients that could get him banged up for a good few years. He's not going to talk, slimy little bastard."

James nodded abruptly, and opened the door for Day and Fitch, who half-carried, half-supported Cann out into the hall and up the stairs, settling him in the front bedroom. James picked up the phone and called Isaacs. The doctor was enjoying a quiet evening at home, and wasn't too keen to come out. A few words about his predelictions soon changed that.

The conversation was short and somewhat less than sweet, Isaacs agreed to come after a little persuasion.

"Your man would be better in hospital if he's really that bad," the doctor said testily.

"Don't fuck us around. Come, and bring some blood or something."

The voice on the other end of the wire was peevish and whining. "What do you think I am, some sort of blood bank?"

"Listen, son, if you don't come, you'll be the one needing a fucking blood bank. Understand?"

James felt bitter when he put the phone down. Everything was going wrong: he wondered how much deeper he would get.

Back in the lounge, McAllister directed his gun towards

Arnie, who was cowering by the overturned chair.

"Now then, you and me need to talk, Arnie. And that's something you seem to be very good at, don't you?"

***

The cabbie seemed to be driving slowly on purpose, to irritate Jack, who leant forward in the back seat and clicked back the catch of the Mauser.

"If you want to drive like you're in a funeral, I could always organise one for you. Know what I mean?"

"Leave it out, squire," the cabbie whined. "I daren't go any faster round here. They've got the old bill out doing speed traps. We've been warned about that 'cause several of our drivers have been caught out in the last week. Be fair, would you want me to get stopped?"

Jack sat back, blowing out his cheeks. In truth, he had no option but to accept the cabbie's word for it: if there were speed traps operating around Bow at this time of night, then it would be just his luck to get stopped by one. From the smell, he was sure that the cabbie had already wet himself in fear. He was too scared to try and pull any kind of stunt. It was a kind of sod's law: when you wanted a copper, there was never one around. When you wanted to avoid them, the area was crawling with them.

So they drove at a steady thirty-five miles per hour through the empty streets of East London, the journey interrupted only by the occasional crackle of static and distorted voices over the cab's radio. One message penetrated Jack's wandering mind: "Ali, come in Ali, are you blue yet?" followed some short time later by "Ali, where the bloody hell are you? We've got a woman in Walthamstow waiting for you."

"Is that you?" Jack asked, the implications dawning on him.

The cabbie jumped. "Yeah. That's me, squire."

"Well you'd better answer." Jack bit his lip, trying to think of a good excuse for the radio silence. He didn't want anyone worrying about the driver. "Tell 'em you've had a flat on your way from the hospital. You've been out of the car."

"But –"

"No buts," Jack said, pressing the muzzle of the Mauser to the cabbie's neck. "You've had a flat. Now do it."

He kept his finger taut on the trigger while the cabbie picked up his hand-set and called in. He told his controller exactly what Jack had told him to say. When he was asked if he needed help, he nervously looked around: feeling the tension in Jack, the bite of the metal in his neck, he replied that he was okay. Really. Just a bit longer, and he'd be back in action. He'd let them know when. He signed off and put the hand-set back on its rest.

"Good lad," Jack whispered. "Just to make sure, though." He leant over the passenger seat and ripped the radio out of its mounting, severing the wires with one strong tug. A shower of sparks accompanied its demise, causing the cabbie to swerve. He corrected it, throwing Jack back onto the back seat.

"Sorry, squire," he said nervously, eyeing the gun in his mirror. "Couldn't help that."

"That's okay. Just get me to the Blind Beggar and you'll be alright."

It took another ten minutes of driving in silence before the cabbie was able to pull over in front of the pub. Jack noted that James's car was parked by the kerb.

Jack opened the back door. "Keep the money, and get the hell out of here."

"That's it?" the cabbie asked nervously.

Jack smiled. "I wasn't going to use this thing on you, son," he said, brandishing the Mauser. "But you didn't know that, did you?"

He slammed the door on the puzzled cabbie, hammering on the roof with his fist. The driver didn't need prompting: he gunned the engine and roared off into the night.

Jack walked up to the front of the pub, making no attempt to hide. It was too late, now, for that: they would have seen him get out of the cab if they were watching – at the very least they would have heard it driving away.

The front of the building was still dark and silent. There was little sign of life. The front windows on the top floor were dark, as well. Had he miscalculated? Had McAllister taken his men somewhere else? But why else was James's car here. . .

There was still the back: Jack walked round to the side door, Mauser dangling loosely in his grip. He tried the door: locked.

Looking up at the glass-topped wall, he regretted leaving his jacket at Errol's earlier in the day. So how was he going to get in?

Jack looked up and down the street. There was a skip about thirty yards away, on the top of which was a length of rolled-up old carpet. It was a clumsy way to do it, but what other choice did he have? He jogged up to the skip, and thrust the pistol into his waistband. Pulling the carpet down, throwing up a choking cloud of dust, he dragged it back to the door at the side of the Beggar. The carpet wasn't tied, and he was able to unroll it until he had a doubled-over length of about six feet square. It was old and threadbare, perhaps lighter than it could have been. Just as well, as he had to somehow throw it up and over the wall. It took him seconds that seemed like hours, but eventually he managed to propel it up onto the glass. The weight of the carpet caused it to unravel with a dull thud, covering the jagged edges.

Jack coughed, hawking up phlegm created by the dust. It would have been easier to take his chances with the glass. He took four steps back, and jumped: his hands grasped the top of the wall, the glass almost coming through the threadbare carpet. With effort, his feet kicking at the wall to propel himself, he pulled himself up and flung one leg over.

He slid down the carpet, landing with a thump on the carpet-covered concrete. He stifled a cough, and crouched low as a cramp flared in his ribs. This was the last thing he needed.

The cramp vanished along with his breath as he looked up: there was a light in the kitchen, and the barmaid he'd seen earlier in the day was standing over the sink, gawping at him in astonishment. For a fraction of a second, Jack gawped back. Then he put his finger to his lips, and she nodded – barely, but enough for him to see. He hoped she'd recognised him. Hoping it was lit well enough for her to see by the light spilling from the kitchen window, he pointed to the back door and mimed opening it. She shook her head – again, barely – and mouthed something at him. He frowned and she mouthed it again: "locked".

He nodded, and pulled the Mauser from his belt. He'd have to go in blazing and hope for the best. Earlier, he hadn't cared;

but now, faced with the prospect of sudden death, his resolve was wavering.

Jack gestured to the woman to get out of the kitchen. She nodded again, and turned her back. She spent a few seconds busying herself with something before disappearing. Jack gulped down the bile rising in his throat, ignoring the fluttering of nerves in his stomach. He checked the catch on the Mauser: it was off. He took one step forward, and fired a short burst at the door. The old wood disintegrated under the impact of the metal-jacketed rounds. He raised a foot and kicked what was left of the door away from the lock, which fell uselessly to the floor.

Then he was in the kitchen.

***

The barmaid took the tray in to McAllister and James, who were sitting at the table. Arnie lay in a corner, unconscious. His face was a mass of bruised and bleeding weals, where McAllister had repeatedly whipped him with the nose of the pistol. He'd held it in Arnie's ear and clicked the hammer back until Shawcross had told him exactly what he'd said to Ross and Goldman earlier that day. Then, enraged, McAllister had beaten him into unconsciousness, kicking him in the ribs while he lay there, listening to the bones snap. Arnie probably had internal injuries, but McAllister wasn't interested: for all that he cared, Arnie could just lie there silently and die.

The barmaid had stood in the kitchen, trying to close her mind to the screams of pain coming from the lounge. She just hoped to get out alive. Seeing Jack slide down the wall had given her that hope, no matter how slim.

She was putting the tray down when the Mauser exploded into life. She yelped and dropped the tray onto the table, the teapot tipping over into James' lap. He screamed as the scalding liquid penetrated his crotch, and scrabbled to his feet.

"Huh?" McAllister was frozen in a moment of indecision, his attention torn between James and the sounds from the kitchen. That moment was enough for Jack to kick open the door from kitchen to lounge. He stood, framed in the doorway, Mauser scanning the room.

"Hello, guv. Bet you didn't think you'd see me, eh? Drop

it," he added, gesturing to the gun hanging limply in McAllister's hand. McAllister let it fall to the floor. James was standing in a half-crouch, hot tea still dripping from him, frozen in shock. "You, too, Laurence," Jack said calmly. "Any weapons, then drop 'em. Otherwise, just sit down with your hands nicely on view, okay?"

James did as he was told. The barmaid sidled past him until she was standing by Jack.

"What do you want me to do?" she said in a hushed voice.

"Get out," Jack replied quietly. "Get out, and run as fast as you can. Stop any woodentop you see, tell him to call C10. He'll know what you mean."

She nodded vigorously, and with one last glance at Arnie, still unconscious in the corner, she ran. Her high heels skittered across the linoleum floor in the kitchen, clattering on the concrete of the yard. Jack heard the bolt on the door being shot, then her footsteps started again, fading into the distance.

"You won't get far with this," McAllister sneered. "Day and Fitch are upstairs. They're tooled up. What you gonna do when they come down, eh? You gonna keep an eye on all four of us? What chance have you got, even with that?" He gestured at the pistol. "We could easily wipe the floor with you, son."

Jack smiled broadly. "I don't think so. Full metal jacket rounds in an enclosed space like this? If the shots don't get you, there's a good chance the ricochet will." He shook his head. "None of you are that stupid."

"I wouldn't bet on it," James uttered bitterly.

Jack looked at him: despite his assurance, he was a little worried by the fact that the other two men hadn't shown yet. Could he trust McAllister that they were upstairs? Any ally could be worth his weight in gold.

"Getting disillusioned, Laurence?" James nodded. Jack continued: "You've still got a chance of getting a lighter sentence, right? Come over to me, turn Queen's evidence."

McAllister snorted. "You still think you've got a chance of pulling us in, don't you?"

"Why not? C10 are on their way."

"You trust that slag?"

Jack smiled. "I don't have to. Errol was wired."

McAllister looked shaken. His face drained of colour and when he spoke it was almost in a whisper. "You weren't on your own. I heard someone scream when I fired at you."

"Got it in one." Jack's attention was taken away from McAllister by the sound of feet clumping down the stairs, and the hushed burble of voices. "Ah, I think this is your version of the cavalry. Tell 'em to come in and put their guns down."

Jack was sure that he was safe: there was no way that Day or Fitch could get behind him, and there were definitely two sets of footsteps. From the hall, the only way they could get into the lounge was by the single door. He had them trapped.

"Day, Fitch," McAllister yelled. "Open the door and throw your guns in, then walk in very slowly. He's got all the aces at the minute."

But if that was so, then why was McAllister smiling that much? Was there something he'd missed?

Jack realised that he'd been devoting all his attention to the men in front of him: he was aware of a faint scraping from behind. He turned quickly; but not quickly enough.

He saw the milk bottle as it descended towards him, but was too slow to stop it landing with a crash on the side of his skull. He felt the blood begin to flow, and the sharp needles of glass splinters in his hair and scalp.

Then everything went black.

***

Ronnie Isaacs was a general practitioner in Aldgate. He'd worked there for over twenty years, since qualifying in 1969. His father had also been a GP in Aldgate and Ronnie had taken over the practice. Unfortunately for Isaacs senior, no-one had told him about Ronnie's little predelictions: high on the list came adolescent girls, and there was no thrill in it for Ronnie unless they were between twelve and fourteen.

He had a lot of patients with children that age, and had first come to McAllister's attention when he instigated a programme at his surgery explaining the facts of life to these girls. Parents who were nervous about handling this were happy to leave it in the hands of their trustworthy GP, little knowing that Ronnie had a few practical lessons lined up for the girls who passed through his surgery.

Most of his victims felt too dirty and ashamed to complain. But not all. One had approached Winston, who was on desk duty at the right station, right time. He'd decided to deal with it unofficially, and called McAllister. A little visit had been organised, and they'd come to an arrangement with Ronnie: he tended to the medical needs of the Avengers, and they let him keep his wedding tackle. It suited both parties, and Ronnie was now far more discreet.

So when James called him, Ronnie jumped. The idea was that he hammered on the back door and they would let him in. Only, when he got there, there was a carpet over the wall, and the sound of gunfire. Ronnie's first instinct was to run and claim he'd been nowhere near the building at any time in his life. But that wasn't really feasible. A sympathetic twinge in the testicles had reminded him of the price he may have to pay for crossing the Avengers.

Praying to a God he hadn't acknowledged for many years, Ronnie had scrambled his way up the carpet, trying hard not to make too much noise with his laboured breathing: it was difficult, as he had his medical bag slung over one arm, and his balance was awkward. But he managed, somehow, and slid down the other side, slowing his descent by digging in his heels.

There were voices from the kitchen, and when he heard Jack tell someone to get out, he hid himself behind the carpet, choking on the dust. He heard footsteps – a woman's, in high heels – and then the back door of the yard was unbolted and opened. He cursed to himself: why couldn't she have done that five or ten minutes earlier?

He waited a few seconds, then crept into the kitchen. McAllister watched him, all the while talking to the man with a gun who had his back to the door. Ronnie felt his bowels churn and he needed to pee. His mouth was bone dry and he thought he might faint. One thing was for sure: he needed a weapon.

There was an empty milk bottle on the drainer. Ronnie gingerly picked it up, then tiptoed behind the armed man.

That was what Jack heard. Ronnie crashed the bottle down

as he turned.

***

When Jack came round, the whole world was turning circles and he felt like he was going to puke. He lifted his head off the carpet and tried to bring his arms around to support himself. They wouldn't move. He tried wriggling his legs. They were fast, as well.

"Oh shit," he groaned.

"So you've come round, eh?" McAllister said from somewhere near his head. The voice was accompanied by a vicious kick in the ribs that made him gasp. It didn't actually hurt until a few seconds later, when the burning afterglow started to throb.

Jack felt himself be grabbed by the hair, and his head lifted up. He could see very little above the level of the carpet. He was lifted higher, trying to suppress squeals of agony as his hair took his weight: it felt like it was being dragged out by the roots.

Blissfully, the pain was eased as another set of hands grabbed him around the body, lifting him higher, until he was on his feet. He didn't have much balance, but he was supported from behind. McAllister was standing in front of him, James just to one side. And there was some guy he didn't recognise on the other side. Must be Day or Fitch – the other one of that pair holding him. But who the hell had hit him?

"You scumbag," McAllister hissed. "I ought to top you right now. But I figure we've got a few minutes, so I want you to suffer."

His fist crashed into Jack's guts, thrusting upwards and knocking the breath from his body. He felt like it had jolted his heart, and he bent double, whooping for breath. His head was pulled up as he still fought for air, and McAllister was looking him in the face. He spat in Jack's eyes. It stung, and he blinked rapidly. He may not have been able to protect himself, but he wanted to know where the next blow was coming from. He could at least tense himself against it.

It was too quick: Day or Fitch – his mind wandered away from pain and idly wondered which one it was – drew back his fist and crashed it into Jack's face. His nose pulped into a mess

199

of pain, his front teeth pushed backwards into his mouth, cutting his lips and slicing into his tongue. The fist muffled the first cry of agony.

Jack's head lolled to one side, and he felt himself being pushed forward into the arms of someone else: it was the precursor to a rabbit punch that made his kidneys burn. His head swirled with the sheer magnitude of the pain, a gigantic throb that pulsed up and down his body in waves, meeting with a clash at the area around his kidneys.

Things were a blur. There seemed to be a lot going on around him, but all he could focus on was the pain. First he heard the sound of cars screeching to halt in the street outside, and the slamming of doors. There were voices, shouting something incomprehensible. Then there was a voice that was much clearer, although he didn't recognise it.

Ronnie appeared in the doorway, excited and scared. "There's loads of people out front. I think we'd better go."

"Fuck it," McAllister exploded. "Let's finish this little shit and get out." He was still holding Jack: he thrust him backwards, so that Jack collapsed onto the table, back painfully arching. He was in no position to move, although he had no inclination or ability to do so at that moment. He was helpless and at the mercy of McAllister.

The fat man delved into his pocket and produced a Smith & Wesson. He pointed it at Jack and clicked off the safety catch.

Jack was only dimly aware of this through his pain. Watching through a mist of colours, he saw two McAllisters draw their gun and point it at him. The words came through as though shouted from a distant mountaintop. He knew he was about to die, but was too dazed to care.

"Bye, bye, fuckhead," McAllister snarled. He began to squeeze the trigger.

"Do it and you're dead, too."

McAllister looked up. There were three men in the doorway: one part-way into the room, two flanking him. All had pistols which covered the room.

Jack was only aware that a noise had come from behind him, and that the two McAllisters let their guns drop to the floor.

Jack giggled through the blood in his mouth. "You're

fucked, McAllister. You're fucked, you fat bastard."

Everything went black again.

CHAPTER SEVENTEEN

It was ten days before Jack could visit Errol: two days of which Jack spent in hospital himself. Three broken ribs, a tendency to pass blood in his urine and persistent dizzy spells led to a series of tests. A few antibiotics and he was released into the custody of the Metropolitan Police.

In a strange way it all seemed like an anti-climax. He'd come within seconds of being rubbed out of existence, and now found himself answering questions about McAllister's activities and the events in Zak's garage. There would be charges, but Zak was willing to testify that Jack and Errol had been attacked, and were simply defending themselves. After all, he reasoned, that was no more than what he'd done himself.

Danny O'Day was buried a week after his death: he had slipped away about the time that Jack was looking down the muzzle of McAllister's gun. There was something almost poetic about that: in their own ways, both men had faced the darkness and won. They let Jack attend the funeral, bruised and battered but nonetheless there. His family treated him like a hero, which left a sour taste. The only good thing was that his ex-wife had allowed young Danny to attend the service. Perhaps good wasn't the word: his son didn't seem to understand, and Jack didn't like him seeing the family's hypocrisy and cant. But when he stood at the old man's grave, and they both bade him farewell in their own way, then it seemed right.

Benny Grazione was finally buried. Jack heard about it when he received a "get well" card from old woman Grazione. The other dead gang members and Courtney Gold were finally laid to rest as well, although no-one bothered to inform Jack about their funerals.

Wendy called round a few times. She had been to see Errol at the hospital. He'd been in a coma for a few days, then conscious but not really well enough to have visitors. Even if he had been, Denise or her brother were hovering near.

"I can really pick 'em," Wendy sighed bitterly when Jack had taken her out for a drink. It was his first alcohol since coming out of hospital and he drank sparingly because of the medication. As they sat in the bar, Wendy continued. "First I pick up on that pig McAllister. I really thought he cared – not that you'd think it to look at him," she said in response to Jack's look of amazement, "but sometimes he was really nice. . . and all he really wanted was to pump me for information. Then there was Errol."

"I didn't know you and him –"

She smiled. "Not for the want of me trying. But he's got someone, hasn't he?"

"What about me?" Jack asked. "You saved my life – that must count for something." He reached out and took her hand.

She laughed sadly. "Trouble is, sweetheart, I don't fancy you at all. . ."

***

Finally, Jack got to see Errol. He limped painfully into the private room where his partner was propped up in bed. Denise turned as Jack entered. When she saw him, she tutted softly, got up, and left the room without a word.

Jack watched her go. "She – er – blame me for all this?"

Errol grinned. "No, 'course not. Just 'cause I did what you asked and ended up full of lead."

Jack sat down painfully on the end of the bed, tossing a box of chocolates at Errol. "Correct me if I'm wrong, old son, but two bullets doesn't constitute being full of lead."

"Pedantic bastard." Errol picked up the box. "These are dark chocolate," he moaned. "You know I hate that."

"Yeah, but I don't." Jack snatched the box back and opened it, picking out a chocolate. "So, how are you?"

Errol shrugged. "Out of action for several months. Still kicking, though. You seen the C10 boys yet?"

Jack nodded. "Several times. They been to you?"

"I still have that joy to come – the doctors have told them I'm too ill. . . that won't last."

"They're alright. Those tapes you got were pretty self-explanatory. You seen Wendy yet?"

"Wendy?"

"Yeah, Wendy Coles," Jack said. Errol shook his head, looking puzzled. "Well you should. You wouldn't be here if not for her." He went through that night in detail, then learned for the first time how Errol came by the tapes and the Mauser. When they had finished swapping stories, Errol looked up at the ceiling, exhausted.

"Why hasn't Wendy been in?"

"Denise warned her off," Jack said through a mouthful of chocolate. "I reckon you're in there, son." When Errol responded with a raised eyebrow, Jack laughed: "Alright, don't trust me then. After all, I fancied my chances with Benny's bit."

"What happened to her?"

Jack shrugged. "Search me. Probably found a nice stockbroker to shag. Had enough of the rough, I suppose."

They sat in silence for a while, Jack slowly working his way through the chocolate box.

"You'll get cavities," Errol said eventually.

"So? I'll get free dental treatment," Jack replied. "Zak's got us off the hook for the garage fuck-up. Reckons it was self-defence."

"So it was."

Jack smiled. "Yeah, sort of. . .anyway, even with that out of the way, I don't reckon there's much of a future for me in the force. I'll be lucky to get an aluminium handshake, let alone gold. It's the dole queue for me, I reckon."

"If you go, I go too," Errol said wryly. "They can't just get rid of one of us. I suppose we could always find something else to do." He grinned at Jack and held up his hand.

Jack returned the smile and grasped it. "Why not? Something always turns up."

Errol chuckled deep and low in his throat. "That, my friend, is way, way more than an understatement..."